HIS COLD BLUE COMMAND

A. J. DOWNEY

BOOK TWO

COPYRIGHT

~

ISBN: 978-1-950222-11-7

Book design by Maggie Kern

Cover art and Indigo Knights logo by Dar Albert at Wicked Smart Designs

Editing by Barbara J. Bailey

Photo by Nathan Hainline

Model Nathan Hainline

Dedication

To Mary Sittu-Kern & Greg Kern, I am glad you are on board. Not a whole lot of swearing in this one Greg, I promise. You've got other problems.

1

___

*Y*ale…

I leaned back in my chair and swiped a hand over my face, glancing at the clock. It was twenty minutes to nine. I had just enough minutes left in the hour to get some decent coffee before the café across from the DA's office closed.

Chrissy Franco tucked a stray lock of her long, dark hair behind her ear. Her tresses were captured in a twist with two pencils thrust through it to pin it. The sleeves of her cream satin blouse were rolled to her elbows, much like mine, as we were both elbows-deep into the Reeves case.

I couldn't help but admire her grace and the beauty of her form as she leaned over the table in my office, shuffling through file folders of affidavits, but she was already taken. Taken by one of my club brothers, Youngblood. I smiled, pleased for them both and a bit wistful at the same time. Again, she was beautiful, but alas, that ship had sailed.

"I'm going for coffee."

"Me, too, please…" she muttered faintly, rapt on what she was reading. I smiled and chuckled to myself, and put both feet flat on the floor from atop my desk, banishing the images I should *not* be imagining from my mind.

"What do you want?"

"The usual," she said, a bit of annoyance tingeing her voice, and that is why we would never have worked. Chrissy Franco was a bulldog in the courtroom, and in some ways, just as alpha as me.

"As the boss, I'm not sure why I am always the one running to get coffee," I stated.

"Because *you* have the crush on the counter girl at the café," she said, shortly. She dismissed what she'd been reading out of hand and set it aside. "And don't think I didn't just catch you looking."

"My apologies," I started, and the word was foreign on my tongue. She raised an eyebrow in my direction. I shut my mouth and smiled genuinely. "Thank you," I said simply, and she gave a nod, the movement graceful on her long neck. She didn't appreciate being lied to as much as I didn't like having to lie, even if it was the politically correct or polite thing to do.

"I know you don't mean it to be uncomfortable," she said. "I also know you're lonely and should ask for the coffee girl's number." I stood and went to the door, shaking my head. One of Chrissy's other qualities I had come to appreciate since she joined the District Attorney's office as a prosecuting attorney was her willingness to be forthright with me. Add to that, her ability to communicate clearly with me without having to say a word? Well, she was an asset to this office I would be forever grateful for.

Granted, I was more perceptive than most, which made it much easier, but all of that aside, she and I had become quite the dynamic duo the last few months. Our styles complemented one another spectacularly.

Another reason that I sometimes let my imagination travel to the land of *what might have been.*

I banished the thoughts from my fatigued mind and made my way to the elevator. When the doors opened at the lobby level, Youngblood looked up from two coffees in his hands.

"Hey, you seen my wife?" he asked. I smiled to myself.

"You aren't married yet, and she's in my office," I frowned, "Come to think of it, have you even asked her?"

"Not formally; at least not yet, but it's going to happen. I just like trying the title on for size."

"Ah, well, in my office."

"Where are you rushing off to?"

"Coffee of my own!" I called back over my shoulder.

"Ah, yeah, sorry! I just brought a couple for me and her, I didn't know you'd be here!"

I waved him off over my shoulder and went out the front doors of the aging government building and down the front steps. The air was crisp and clean with the smell of ozone and fresh rain. The ground was wet, darkness rising up from the streets to meet the sky. The fiery orange glow from the setting summer sun was barely a glimmer between the buildings where you could catch a glimpse of the horizon.

I got to the doors of the café and tugged on them to find them locked, muttering, "Ahhh… damn it!"

Movement caught my eye as I went to go back across the street. and I turned. Ally, the morning coffee-girl, came to the door and unlocked it.

"Working late, Mr. Parnell?"

"As, so it seems, are you."

"Right, yeah… Come on in. I already shut down the till and counted it out, do you have cash?" she asked meekly.

"No, I'm sorry I was going to…" I held up my phone, and she bit her bottom lip.

"That's okay; I'll take it out of my tips."

I smiled as she turned around and set her mop aside. She went behind the counter and began making my coffee without asking. She knew what I liked. I stood, hands in my pockets, and vowed to tip her the cost of the coffee plus more, the next morning.

"How come so late?" I asked.

"Millie needed someone to close, and I could really use the extra hours, so I volunteered to stay and work straight through."

She poured the shots of coffee into a paper cup and smoothed her hands along her long, baseball tee over a pair of form-fitting black leggings. I let my gaze linger, as she added hot water to the cup to make my Americano.

"How about you?" she asked.

I cleared my throat and tried to decide what to say. The case we were working was horrific. Jordan Reeves, an eighteen-year-old high school student, had buried her baby alive in her parent's backyard. Her mother had discovered the nineteen-day-old remains when tilling her rose garden. The family had circled the wagons, and their high-priced attorneys were stonewalling. We were in the midst of trying to have some of their motions quashed, and it would, honestly, be a near thing. This case was proving to be a nightmare, and we were barely past arraignment. Still, none of that was anything to burden Ally with, so, "Tough case," I finally settled on, lamely.

Ally's face softened, her expression empathetic, green eyes searching mine. "The Reeves thing?" Her voice was soft. Delicate and gentle, sensitive, it was a soothing balm to the burns caused by the utter depravity I waded through on a daily basis.

"You know about that?" I asked, taking a careful sip of my coffee. It was good. I always appreciated how Ally made it.

She leaned a hip against the counter and sighed, hugging herself. Her long, stiff, blonde hair with dark roots fell around her pale face, making her green eyes shine that much more. I didn't typically like it when women processed their hair, but Ally's white-blonde hair with their dark roots worked well for her.

"Hard not to know about it, it's been all over the news."

"Ah," I said, nodding. She'd likely seen the press conference on the courthouse steps that morning. I'd had to speak. It wasn't my favorite thing, dealing with those jackals. The media always left a bad taste in my mouth, one I attempted to wash away with another sip of coffee.

I swept Ally with my gaze and decided that as much as I would like to sully her in other ways, I didn't wish to defile her with anything pertaining to any one of my legal cases. I smiled slightly, feeling the weight, the mantle of responsibility, return to my shoulders. The scales of justice were attempting to balance and needed my attention. So too, did my scales.

"I should get back," I said, and she nodded, smiling.

"Good luck," she murmured, and followed me to the door.

"I'll see you tomorrow, maybe?"

"Tomorrow," she agreed. "Have a good night."

I nodded and waited until she locked the door behind me. I turned to the curb and waited for traffic to pass, and once I was across the street, gave into the urge to look back. She stood in the center of the café, the chairs up, their seats resting on the table tops, swiping the string mop back and forth across the floor. She concentrated on her task, making sure she was being thorough, and I could appreciate that.

I turned and went back up to my office, those smiling-yet-somber green eyes haunting me.

For some reason, I couldn't look at Chrissy Franco twice after that encounter. Every time I even tried, Chrissy's brown eyes morphed to green, her dark hair to blonde, and her olive complexion became kissed by the moon.

2

*A*lly…

I swept my wild mane of hair over my shoulder and nodded, my eyes beginning to fill with tears even as I tried my best to fend them off.

"I understand," I said quietly into the receiver.

"It's honestly for the best, Ms. Blaylock. Your grandmother just can't be on her own for any length of time," the social worker's tone was conciliatory, and I swallowed past the lump in my throat. I wanted to argue with her. Wanted to say *'But she's not alone! She has me, she's with me!'* but I couldn't argue because nothing would change the fact that my grandmother had fallen and broken her hip while I was at work. I hadn't been there; she wasn't with me; she had been by herself and nowhere near the phone, and I hadn't known anything was wrong, and she had lain there for four hours before I had come home.

I nodded, realized she couldn't see it, and cleared my throat, my voice coming out deceptively strong even as my brittle heart was breaking.

"What happens now?"

Her voice buzzed calmly in my ear as she laid everything out and I felt myself nodding dumbly. They would move my grandmother into an assisted-living facility. She would be taken care of, but at what cost? Those places were expensive. We weren't rich by any means. I would have to move! The apartment I grew up in was rent-controlled, but under my grandmother's name, not mine. If she no longer lived there...

"Yes, I understand," I said numbly and shivered in the warm sunshine. People walked to and fro, and someone stepped past me into the coffee shop. I glanced back over my shoulder at Millie, my boss, and she waved me off. The shop was busy, though.

"Ms. Blaylock?"

"Yes, I'm sorry, I'm here. It's very busy here. I'm at work."

"I understand, Ms. Blaylock; we can finish discussing this later this afternoon."

"Yes, I'll be over as soon as my shift is over, say around three?"

"I look forward to seeing you then."

"Okay, thank you. Bye."

I turned and looked at Millie whose face was crushed with sympathy, and I sighed. I wiped under my eyes and checked my reflection in the glass of the door to see if I needed to fix my make-up or if I was okay to just go behind the counter.

"Take five in the back," Millie ordered. "I have it out here."

"Okay, thank you!" I called, grateful for her.

I went to the bathroom, fixed my makeup, took a good hard look in the mirror and nearly broke down – but I couldn't. I needed to work, I needed to go to the care facility they had Gran in, and I needed to make all of the arrangements. I went back out and slipped behind the counter, tying on my apron.

As luck would have it, my favorite customer, Mr. Parnell, was standing next in line. I smiled at him, and he looked me over. His eyes were lovely, dark and deep, framed in long lashes any woman would kill for. I don't know what it was about him that I found so attractive. By all accounts, his affect was cold, almost heartless, but something about those deep, soulful eyes called to a piece of me.

There was just something about him I found alluring. Maybe it was the way it felt like he saw right down to the deepest parts of me. Like now, the first words out of his mouth were, "What's wrong, Ally?"

"Nothing," I lied, putting on my best and brightest customer-service smile. His brow crushed down and it made him look so fierce and so angry. I tried to deflect even more and asked, "The usual?"

"And Ms. Franco's order, if you please."

"Sure thing!"

I began making the two coffee drinks, and he leaned in saying low, as to be barely heard over the grinder, "Please, don't ever lie to me again."

I froze, and the breath was stolen from my lungs as he caught my eyes with his, the intensity of his look as he searched my face causing my own eyes to go very wide.

"I'm sorry," I murmured. "I just… it's..."

"Private?" he asked with a chilled, but not unkind, little smile.

"Yes," I breathed.

"That's fine, I don't want or need to know, but I value honesty above all else."

I gave the portafilter a twist onto the machine and hit the two switches, waiting for the moments it would take for the two heavy shot glasses to fill.

"I'll remember that," I murmured.

He smiled, and this time it was kinder, gentler as he said, "Just remember that it's okay not to be okay."

I looked up sharply at where he'd stood at the corner of the counter, but he was gone. He'd moved to the register to pay for the drinks. He looked over at me and winked and thrust some money into the tip jar. I set his two cups on the round drink station, and he swept them into his hands and backed out the front door. I couldn't help it, I sighed and watched his ass in his slacks as he jogged across the street. It was a guilty pleasure of mine, what could I say?

I may have been too busy with life to add a relationship to it right now, but I wasn't dead. Not that I thought anything would happen with the city's best ADA. He was way out of my league. I was just a poor inner-city girl.

Business picked up and I banished all thoughts of Damien Parnell from my mind as it became everything I could do to keep up with the flow of orders. Before I knew it, it was time to face the music – I counted my tips and felt a slight rush of relief. I could afford a cab to make the appointment with my gran's social worker. I didn't have to worry about if I would make it or not by taking the two buses it would take to get there.

At least that was something.

3

$\mathcal{Y}$ale…

She was crying again, waving papers in front of her and practically begging her boss for something when I walked through the door that morning. I paused and looked around but it was still early, and I was the only customer.

"What seems to be the problem?" I asked, and let my gaze bore into hers.

"I'd rather not say…" she murmured, but I held my hand out for the papers. Reluctantly, she handed them over. Her boss wasn't unsympathetic, in fact, her blue eyes said that her heart went out to the girl, but there was nothing she could do.

I raked my eyes over the pages for an assisted-living facility and frowned. I looked back up to Ally and asked, "Who are these for?"

She swallowed hard, "My grandmother."

"I was telling Ally, I can't afford a raise, but that I could give her as many hours as I could…" I let my eyes go back and forth between the two before I made a snap decision.

"Do you clean?" I asked Ally, and she blinked.

"I… I can," she said cautiously.

"I'll be right back." I turned abruptly and returned to my office.

"What happened to the coffee?" Chrissy asked when she saw me return empty-handed. I didn't want her in my business, and though I valued honesty, I lied.

"Forgot my wallet."

I went to my desk and found the papers I needed, and returned quickly to the coffee shop. I handed them to Ally.

"Fill these out; I'll be back for them this afternoon."

She stared at me with wide, clear eyes and looked down at the background-check papers in her hands.

"Okay," she said faintly.

I caught her eyes with mine and gave her a curt nod. She straightened up a little and gave me one back, and I got the drinks and left.

She was in the back of my mind for the rest of the day. I wondered if she would fill them out, but more importantly, I wondered if I had lost my mind. I could afford a housekeeper; in fact, I already paid a service to clean my condominium once a week. Depending on what the background revealed, though, I would be canceling that service and, likely, would be paying Ally a little bit more besides.

I kept thinking to myself, *she's beautiful, but not a stray, and you're a sick son of a bitch. You shouldn't be doing this. You shouldn't even be entertaining the idea. So much could go wrong.* I kept all of this to myself and after court was adjourned for the day, made my way back to Mildred's Café to see if Ally had followed my instructions.

Millie, the café's owner, looked up from behind the register when I came in. She smiled kindly and said, "You just missed her, but she asked me to give these to you." She pulled a plain manila file folder from beside the register and handed it over to me. I smiled, tapped the edge against my fingers and finally nodded, turning to go.

"She's a good kid, Mr. Parnell. I'll give you any reference to that fact that you require, written or otherwise."

I turned, nodded briefly, and went back outside. My fingers itched to flip through the papers and rifle through the information they contained. I was curious about her – wanted to know more, but I didn't trust myself to ask. I didn't want to encourage her, or any woman, into thinking that I had time for a relationship. I didn't.

I went back to my office and closed the door behind me, wanting a bit of privacy for this. I sat down and flipped open the file.

Blaylock, Allison Kay, born November 22nd, 1994. She was twenty-two, would be twenty-three in a few months. I'd known she was young, but I didn't think *that* young. She was petite, which could be deceptive, I knew. Ally was shorter than me, her body still holding the alluring curves of a woman despite how tiny she was. I was not what could be considered a large man, at five-foot-five; it had proven to be a slight challenge in both my personal and professional life.

As an unfortunate result of my genetically given physical stature, I was required to cultivate a presence that relied on things other than my size. For instance, I kept a neat, trim beard; without one, I looked twelve. Add to that, I dressed extremely well and had my clothing tailored so that it fit properly. When you were a man my size, people tended to dismiss you out of hand. Wearing what looked like your father's suit did nothing to dispel that notion, so I made sure I didn't give them the option to judge me on that front.

I made up for my lack of height and bulk with speed, agility, and knowing where to strike, as opposed to relying on brute strength for anything. I also kept extremely fit to maximize what strength I did have and to keep my endurance unparalleled.

I cleared my throat, and read further down the page. She had only had one job since high school, the one she had now, and lived in the Point Side projects with her grandmother. I noticed writing on the other side of the sheet from where the afternoon light came through the blinds over my single office window and frowned. I turned the sheet over, and in delicate cursive Ally had written.

Dear Mr. Parnell,

I have written down everything this sheet has asked, however, I will not be living at my current address much longer. I don't know where I will be, yet. So Millie said that if anything needed to be mailed to me, I could have it sent to the café. I hope that is all right with you.

Sincerely,

Ally

Dammit. It wasn't bad enough that her grandmother had been placed in a too-expensive assisted-living home, it had ensured Ally would lose hers. I didn't know what I was playing at here, but I couldn't let that stand. I let out a frustrated sigh and returned to her particulars, glancing over everything and hitting a key to wake up my computer's screen.

I typed in her name, date of birth, and social security and ran her information. An even sadder story emerged on my screen.

Orphaned at age six, her mother had been a junkie in and out of the system from just after she was born until her death. No known identity for her father. Ally had been placed with her maternal grandparents at the age of two after children's services found her living in squalor. It was a clear case of neglect, and I wondered briefly if, at that age, she remembered any of it.

Her grandfather, her grandmother's husband and father to Ally's mother, died of a heart attack when Ally was eight years old. It had been her and her grandmother ever since, until units responded to their apartment, close to three weeks ago. Sylvia Blaylock had fallen and broken her hip while her granddaughter had been working at the café. She'd been declared medically unfit to return home, and it had been recommended she go to a residential care facility.

I sighed and leaned back in my seat. Everything I was seeing would tug on one of my brother's heart strings, and it did mine, too, but not in the way you would think. I wanted to help Ally, but there was a dark part of me who wanted to do it for all of the wrong reasons. She was easily something, someone, I could control, and that appealed to me, called to that visceral part of me that wanted to claim her… and that simply would not do.

What are you doing, Parnell? I asked myself. I flopped the papers back in their file folder and propped my elbows on the desk. I breathed out and scrubbed my face with my hands, at total war between what I should and should not do here. It was a bad idea, letting her into my life, into my home, even if it was just to clean. A slippery slope, but one that was manageable with careful navigation. A double knock fell at the door, and before I could answer, it opened. Chrissy froze halfway through and dragged her keen eyes over my face.

"Rough case?" she asked, spying the folder on my desk. I flipped it closed before she could come near enough to see what was in it.

"Not exactly, what can I do for you?"

"Everything all right?" she asked, and I gave her a look. She raised her hand and the file folders she had in the other in surrender. Changing the subject completely she said, "There may be a problem with the Bardem search, the defense has filed a motion." I closed my eyes and pinched the bridge of my nose as she laid out the scenario, and for the time being, Allison Blaylock's problems were chased from my mind while I switched gears to deal with this.

It wasn't until I was packing up my briefcase at the end of the day that

I stumbled across her report again. I stared at my computer screen where her sad background glowed, and sighed. I hit print and waited for the high-capacity laser printer by the window to spit out the pages while I finished putting things into my Swiss backpack.

When it was done, I thrust the pages in the manila file folder, along with her handwritten background check, and shoved it into the backpack along with the legal folders I had to take with me.

I went down to the street, night rising from between the buildings and falling from the sky to meet somewhere in the middle. I was tired of compromising today. I needed something to eat, something to drink, and I wanted it in short order, so there was only one place for me to be. I hailed a cab and directed it to 1013 Muller St. in Old Town.

The 10-13 was busy, and I asked the hostess to direct me to one of the back booths for some privacy. Not only so I could go through some of the papers I'd brought with me, but also as a signal to any of the other Knights that I just wasn't in the mood tonight. Which, I had about a fifty-fifty shot of them actually paying attention to.

Skids came by and dropped an Old Fashioned on a bar napkin within my reach. I looked up at him from where I had been rooting in my backpack between files, looking for Ally's. I raised my eyebrows, asking without asking.

"You show up in a cab; I know you're drinkin'. Rough day, Prosecutor?"

"After a fashion," I responded, and waved a hand, inviting him to take a seat. He slid into the booth across from me, blue eyes sharp.

"Had an adventure of our own around these parts this morning," he said, with a smile and a hitched laugh.

"Oh yeah?" I eyed him, inviting him to tell his tale; usually, they were pretty good.

"Had a break-in," he said.

I scowled, "What, here? What'd they take?"

"That's just it, nothing! They were running from someone, came up through the basement hatch. You know Old Town, riddled with basement and subterranean tunnels."

"Dating back to Prohibition, right. I didn't think this place sat on top of one."

"Heh, shit yeah. Even *your* building has them."

He had a point. My building actually took advantage of one such old basement tunnel in that it opened up to an underground garage next door, behind my building. I had actually known that it was a Prohibition-era doorway into what had once been the basement of the building behind mine. It had been one of the interesting historical talking points when I'd bought the condo for myself.

"So, what happened?" I asked, and Skids shrugged.

"I let 'em through and called the real cops in."

I frowned, "How magnanimous of you." I meant it, too. Skids didn't just let people go like that. He raised his eyebrows and changed the subject.

"So, what about you? It ain't shop, I see." He nudged the plain manila file folder I set in front of me. Typically the files I laid out on the table were more of a maroon color, stamped on their label in bold red letters, '*Property of Indigo City's District Attorney's Office.*'

"What's the deal?" he asked when I didn't immediately launch into my day. I tilted my head and let it go. Whatever reason he had to give the people breaking in here passage was his own.

"I'm looking at hiring someone to clean my condo," I said.

"Eh?" He looked me up and down and nodded, asking, "Is she pretty?"

I scowled, "It's not like that. I won't even be home…"

"Ah huh… background check?" he asked and I slid the folder over to him without being asked. He looked through it, nodding to himself, scanning through the data there.

"Seems legit. I thought you had some kind of a service, though."

"Expendable." I dismissed the notion out of hand and took a sip of the drink.

He looked up and said, "Well, sounds like you've made up your mind."

I bobbed my head. "Looks like I have," I agreed, and stopped myself just short of thanking him. I mean, he didn't know he'd helped me decide by pointing out that I already had.

"Doesn't look much like she's got anyone aside from her grandma."

"She has a boss who cares."

"Friends?"

"That I don't know."

"So how is one little girl gonna move a whole apartment full of furniture?"

"Hadn't thought that far ahead, Skids."

"Bullshit, Yale. You think of everything."

Actually, I hadn't thought of that, but if I knew Skids, the problem would already be solved. That's the kind of community outreach the Indigo Knights was known for. I took a larger swig of my drink, savored it and swallowed without making a comment.

"Mm, you know what you'll have?" he asked, the subject tabled for now.

"Yeah."

I placed my order, and he went to put it in, leaving me in peace. Once a cop, always a cop. Skids didn't make it a habit of serving me personally when I came in like this. I must have been wearing a permanent frown. I passed a hand over my face and met my own dark eyes in the night-darkened glass of the window beside my booth.

With a sigh, I pulled out my personal phone and entered Ally's number from her background check application. I shot off a text.

You're hired. We will discuss the particulars tomorrow.

A few moments later, my phone buzzed, the screen lighting up with her number and a return message.

Thank you, Mr. Parnell… I really appreciate it.

I scowled at the message, not upset that she'd been polite, but not happy that she'd been desperate enough to accept the position without knowing any of the particulars. That wasn't safe.

You're one of the city's best ADA's; she knows that. ADA's are supposed to be the good guys.

Which was true, but then again, so were cops. Cops were supposed to be the good guys too, but the DA's office was well aware there were some really bad apples in among the ICPD.

I sighed as the waitress dropped my food off at my table, setting it down gently in front of me. I looked up and thanked her, and she smiled coyly, and it made me think of Ally again. When she smiled at me, it was shy, with no ulterior motives. While the light blush that I'd caught on her cheeks told me that she found me attractive, she seemed honest about it. Not likely to pursue it, though, and that appealed to me for a whole host of other reasons.

Shit. This may have been a bad idea. I took a deep breath and let it out slow, and resolved to see it through. I mean, I had already offered her the job. It wouldn't do to take it back, now.

I finished my meal and a second drink and caught a cab back to my apartment. I collapsed on my bed, intending to only lay there a moment before getting up and grabbing a shower before bed, but apparently, my exhausted mind had other plans. When I woke again, it was to the screeching of the alarm. I hadn't moved an inch.

4

*A*lly...

Mr. Parnell was hidden behind a much taller, much larger customer named Butch. Butch was in construction and had been here faithfully for the last two months while his work crew renovated a building a-block-and-a-half down from the café.

The look in Mr. Parnell's dark eyes made my heart both plummet and soar at the same time. Soar because I would be finding out more about the job, but it plummeted at the dark and tempestuous look in those very same eyes I could have stared into all day. They were just so beautiful.

He handed an envelope to me after placing his order and I tucked it into my apron pocket, then set to work making his drink. When I went to hand him his coffee, he paused and said, "Be at that address at six pm. If you can't make that time for whatever reason, please message me. You have my number."

"Yes, sir," I said quietly, and he froze for half a second, his eyes drifting shut. He swallowed hard, and I frowned.

"Is everything all right?" I asked.

"Yes. Just continue calling me Mr. Parnell," he said and I nodded.

"Of course. Thank you again for the opportunity, Mr. Parnell."

He smiled and inclined his head, and I started in on the next order, smiling at the next customer in line. It was the morning rush, and I spent the next hour too busy to read the card which was burning a hole in my pocket. When I finally did get a moment, it was only long enough for me to read it and thrust it right back into my apron pocket.

Ms. Blaylock,

Meet me in front of the Calvert building.

2246 Newsman Street

We will discuss the rate of payment and expectations upon your arrival.

-Damien Parnell

I nearly sagged with relief when the rush was over and immediately put in my headphones and called Dawnie, my best friend. She answered on the first ring.

"Well?"

"I have to meet him at six."

"Oh, so you still don't know anything yet?" she asked.

"Not yet," I picked up a bus-tub and went around the tables, picking up as we talked. "I told you, as soon as I know, you will know everything, I promise!"

"Girl, you better not hold out on me. I live vicariously through you." She gave a long-suffering sigh, and I felt for her. Dawnie had gone blind in a car accident when we were fourteen. Her dad had been drunk-driving and had nearly killed her. Her mom had never let him see Dawnie again. It'd been a brutal adjustment for her. She lived with her mom and stepdad and they were a happy family, but it was a hard-won happy.

Me? I had stuck by my friend, had never given up, even when she pushed me away. We were sisters, had been sisters since the first grade. You didn't give up on things like that, no matter how bad it got.

"So do you at least know how much you're getting paid?" she asked and I laughed.

"I don't know anything yet, other than I have to cancel on you so I can go to this meetup and find out and I feel really bad about –"

"Don't!" she cried. "Seriously, Ally. I understand. You can't do this all by yourself, and I will always be here. I mean, seriously, best friends forever means *forever*."

"I love you," I said, feeling more guilty, not less.

"I love you, too. Find out the details and call me immediately. I want to know everything."

"I'll tell you what I can," I promised.

"Like, all the gory details, Ally!"

I laughed, "Okay, like what could be gory about the DA office's best attorney?" I asked.

"I don't know; maybe he leaves skid marks in his underwear."

"Dawnie!"

"Oh, that's a thing. I mean what kind of underwear does he wear?"

"Dawnetta Marie! I am not telling you what kind of underwear my boss wears." I hissed and glanced around the café to make sure no one had heard me. Millie was laughing at me behind the counter, but the rest of the shop was empty.

She put on her best Yoda voice and said, "Mmm? Oh, you will; you will…"

"Right, okay, Yoda."

She nearly had me in stitches and I could hear her smiling when she said, "I'll see you soon, though?"

"I promise. We have a date at the city's talking book and braille library. Remember?"

"Yeeeah, I am really liking the talk-to-text feature on the Kindle you got me for Christmas. It's just a bitch I have to have somebody start it for me."

"I know, you would think they would have worked up something for the blind by now."

"Meh, a big company like that doesn't care about us," she declared, and I sighed.

We chatted for a little while longer and I managed to have the café cleaned up just in time for the lunch rush to start trickling in.

"I've got to go, Dawnie."

"Fine!" she declared, following a melodramatic sigh.

I pulled my headphones out of my ears and shoved them into my apron pocket, greeting the customer who had come in. "Hello! What can I get for you?"

"See you tomorrow!" Millie called, and I waved over my shoulder as I went out the door. I had looked up where the Calvert building was, surprised to find it on the nicer edge of Old Town, across the city. It would take three buses to get there, and I needed to leave from the café and go straight there. It was only two-thirty, and barring any catastrophes changing buses, it should only take forty-five minutes or so to get there.

Still, I would much rather be early than late. I didn't think Mr. Parnell would appreciate late.

5

*Y*ale…

I'd taken a cab that morning since my Mercedes was parked under the DA's office, and then had completely forgotten that it was there and had taken another cab home. It pulled up in front of the green carpet, under the matching green awning that was trimmed in gold, leading into my building. Clive, the doorman, opened the back door of the car for me. I stepped out, but my eyes were on Ally, sitting on one of the stone benches flanking the door.

"Mr. Parnell," Clive said with a nod.

"Hello, Clive. How long has she been here?"

"A little over two hours, sir. She said she had a six o'clock with you?"

"Yes. Yes, she does."

"Very good, sir."

The Calvert building was way above the pay-grade of a city-waged prosecuting attorney, but money hadn't been why I'd taken the job. I had money, in spades. Granted, it was mostly my father's money; when

I'd turned twenty-five, he'd put me on a sort of payroll-without-conditions. His companies ran themselves, and I got a pay-out that was far more than enough to live on even for the Calvert building.

I believed in living below my means, and for the fully-restored 1920's building to be below my means? Well, that gives you an idea of just how much money I had at my disposal on a monthly basis.

My father wasn't greedy. My mother, on the other hand, loved to threaten to get my father to stop handing me a free paycheck anytime I displeased her – which I believe I did just by virtue of drawing breath.

Ally had her headphones in her ears and was reading on some sort of tablet device intently. I took a moment to take her in and admitted to myself that this was, very likely, one of the worst ideas I had ever impulsively decided to follow through on, which was so very unlike me.

"Ms. Blaylock." I called and didn't receive any sort of answer. Clive and I exchanged a look of amusement before I strode up the green-carpeted walkway to put myself in front of her. My shadow fell on her, and she jumped, looking up guiltily from her e-reader.

"Sorry," she said, and popped the earbuds out of her ears. Music blared from them, and I raised an eyebrow.

"You're early," I declared.

"I'm sorry… it takes three buses to get here from the café; I didn't want to be late," she said defensively, coloring. I dismissed both the apology and the excuse and held out a hand. She took it, standing, and I gave it a firm but gentle shake.

"That's all right; I want to introduce you to Clive; he's the doorman for the Calvert building. Clive, meet Ms. Allison Blaylock. She will be cleaning my place. I will be giving her a key and access to my security system so that she may come and go as she pleases and as it fits her schedule."

"Pleasure to meet you, Miss Blaylock," Clive said politely and shook Ally's hand.

Ally smiled and said faintly, "Please, call me Ally."

Her shyness was absolutely adorable. As I watched the interaction, I realized how I, perhaps, took Clive's presence here for granted a bit, realizing that Ally and he were almost on the same level, both of them hard-working, blue-collar individuals. Clive smiled and returned his white-gloved hand to the back of the other, equally white glove, clasping his hands neatly in front of himself as his position with the building dictated.

"Come with me," I murmured, and Clive opened the polished, brass-handled, glass-and-wooden door for Ally and me.

She smiled at him and murmured a nervous, "Thank you," and Clive beamed.

"Not at all, miss."

I gave Clive a nod and followed her into the building's ornate lobby. She froze, open-mouthed, and I nearly crashed into her, stopping short so I wouldn't. I waited patiently for her to drink in all the brass and bronze. The walls glowed with a light golden paint past the fittings, the floor; a highly-polished honey oak parquet done in a chartreuse pattern.

Of course, the only reason I knew that was because the real estate agent I had secured my condo through had used it as one of her selling points. I resisted the urge to tell Ally, though she struck me as the kind of girl who would both appreciate and absorb the information like a sponge. I had watched and listened to her exchanges with other customers in line at the café, and she always seemed genuinely interested in what they had to say, especially if it was a piece of information she hadn't previously known.

Not why she's here, Parnell... Stick to the plan.

I moved to the ornate stairs leading to the second floor and started up them. I preferred them to the old elevators by virtue of being somewhat of a fitness junkie. I had expected her to follow, but she was transfixed, her gaze thirsty for the beautiful things inside its reach. I let myself get nearly halfway up the staircase before I stopped and watched her look. Still, the spell must be broken; regrettably, I didn't have all night, although I could surely watch her look at the building's lobby for that long and more.

She held such a beautiful and whimsical innocence to her and it exacerbated the urge to open her eyes to new things, darker things that held no less beauty to them, all the more. I frowned at myself, I couldn't help it; and before I could stop myself, I called down to her.

"Ms. Blaylock, if you will come this way?"

She shook herself as if waking from a beautiful dream and looked up at me sharply. She blushed, flustered and stammered out yet another apology and said, "Of course, I'm coming right now."

She moved up the stairs with a feline grace that I secretly took pleasure in watching and when she was but two steps below me, I turned and put myself into motion again. I bypassed the landing on the second floor, taking the switchback to the next set of stairs leading to the third floor.

Ally drifted up behind me nearly silently, following me along the hall, our footsteps hushed on the thick forest-green carpet with golden trim along the polished wood baseboards. She stopped with me at the heavy, dark wooden door under the Art Deco stained-glass light. Matching stained-glass sconces flared upwards like torches on the walls to either side of every door along the corridor, each portal labeled with bronze number plaques. Mine happened to be '3A.'

I held out a ring with two keys on it to Ally; she blinked those brilliant green eyes and reached out a hand, grasping them lightly. I didn't let go of the ring, not just yet.

"You can come whenever it is convenient for you. I will leave an envelope with money on the dining room table. One hundred dollars a week for you, plus more for whatever incidentals you may need. Cleaning supplies, for the dry cleaning, et cetera. Do you understand and agree to these terms?"

She blinked and nodded dumbly for a moment, in total shock and surprise, before her voice caught up and she said, "Yes! Absolutely."

I turned back to my door and stuck the key in the top lock, sliding back the bolt. I did the same to the lock in the doorknob, and, with no hesitation, opened it for the both of us, letting her into my home, my private space, my sanctuary.

6

*A*lly…

His apartment was a near-seamless blend of the 1920's décor of the building and the convenience and sleek lines of the modern day. The hardwood floors were deep, dark, and rich; the floor plan open. I turned to address the keening beep flowing from a little silver control panel on the wall behind the door as Mr. Parnell waved me forward to look.

"The code is 092715, but you press this first," he said indicating a button with a shield symbol on it. I scrambled through my purse at my hip.

"I should write all of this down; I'm not familiar with alarm systems."

"Don't bother," he said. "I've taken the liberty of doing it for you, but you need to commit the code to memory, now. I won't have it written anywhere."

"What is it?"

"Zero-nine-two-seven-fifteen," he repeated, and I frowned.

"A date, it's a date... I don't want to pry, but it might help me remember if I knew –"

He held up a hand and nodded, "That's fair. It's the date a friend of mine died in the line of duty; it was his birthday."

"Oh, a police officer?"

"Fire," he said shortly, and I shut my mouth.

"Oh-nine, twenty-seven; fifteen." I repeated solemnly. His gaze remained cold but he nodded, and I realized it was so he would never forget. So he would remember, even subconsciously, every day. That was deep, but then again, I always suspected that he'd had hidden depths to him. It was part of his mysterious appeal, I guess.

"What would you like me to do?" I asked.

"I've put that in writing as well. Come with me; I'll show you around."

Truthfully, I could see most of the apartment from where we stood. Straight ahead as you came through the door, the dining room table stood on a fancy, big, red-and-gold scrollwork area rug. The table was massive, seating eight people. To the right of it was the kitchen. Four tall barstools, all sturdy wooden legs and rich, padded black leather seats, were tucked up under the high granite breakfast bar.

The kitchen alone, with its cool gray glass-tile backsplash and modern stainless steel appliances, was easily the size of the entire kitchen, living room, and dining room of my gran's two-bedroom apartment combined. To the left of the table was a living room area: a deep brown leather couch against the bank of windows, the back of a wingback leather chair faced the dining room at one end of the heavy, dark wood coffee table. The chair had a matching ottoman and faced the television and heavy wooden entertainment center against the brick wall. The television felt larger than a movie theatre screen to me, and was easily visible from the kitchen stove.

To the left, recessed into a nook, was a wooden desk, large, heavy, and old in that 1920's style, the wood glowing and lighter than the rest of the apartment. There was a step up – to reach it and the surrounding filing cabinets surrounding it – also made of the same rich, glowing wood. The only modern concession to the look was the laptop dock on its surface and once again, the design was perfect; everything modern and old fitting into their own spaces. Even though the floor plan was so open, it felt as if everything was its own room with walls like I was accustomed to; each space had its own personality.

He stood, stock-still, behind me as I ranged cautiously into the center of it all, turning slowly, taking it all in and I felt star-struck. It probably looked completely unprofessional, but I had never been in the center of anything so posh or so nice, not even standing in the middle of furniture displays in the store.

"You have a very lovely home," I said nervously, suddenly self-conscious.

He smiled, and it reached all the way into his eyes and put my heart at ease. I was struck by how he managed to do that with one look, and it caused me to give a tentative answering smile of my own, "Thank you, Ms. Blaylock. This way and I will show you the rest."

He jerked his head past what I presumed to be a closet or pantry and down a hall to the right, past the kitchen. Behind the kitchen, on the left down the hall, was a small guest bathroom – just a toilet and sink, and a narrow, glassed-in shower past them both. It didn't look like it received much use. In fact, I spied some plaster dust in the corner of the shower and realized that it probably had never been used. The toilet and sink were tidy and clean, but could use some attention and the towel on the towel bar could stand to be changed.

Past the little closet door were some massive, shuttered folding doors on rails. He opened them for me, to reveal the front-loading washer and dryer and a shelving unit to the left of them that was fairly spartan, save for the home's linens on one set of shelves. The other set of shelves contained toilet paper, paper towels, laundry detergent and the like. It was pretty barren of the other cleaning supplies I would expect to be there, but before I could ask, Mr. Parnell was speaking.

"I will give you an allowance to start for cleaning supplies. I appear to be rather limited. Don't bother with anything bargain-basement, unless it's something that you know works, and works well. I prefer my home clean."

I didn't let his words sting. After all, they weren't geared towards my status as one of the city's working poor. My gran liked our apartment clean too, and I had learned plenty of things from her, old-time things that got the job done with fantastic results and at an affordable price. Some of those things could clean twice as well as the biggest and best brand-name cleaners without nearly as many chemicals.

Past the guest bathroom was the guest bedroom, which also looked as if it had never been used. I made a mental note to get in here and give it a thorough dusting, even though it didn't look like it was too bad, but I didn't have too much time to assess because he was already closing the door, and we were off to the door set into the wall at the very end of the hall. He opened it into the very spacious master bedroom.

Cool gray walls, deep dark wood that gleamed, and a bed that was the size of my entire bedroom back home. The furniture was all very modern, and there was a walk-in closet across the plush, thick carpet to the right and a dark, open doorway set in the wall to the left, leading into a spacious master bathroom.

The bathroom was incredible, the shower as big as my kitchen at home and lined on two sides with gray river-stone tiles, some long, some square, all grouted together. The other two walls out into the room were clear tempered glass and it looked like a massive undertaking to keep clean.

The vanity was meant for two and there was a deep bathtub that looked more like a hot tub, with jets and all, in the corner beyond the vanity. This was easily going to be the room that took me the most time and effort.

"I may need to come twice a week," I murmured.

"Would you require more pay?"

"What? No! No, no… that wasn't what I was saying at all. It's just so much bigger than I imagined."

"Twice a week would be fine if that is what you require."

"I can come Mondays and Fridays, after my shift at the café."

"As I said, whenever is convenient for you. I more than likely won't be home."

I was vaguely disappointed by that, but didn't let on. I smiled and said, "I'll get started this Friday if you'd like."

"That would be fine. I will leave your money on the table. For now," he pulled his wallet out of the back pocket of his suit pants and opened it, shelling out two crisp one-hundred-dollar bills, "this should get you the supplies you need. You needn't worry about receipts or change."

He held out the money to me, and an odd sort of anxiety flitted in my chest. I don't think I had ever held such high-denomination bills in my life. The amount, close to it, yes, but in twenties. I mean, Millie did the deposits at the café.

"It's not going to bite you, Ms. Blaylock," he said gently. I swallowed hard and took it.

"I'm sorry, I'm just nervous, I guess… I'm not used to people just handing me that kind of money."

He smiled. "I find you trustworthy. That trust is not misplaced, is it?" he asked and I felt my eyes go wide.

"No!"

He chuckled, and I realized he was actually teasing me. I blushed, and he laughed outright. It was a good sound, light and airy and he said, "I'm sorry," and I knew he meant it.

"It's all right."

"May I give you a ride home? It's getting late."

The sun was beginning to set, the days growing longer. I shook my head, suddenly very embarrassed by the prospect of him seeing where I lived. I mean, I know he knew, I'd had to put it on my background-check application, but knowing and seeing the deplorable, shabby conditions of my building and neighborhood were two different things.

"Oh, no, thank you. I'll be fine."

"At least let me hail you a cab," he said, and I thought about how much money I carried. I did the math in my head, trying to figure out if I could afford one and he saw me do it I think because he smiled and said, "My treat."

I pursed my lips and nodded, and we went back out into the living area. He stopped and reached into the side of his briefcase and handed me a manila folder with a sheaf of papers inside.

"How to disable the alarm, plus other incidentals and peculiarities of mine."

"Oh, okay." I took the folder and clutched it to my chest, the money all but burning a real, physical hole in my pocket.

We went downstairs and he had Clive hail a cab for me. As I got in, he leaned in the door and said, "If you need help carrying supplies, have Clive call Jimmy, the building steward, to help you."

"Oh, you have one of those too?" I asked and immediately wanted to clap a hand over my mouth. In fact, I did and closed my eyes. He laughed again and I uncovered my mouth and said: "I am so sorry, that didn't come out right at all!"

I felt my face flame, and he replied, "It's all right Ms. Blaylock. Until Friday." He shut the door and I think I heard him mutter something about my being adorable and I felt a resurgence of heat in my cheeks as the cab pulled away from the curb.

The curb at which Mr. Parnell stood, hands in his pockets, until I was no longer in sight.

~

"Seriously?" Dawnie asked, one hand on the handle of the shopping cart as I wheeled it along the aisle. Her cane was clutched to her chest in the other hand.

"It was in the papers he gave me. He says he's a very private person and asked I not share anything about his habits with anyone. He also said it was a matter of his personal safety, which he's a prosecutor, so I can believe that."

"So you're not going to give me *anything*, not even as your best friend in the whole wide world?" she asked, but her voice was half teasing.

I laughed and said, "I'll give you this, his apartment is like one entire side of the building, and the lobby was gorgeous. Seriously. It was like three, maybe even four, of our apartments combined!"

"Wow," she said.

I wished she could have seen it for herself, but I would never, ever say as much out loud. She sighed and said, "Tell me more about how hot your boss is. I mean, you already told me once before, so it's not like you're giving out any new information. I do love my re-reads of my favorite stories, so this is no different."

I laughed, putting a bin of laundry detergent pods, the kind his washing machine took, into the cart. Sighing, I reluctantly agreed with a long, mock-suffering, "Okay…"

I completed the shopping I needed to do and we went to the checkout, both of us dissolving into peals of laughter. The girl behind the counter rang me up and said, "Okay, your total is $132.08."

I swallowed hard and handed over the two one hundred dollar bills, and she tested them with that pen for counterfeit. I couldn't blame her, I mean, my clothes, while not shabby, were from the local discount fashion store and cheaply made. I felt self-conscious but tried not to let it show. Dawnie held around my arm after I took the change and the girl asked, "You want your receipt with you or in the bag?"

"With me, please."

She handed it over, and I wrapped it around the money and put it in an empty pocket of my purse. Dawnie held my arm and carried some of the bags with me in the other hand.

"You should totally take me out to dinner with the change," she said, and I made an exasperated sound.

"I can't," I said. She smiled and turned her head, chin tilting slightly up in that way she'd acquired after losing her sight, a cross between listening to what I had to say and a signal, to me, that said she wouldn't hear it.

"Look, I shouldn't even be taking you with me to drop this stuff off!" I cried.

"I said I would stay downstairs, not like I can see where we're going, either," she said dryly. I was silent too long and she laughed, "Oh come *on*, Ally-cat! You said there was a bench and a doorman out front. You're going to be what? Twenty minutes, tops?"

"Maybe a half an hour, I have to put all this stuff away. It's not like I can just drop it on his dining room table until tomorrow."

"I'll be fine. Set me up on an audio book and do your thing, sister."

We went out to the street and up the block to the bus to wait, laughing and talking. I was uneasy. The city could be a dangerous place, and two young girls, one of them blind, hampered by a bunch of heavy grocery bags were a prime target out here. The bus came and we were on a route that would take us to Mr. Parnell's street, dropping us a block away. I'd plotted the route carefully, and was grateful I could not only spend time with Dawn but to have the help schlepping this stuff to the Calvert building's front door.

We got off the bus and had a block to walk: half a block to the corner, then half a block more to the Calvert building's door. Clive greeted me when we were within calling-out distance with, "Ms. Blaylock! Back so soon?"

"Uh, yeah! I had to buy some supplies and bring them. Clive, this is my best friend, Dawnie. Is it all right if she sits on one of the benches here with you while I run upstairs?"

"Sure, sure!" He eyed my best friend up and down and smiled, "Pleasure to meet you, miss."

"Likewise," Dawnie said, and let her cane unfold, letting my arm go.

"Oh, hey! Why don't we put these down over here, Jimmy's helping Ms. Fournier right now, but as soon as he comes down, I'll have him bring these up to Mr. Parnell's." He took Dawn's bag and she followed the sound of his voice as he went over to the bench and set the bags down off to one side. He was kind to her, putting his gloved hand under hers and saying for her benefit, "Turn right here, that's it, and sit down. Good, good!"

I smiled and standing near the jovial older gentleman and my bestie said, "I'll be down as soon as I can. Do you want me to hook you up?" I asked.

"Nah, I think I'll keep Clive here company. I'm sure he has some stories to tell." Clive smiled and nodded, realized she couldn't see it and said, "That I do! Let me get the door for you, Ms. Blaylock."

"Ally, please!" I said laughing, and he chuckled.

"Force of habit, Ally. My apologies."

"Thank you," I said, slipping past him into the lobby, calling out to Dawnie, "Be back in a minute!"

"Take your time," she called back, "Clive's got me covered!"

I laughed and had to admit since she lost her sight, Dawnie had a way with people. She was shrewd before, even at fourteen, but now? It was like she had a radar, a sixth sense about people. Like she detected their energy or something. Her instant liking to Clive told me something I already knew. He was good people and a nice man. I would have to do something to say thank you for looking out for her while I got this done.

I hauled as many of the bags as I could up the stairs to the third floor and went to Mr. Parnell's door and unlocked it. Stepping inside, I stopped at the panel, realizing the alarm had already been deactivated. I heard his voice from his study area a moment later.

"Hold on a moment; someone is here." He peeked around the corner and I waved my hand in a halfhearted wave. He held up a finger, asking me to give him a moment. I brought the bags in that I'd set down out in the hall to unlock the door and held them up, waving them in the direction of the pantry. He nodded and went back to his call.

I shut the door, drifting up the hallway to the linen closet and laundry, sliding open the doors. I worked quickly to put everything away neatly in an order I liked and heard his smart dress shoes clicking up the hall. I leaned back to see him.

"I'm sorry," I said. "I didn't mean to interrupt; I just will need this stuff for tomorrow."

"Don't apologize," he said.

I fished in my little purse at my hip, the strap crossways over my chest and body. I came up with the receipt and change from my purchases and held it out. He curled his hand around mine, pressing the paper and coins into my palm firmly, but not painfully.

"I told you to keep that," he said.

My heart seized in my chest; he was close. Stepping into my personal space with the action and I swallowed hard. Not because I was intimidated by him, though there was a slight touch of that, too. It was more because I *liked* having him this close. The moment was dispelled by a knock at the door.

"That must be the rest of the bags," I breathed, "and thank you," I said, unwilling to reject the money a second time. "I can take Dawnie to our favorite noodle shop to make up for not spending time together yesterday."

He stepped back with a nod and went to the door, but his eyes had hardened and turned chill in the light cast from the laundry area. I swallowed hard; had I said something to upset him? I couldn't for the life of me fathom what.

I went out to the front door, stuffing the money in my jacket pocket this time, and reached for the bags Mr. Parnell had taken from the mysterious 'Jimmy', who turned out to be a gentleman even older than Clive, who I thought was somewhere in his fifties or sixties. Jimmy was a black man, his brown eyes cloudy and almost tinged blue in that way older people sometimes got. He smiled and said, "You all have a nice night, now."

"Thank you, Jimmy," Mr. Parnell said kindly and I felt so guilty.

"I didn't realize that was Jimmy," I said. "He was busy helping someone else when I arrived."

"And?" Mr. Parnell asked, perplexed.

"And if I'd known, I would have run right back down to get them," I said. Mr. Parnell smiled.

"Jimmy has been with this building since before time, Ally. He's still here because he wants to be here and none of us have the heart to make him retire. He likes to help; this place gives him purpose."

I considered what he was saying, twisting my lips in indecision. Finally, I nodded. I took the bags from him, and he let me, saying, "I need to return that call, you can see yourself out?" he asked and I nodded. "Have a nice dinner," he said and I swear I could detect a hint of displeasure, that he had forced the pleasantry out.

"Thank you," I said faintly.

I rushed to finish putting everything away and slid the doors on to the laundry room closed. I blinked, something just dawning on me, and slid the doors open again. "How cool," I murmured to myself and slid the doors closed. The recessed lights in the ceiling above everything turned out, like a refrigerator. I hadn't realized they'd done that.

I jammed the bags into the trash can under the sink labeled recycling, closed those doors, grateful that he'd laid things out in great detail in his written instructions as to where everything was and how he liked things done. I peeked around the corner into his recessed office space and raised a hand, curling my fingers in goodbye. He was scowling at whatever the person on the other end of the line was saying and gave me a curt nod.

I backed out silently and beat a hasty retreat to the door, letting myself out. When I got back downstairs, Clive was laughing at something Dawnie had said, his white gloved hands clutching his belly beneath his dark green coat, with its gold trim and twin rows of brass buttons. I opened the door, and he jumped, looked startled and rushed to hold it open for me.

"It's fine," I said and he shook his head.

"No, Miss. It's my job."

I smiled and nodded graciously, saying, "Then I'd best get Dawnie out of here before she gets you into any real trouble."

Clive grinned, and Dawnie got up her white, red-tipped cane unfurling. "Homeward bound?" she asked and I smiled.

"Actually, I can afford dinner after all. Noodle shop?"

"Ooo, yeah! You're on, Sister."

"I'll see you tomorrow, Clive."

"I look forward to it, Miss Ally."

I smiled; I supposed 'Miss Ally' was an improvement from 'Ms. Blaylock' and I would take it.

Dawnie and I drifted up the sidewalk, back towards the bus stop. She heaved a melodramatic sigh and said, "Spill it, girlfriend."

I smiled, "I'm not sure," I said.

"About what?"

I looked up and back at the building one of the windows on the third floor held an indistinct figure and I paused. Was he watching us? I dismissed the notion. I probably had the wrong set of windows.

"I don't know," I said honestly. "It was almost like he was upset I was taking you to dinner."

She laughed at me and asked, "How did you phrase it?"

"What?"

"How did you say it? 'I'm taking my best friend, the Queen of my universe, my absolute soul sister, out to a fabulous dinner of her favorite pho in the whole wide world' or 'I'm taking my friend Dawnie to dinner?'"

"I don't know, does it matter?" I said when I could catch my breath from laughing. That was Dawnie, ostentatious as always.

"Oh, it matters. Seriously, think about it."

I did and finally said, "The latter, I think."

She got all excited and squealed as we reached the bus stop, "Oooh, your new boss has the hots for you!" she declared.

"What are you, nuts?" I cried.

"Not at all," she said. "Girl, you tell a man 'I'm taking Dawnie to dinner,' they don't hear 'Dawnie' and picture a hot blind chick. They hear "Donnie" and picture Donnie Wahlberg. Dude got pissy because he was jealous."

I scoffed at the notion. "You've been reading way too many Timber Philips novels," I said.

"They don't come in braille; she's indie published. I listen to her books; she has them in actual audio now. So much hotter than the mechanical voice."

I rolled my eyes and said, "Bus is coming."

"Excellent. Favorite noodles here we come!"

I loved my crazy best friend.

7

*Y*ale…

I checked my phone after court, and there was a text message from Ally…

Mr. Parnell, I have to move this weekend, would it be all right if I came Wednesday or Thursday rather than Friday?

I sighed and felt my shoulders drop. She didn't know how appealing it was that she asked permission for just about everything, even things I had already told her time and again. I felt my return text was a little short to her when I said, **at your convenience still applies, Ms. Blaylock.**

I put my phone away and moved through the courthouse lobby, across the marble mosaic compass set into the floor, and a little bit of something – guilt, maybe? crept in. I stopped just inside the doors and pulled out my phone.

My apologies for the abrupt reply. I have been very busy. Not much time to spare today.

My phone buzzed in my hand near immediately, and I read the message, **I'm sorry to bother you, the good news is that the only part of my address to change will be the apartment number. Mr. Comey, the super, found me a studio.**

I wasn't sure what she wanted from me, and I realized that perhaps it was some kind of approval, which made me want her with a savage ache. There wasn't much more alluring than the sense of power that gave me. I let out a breath and rolled my shoulders and neck to rid myself of the sudden tension there.

That's good, very good.

She'd been working for me, officially, for two weeks now. I received text alerts on my phone every time she disabled the alarm, and the first night, when I had come home, the entire apartment had felt lighter, the air fresh and clean. I had stood in my entryway, eyes closed, breathing in deeply, trying to catch the subtle scent of her perfume among the disinfectant scent of cleaner.

I had gone from room to room inspecting her work, pleased beyond measure that she had executed all of my demands, some pithy, some not, to absolute perfection. I'd sat sipping whiskey for an hour or two, imagining her moving through my space, soaking in the ghost of her presence and fighting my so-called perverted urges. You can't always stop your imagination from taking you places, and resistance had definitely been futile that first night.

Back at my office, I checked my phone once more to see her last text message…

Thanks, it may take me all weekend, but I'll get it figured out!

She'd meant the message to be upbeat and plucky, it was who she was, after all, but I read it as something else entirely… I read *I'm alone, I'm a little scared, I don't know how I am going to move it all by myself.*

I pursed my lips and didn't reply. Tonight was the club meeting at the 10-13, and I – maybe– had a solution.

~

"I have something," I said when we were all seated around the table. The ride here had definitely helped, and I realized I was in need of some real wind therapy, a much longer ride, very soon.

"Oh yeah?" Skids asked. "What's up?"

"The girl I hired, she's moving this weekend." I frowned. "I am under the impression that she has little to no help."

"What girl?" Oz demanded, scowling at me.

Youngblood was grinning, "You totally hired the coffee shop girl, didn't you?"

"I did; she needed the help, and I felt I was in a position to pay some kindness forward." My remarks were cool, and he grinned.

"Where she moving from, to?" Oz asked.

"A two-bedroom in the Point Side project building to a studio in the same building."

"Hoo, Point Side? That's not a good place for anybody."

"She grew up there," Skids remarked. "Kind of amazing she's stayed out of trouble."

"She's tenacious," I agreed.

"So, boys, who's up for some community outreach this weekend?" Skids asked.

"There's a slight problem," I said, shifting uncomfortably. "As her boss, I don't feel it would be appropriate that I go."

"Aw, hell, didn't expect you to," Reflash chimed in. "That would just be… weird."

"Reflash is right," Skids said. "If it were one of our employees," he looked out of the glassed-in box over the busy floor of his restaurant and bar outside, "I'd do the same thing. Ask for help, but stay the fuck out of it. Some lines shouldn't be crossed."

I was relieved to have allies on the matter in the president and vice-president but didn't expect to escape the reminder that I would owe the brothers who went to help. Youngblood killed two birds with one stone for me.

"Call us even for all your help with Chrissy and I'm in." He winked at me and I gave him a stiff nod.

"Shoot, I ain't got nothing planned," Oz chipped in.

"Wish I could, but I'm on shift," Golden griped, and Angel, his twin, echoed the sentiment.

"I don't think she needs all of us," Skids said. "I'll go, the bar is pretty dead during the day on a Saturday. As long as I'm back in time for the evening rush, I'm good."

"It's a girl and an old lady's two bedroom apartment. Where is the rest of her shit supposed to go?" Oz asked.

I shook my head and shrugged, glancing at Backdraft, who had a sour look on his face. "What's the matter with you?" I demanded.

"Is it bad I'd rather move a strange girl's shit rather than do what I'm supposed to be doing on Saturday?"

"Depends on what you're supposed to be doing," Blaze said.

Backdraft sighed. "Torrid and I are trying to sort our shit out. We're supposed to go for a ride and maybe hit up one of the local farmers' markets or something."

"Eugh," Oz made a noise and visibly cringed. Backdraft scowled and opened his mouth to say something but Skids cut him off.

"I think Youngblood, Oz, and myself will be plenty. Don't want to overwhelm her."

"Thank you," I said, and we moved on to the next order of business.

The meeting felt like it dragged, and by the time it was over, despite how grateful I was to my brothers for their help, I just couldn't wait to get back out to my bike and ride home. Youngblood came around and knocked his shoulder into mine.

"You good, Yale?"

"Yeah, I'm good."

He chuckled, "Liar, what's going on, brother?"

"Between you and me? Definitely can't get back to Chrissy."

Youngblood frowned and searched my face. Finally, he nodded slowly. I sighed and stated bluntly, "I want her."

"Chrissy?" he asked scowling.

"No, dumbass! Ally."

He looked surprised for a second and then his brow crushed down. I huffed a little bit of a laugh and said to him, "Exactly."

"That's on you, brother… you're part of the system, hell, your whole world – it's not like ours. You don't have the same kind of luxuries that we're afforded."

"Tell me about it," I said, and he shook his head.

"Be careful," he admonished, and I nodded.

"Always am."

I knew precisely what he meant. I wasn't just a prosecuting attorney for Indigo City; I was also one of the wealthy set. We were under a microscope, not only for corruption of any kind but also any image of sexual impropriety. I was a fucking deviant on the inside, never felt freer than when I had a beautiful woman under my control. The sweeter, and more innocent, the better… but I was Ally's boss, her employer, and that fell under current sexual harassment laws. But by some older laws, it could, given the circumstances – me being in a position of power over her – be considered a statutory rape charge. If the wrong people with the right kind of hard-on for me got wind of it, there would be a lot more than just my job at stake. My reputation, my entire livelihood as a prosecutor, could and, most likely, *would* go up in smoke.

If I went anywhere with Ally, I had better ensure she was trustworthy – implicitly so. Which is precisely why I shouldn't go there. Why I wouldn't be going anywhere near that girl, no matter how much she lit a fire inside me when she looked at me with those hallowed green eyes.

8

*A*lly…

A knock fell at my door, and I got up from the living room floor where I was wrapping the last of the dishes and boxing them. I opened it, expecting Mr. Comey but that wasn't who was on the other side. My eyes widened and I went to slam the door shut, but the big biker stuck his booted foot in the way.

"Ms. Ally Blaylock?" he asked, and I stammered out a careful, "Y-y-yes?"

"We're the movers." A bald black man with wraparound sunglasses, in the same imposing leathers, said from behind him.

"Movers?" I squeaked.

"Relax, honey. We're police," the third man, probably between the two in age, with kind blue eyes, said to me.

"The police?"

"Yeah, the police. We're here to help you move."

I frowned, and let my natural suspicion of my surroundings prod me into asking, "Can I see a badge or some ID or something?"

The younger white guy pulled out his badge and showed it to me, Tony McCormick, a homicide detective. The other two pulled out identification cards. The black man, Hector Jones, his ID said he was a correctional officer with the ICPD city jail, while the oldest man was an ICPD retiree.

"Don't you be callin' us by those names, either," the black man said as he took his ID back. "I'm Oz, that's Skids, and this here is Youngblood."

"How did you know I was moving?" I asked, and Skids said gently, "Best have that conversation inside if you don't mind?"

I nodded and wished that Dawnie were with me; she would know if these men were trustworthy or not, but for now… I opened the door and let them in, but then I kept the door open to the hall and stayed near it.

When they passed me, I saw the backs of their leather vests, and something about the design, the knight's chess piece picked out in indigo thread against a silver shield background, tickled my memory. Whatever it was, it set me further at ease because I remembered seeing it, and I remembered that wherever I'd seen it, I hadn't felt frightened.

"So, where is all this stuff going?" Oz demanded.

"Um, some of it is going to storage in the basement, some of it to the new apartment on the sixth floor."

"Shit, we gotta take all them damn stairs?" he asked.

"No, Mr. Comey said I could use the freight elevator."

"Okay," Skids said, "Where's that at and where did you want us to start?"

"Allison, are you okay?"

I jumped and whirled, Mr. Comey startling me. Dawnie had a hand in the crook of his elbow and said, "Woah, who's in here with you, Ally? Two of them smell great."

I laughed nervously and squeaked out, "Um, three men from the Indigo Knights motorcycle club?"

"Shut the front door!" Dawnie cried.

"We're here to help get this stuff moved," Skids said behind me, and Dawnie cocked her head.

"Oh yeah, who sent you?" she demanded.

"A friend, that's all you girls need to know," Oz said curtly. Dawnie frowned and said, "And what about you? Dude with the girlfriend. She's got a nice perfume."

Youngblood laughed, "Here to help."

"Uh huh…" she pondered a minute and sighed, "You look at their ID?"

"Yes, of course!" I answered.

"And?"

"I think they're legit, Dawnie."

"Her boss is an ADA, you know."

I blinked, long and slow, and realized where I had seen the logo on the back of their jackets. It'd been hanging in Mr. Parnell's hall closet.

"I think they know that," I said abruptly. "They're the police."

"Oh, well… The police don't necessarily equate good things in the Point Side," she reminded me.

"No, seriously, Dawnie, it's fine now." The three men exchanged a look and Dawnie, ever on the defensive when it came to outsiders said, "Okay, girlfriend… Spill."

"I can't," I said pointedly, and she got it right away.

"Oh… *oh!* In that case, where are we starting, Mr. Comey? I'm your lead stupid-visor!"

The guys laughed a little and I blushed furiously. I think they knew I'd figured out where they came from, but why wouldn't they say? It was another strange kindness Mr. Parnell had done for me, and I didn't know why.

I didn't get to think about it, either. We had a lot of work to be done and a lot of stuff to move, the vast majority of it being my grandmother's furniture to the basement. Her bedroom, most of the living room, and the dining room set all had to go. I just had room for my cast iron daybed, the television and its stand, and one tall dresser in the single-room little studio downstairs.

I had been slowly moving boxes down there and stacking them. At the last minute, I decided that one of the tall book cases *would* fit, and the guys were nice enough to go all the way back down to the basement to get it for me.

Mr. Comey was kind and no one judged when I cried at having to let this place go. I mean, I had grown up my entire life in this little apartment; just me and my gran for the most part.

"It's okay, Ally Cat," Dawnie whispered, hugging me tightly.

"I know, goodbyes are just hard."

"Well, you ever need anything else, you call one of us, okay?" Youngblood asked, and he, Oz, and Skids all handed me their individual business cards with their contact information.

I nodded, and Dawnie said, "Cool, thanks, now, no offense, but try not looking like cops when you get out of here. The last thing we need is anybody thinkin' Ally Cat's a snitch."

"Dawnie, don't be rude!" I snapped.

"Look at them; I'm sure they get it."

I did, and they all traded guilty looks. I smiled half-heartedly and Oz said, "I grew up on a block just like this. I *do* get it. Come on boys. Skids, you're buyin' our lunch."

Skids laughed and said, "Reflash is fixing us all food, come on down to the 10-13."

"Thank you all so much," I said and they each took my hand and nodded and left, out my tiny studio's front door.

"They're good people, but we live around a whole lot of people who *aren't*," Dawnie said, worriedly. I looked at Mr. Comey who scratched the back of his balding, gray fringed head, his thick gray mustache twitching as he twisted his lips back and forth.

"She's right, Ally."

"The cops aren't the bad guys though," I murmured.

"We know that, but the ones who cause trouble?" He waved his hands back and forth, "They'll cause it and make us the victims, guilt by association, you know how it is."

I did, and it made me tired.

"It was nice to have the help, but if they want to hang out or whatever? They should do it at that cop bar in Old Town." Dawnie shuddered.

"I didn't know they were coming," I murmured, suddenly feeling like they were mad at me for the men's presence.

"No, I know, girl... but you don't need anyone around here figuring out who you're working for; it could bring a whole gang of trouble to your door."

"Right, you're right."

She sighed, "I've harped on you enough. Let me get used to moving around this place…"

I smiled, "I want to get some of this put away."

"Cool, Mr. Comey, thanks for everything, but I'm kicking you out. This is officially girl time."

Mr. Comey laughed and said, "Okay, girls… Dawnetta, remember, you are on the sixth floor, now. You must find the stairwell and go up, not down."

"Thanks for the reminder. I'm making Ally walk me the first couple of times."

"I'd be happy to."

9

*Y*ale…

"I thought for sure you'd be here waiting for a full report," Youngblood said jokingly, through the receiver. I leaned back against my bike and answered.

"Nah, I wanted to be there, but I needed to get out of the city at the same time."

"So where you at?" he asked.

"Burnside's Bridge."

"Jesus!"

"Yeah, I need to head back."

"Good thing it's Saturday, you got most of tomorrow if you're gonna recover from that ride."

"Yeah."

"Yale?"

"What?"

I was staring sightlessly at the picturesque bridge; the light hadn't begun to fail yet, but it would, soon… I really should get back.

"You need to make the leap, my brother. You're torturing yourself."

"I can't, Youngblood. There are too many reasons why."

"You don't, you're gonna make some kind of a piss-poor decision in the moment."

"I believe I've already done that by hiring her."

"Then fire her."

"I can't do that, she needs the money and she won't just take it, she's not a charity case. Work, I could see her doing; handouts, I could not."

"Tell me about it. She gave us a hell of a runaround when we got there, but I'm pretty sure she put two and two together, man. I could see it click, and then there was no more resistance. She fell right in line and let us help."

"Shit," I muttered.

"She's a smart girl, Yale. She was bound to figure it out."

"Right; well, I'll deny it."

"Dude, you're a big fuckin' boy. You'll figure this shit out. Just know it doesn't matter what you do or what happens, we're here for you. That's how this whole thing works."

"Yeah!" I heard Oz in the background, and I chuckled.

"You shut up!" I fired one of his signature lines back at him.

Youngblood laughed and said, "Ride safe, brother. See you next week."

"Yeah, thanks. Next week for sure."

We said our much shorter final farewell and I hung up the phone, returning my gaze to the idyllic scene in front of me: the old stone bridge, the water beneath it reflecting the sky. I sighed and pressed my fingertips into my eyes, rubbing before standing up. I turned back to my Harley Softail Deluxe and pulled on my gloves. I let out a hard, frustrated rush of breath before putting on my helmet with its full face mask and sitting astride the bike. The tank was a silky matte black and deep blue, the same with the tailpipes. I didn't go for a lot of shiny chrome or flash. I liked keeping my profile low and my private life private.

I'd already taken a risk in trusting Ally with my privacy, but a risk that to date seemed to be well-founded. She had followed my instructions to the letter and I appreciated that.

Good behavior should be rewarded...

The inner voice was from the darkest part of me, and I resolutely ignored it. There was a difference between privacy and intimacy. A vast one. Still, I don't think a day went by where I didn't picture her nude and spread beneath me. It was wrong, for certain, but what would be really wrong would be acting on those urges. I leaned the bike up, heeled the kickstand back into place, and started the bike all in one smooth motion.

The rushing pavement did nothing to soothe me like it usually did: the wind, which normally calmed me, wasn't up to the task. All I could think about was the curve of her cheek, those bright green eyes, and those pouty lips... which inevitably led to my imagining them wrapped around my cock, taking me deep until I hit her in the back of her throat. I couldn't stop thinking of her long hair sliding through my fingers, of clenching it in my fist to control her head. Of the inevitable gasp, her breath coming shallow, her perfect tits rising and falling...

Fuck.

I would be riding all the way back to Indigo City with a raging fucking hard-on... but I couldn't help it. I couldn't stop thinking about her.

About what it would look like when her eyes fluttered shut in perfect trust. Of moving over and inside her.

Damn it. I had it bad for this woman, like nothing I'd ever experienced before. The urge to make her *mine,* to have her acquiesce and submit to everything I wanted to do to her, to let me take her, body, heart, and soul to places I know she'd never been – it was a siren's call. She had no idea how alluring she was. None, whatsoever.

It was killing me.

10

$\mathcal{A}$lly…

I had fallen into an easy routine the last few weeks. Sunday was always dinner with my grandmother at the nursing home. It wasn't an 'assisted-living' facility like they claimed. I think they just thought it sounded better, made it easier to assuage the family's guilt, but it did no such thing for me.

Anyways, every Sunday, for a nominal fee, of course, I could join in on the slop they served the residents and have dinner with my grandma. I was allowed to bring outside food, and so it had become a custom that after dinner I would bring a treat for dessert. We would go back to my grandmother's room to enjoy it because, sadly, I couldn't afford to bring enough for everyone.

Everything I had that came from Mr. Parnell, and even some of what I earned from the café went to make sure my grandma was taken care of here. Even with her social security income and grandpa's meager pension going to this place, it was amazing the costs associated with her being here and it had to come from somewhere.

"I wish you would work less," she said, with a heavy sigh, and I snapped out of it for the moment and smiled at her across our cafeteria trays.

"I'm okay," I said brightly. "Millie has been great, and Mr. Parnell is really flexible. As long as I get my work done, he doesn't care what day I do it on."

She frowned slightly, and I knew what was coming but didn't say anything, letting her go on ahead with, "I don't know if I like you working alone for a man like that," she said.

I smiled and picked at my mashed potatoes from a box. "He's never even home when I'm there, Grandma. He's a busy man and still at work when I am there. He just leaves the money on the table."

"Humph, it doesn't sound proper for a young lady to be in a man's house alone like that. Not when he's not married."

I gave a gusty sigh, "Times have changed a lot, Grandma. Things just aren't like that anymore."

"Well, maybe they should be!" She sighed too, an echo of mine and said, "I just worry about you. That's all."

"I know, Grandma, and I'm *fine*. I swear, Mr. Parnell is a perfect gentleman."

"Hah, they don't make them like your grandfather anymore," she said in a conspirator's whisper.

"I don't know, how gentlemanly was it that you almost got arrested for prostitution?" I asked.

"Allison Kay!" she cried. "That was only because he couldn't stop laughing long enough to tell the policemen that I was his wife!" She and I broke out into a peal of giggles.

The story went that my grandfather was a troubleshooter for one of the city's hotels. Nowadays, he would be considered hotel security or a bouncer. Anyways, a girl at the hotel had borrowed a few dollars from my grandmother, who had been a seamstress for one of the city's tailor shops. So my grandmother, after work, went down to the hotel so the girl could pay her back and there they were in the hotel bar when the police had swept in to bust all of the prostitutes.

My grandmother had no idea that Maura had been, as she called it, 'a lady of the evening' and had been swept up right along with her. My grandfather let my grandmother be taken all the way to the paddy wagon and had stood outside laughing so hard as she'd screamed at him, 'Mace! Tell them I'm your wife! Oh, my god, Mace! It's not funny!'

It's one of my favorite stories of them. She and I laughed and laughed about it until we had to wipe tears from our eyes. She looked at me with such fondness, her green eyes going milky with age, and patted my cheek. The guilt of having to keep her here overwhelmed me for a moment.

I smiled through it, and she asked me quietly, "What did you bring us this week?"

The change of subject was a welcome one, and I said, "Those chocolate peanut butter bars. We'll have to go through your recipes… I am running out of ones I know."

She smiled with glee and wrinkled her nose, shrugging her shoulder, and I swear let out the most adorable little cackle, and the sadness of a moment before left me.

When I got home that night, I brought out the recipes I had carefully copied out of grandma's recipe book, which she had me bring her, along with a few other personal items. Her clothes, obviously, as well as photographs, a few important documents she wouldn't live without, and some other things; I would bring a little more for her each trip, and it had become a habit of ours to sit with magazines and flower catalogs and cut out flowers for the wall beside her bed.

Back at the Point Side, there was a courtyard. Down, way down, in the center of the building which ringed it, there had been a fountain but it hadn't worked for years and years and years. One summer, my grandmother had gotten together with a bunch of the neighbors and every payday for weeks each neighbor had brought home a big bag of cheap potting soil for her. She dumped them in the dry and empty fountain and ordered bulbs from a catalog.

She, my grandfather, and I had turned that fountain into a flower garden that summer, planting lilies and roses, tulips and daffodils, so that there would be blooms all year around. It was the nicest thing that the Point Side had seen in so long, and the good residents of the project loved her for it. It was one of the odd little things that even the thugs of the building, the gangbangers, and never-do-wells respected, mostly because when one of them fell, it turned into an impromptu shrine at one end with candles and pictures.

My grandmother tended her garden faithfully, and I tried to do what I could, but it had been Mr. Comey, the building's super, who had been keeping it up for her when I just didn't have any energy left to do it.

Anyway, the moral of my rambling story is that out of everything my grandmother missed the most out of her home here, her garden was it... aside from me, of course. Hence all the work carefully snipping catalog and magazine pictures for her wall. She said if she couldn't go to her garden, she demanded that her garden be brought to her. So I did my best.

Now, sitting on my bed, I went through dessert recipes trying to decide what to make for next week. I landed on an old favorite and chewed my bottom lip. It made so much... I thought about it and looked at my tiny kitchen and then had a brilliant idea.

Mr. Parnell's kitchen was huge and making these cookies required a lot of counter space for cooling. My grandmother and I couldn't eat them all, and honestly, what better way to say thank you? I smiled to myself, and, a decision made, went to bed that night smiling.

The next morning was a flurry of activity. I nearly slept through my alarm! I dressed quickly, forgoing my shower, grateful that it was Monday. Every other Monday I tackled the monstrosity that was Mr. Parnell's shower in his master bath. Best way to clean a shower? Get in it after applying cleaner and apply liberal amounts of elbow grease with a scrub brush… which was the plan, *after* cookies!

I grabbed my tote, with the majority of the ingredients from by the door and practically flew to work. I was a little disappointed that Ms. Franco, Mr. Parnell's 'second chair', whatever that meant, was the one to come get their coffee that morning. I was also a little sad I wouldn't get to see Mr. Parnell's reaction to the cookies. I mean, I would be gone before he got to them.

The day dragged so slowly, but finally, it was time to put my master plan into action. I waved to Millie as I left, and stopped at the corner store for the fresh ingredients I would need before boarding my first bus.

Traffic was immense, but eventually I made it, smiling and waving to Mr. Clive as I made my way up the block.

"Hey, Ms. Ally!" he called back, and I let him open the door for me.

"Stand by, Mr. Clive. I'm going to make some cookies; I'll bring some down for you and Mr. Jimmy on my way out."

"Oh! Why, thank you!"

I took the steps two at a time and reached Mr. Parnell's door, sticking my key in the lock. I would sometimes bring pastries from the café to Mr. Clive and Mr. Jimmy. They wouldn't hear of just calling me 'Ally' so it'd become a sort of informal greeting over the last month or so to include 'Mr.' and 'Miss or Ms.' in front of our first names. It kept the snootier residents of the Calvert building happy and it just seemed… I don't know… happier for us. Special, almost.

Everyone needed to feel appreciated and special sometimes. Even for the little things that everyone else just took for granted on a daily basis. Opening doors, holding elevators, assisting with bringing groceries to the door, building gardens out of defunct water features or, like Mr. Parnell, taking a chance on a girl he barely knew and giving her a job cleaning his expensive apartment.

I'd cleaned his kitchen enough times that I knew where everything was. I preheated the oven, laid the wax paper I'd brought in long sheets over his stone countertop, liberated his baking sheets from their cubby and set to work unpacking my grocery totes.

I spent the eight minutes between putting batches in the oven cleaning the easy things. The timer on my phone would go off; I would return to the oven, smoosh the Hershey Kisses into the center of the peanut butter cookies and then let them go for a minute more. Then out of the oven, rest for a minute, and off the sheet and onto the waxed paper to cool.

I put some on a plate for Mr. Parnell and set it on the dining room table with the simple 'Thank you' note card I had picked up from the dollar store. I put the rest into three different Tupperwares I'd brought. One for me and Gran, one for Mr. Clive, and one for Mr. Jimmy. I repacked up my bags, washed all of the dishes from my kitchen adventures and went in to tackle the main event: Mr. Parnell's giant, stone-tiled shower.

I sprayed the special cleaner for it, stripped down and folded my clothes neatly on the corner of the vanity, and started the shower, stepping into it. I scrubbed, rinsing the walls and floor as music played from my phone, laying on top of the pile of clothes. I hadn't taken into account the time – the cookies had drawn it out much later than I'd expected.

The next thing I knew there was a sharp clack of the shower door opening. I shrieked, jumping and covering myself, meeting Mr. Parnell's tempestuous gaze. He kept his eyes fixed on mine, and they weren't happy. At all. He snatched the towel off of the bar and threw it at me. I caught it reflexively.

"Get dressed, meet me in the living room." His cold blue command rang off the tile, echoed in the space that he'd been in. He was already gone, striding through the door, turning sharply to leave his bedroom and march up the hall, his angry strides fading.

Oh, shit… what had I done?

11

*Y*ale…

When I unlocked my door, the first thing I realized was that the alarm panel didn't make so much as a sound. The second was that it smelled *fantastic* in here. Ally's bag sat beneath the panel – which was unusual. She was never here when I came home.

"Ms. Blaylock?" I called out softly, and went to my dining room table. A plate of cookies rested on the corner I usually left her money on. I set my briefcase in the chair and plucked the white card off the table where it sat beside the plate of cookies.

Thanks, all lower-case letters in silver foil emblazoned on its front, decorative scrollwork above and below it, classy, simple, elegant… drawing attention to the one word. I opened it to equally-beautiful and delicate cursive writing done in blue pen.

Mr. Parnell,

I wanted to thank you for sending your friends to help me move. I know it was you, and we don't have to talk about it. I just wanted you to know that I know and that I am grateful. I am also grateful that you took a chance in helping me, in giving me this job. There aren't enough words, really, and 'thank you' doesn't really seem to be enough... so I baked you these cookies. They're peanut blossoms, my grandmother and I make them every Christmas. They're special in our family.

Yours,

Ally Kay

Shit. I rolled my lips together and set the card down.

"Ally?" I called out a little stronger and made my way down the hall, towards my room, to investigate her whereabouts. I heard the shower running, music playing from my bathroom, and pushed open the door.

The shower was running; the glass steamed giving a blurred glimpse of Ally's lean figure. I felt my body immediately respond and I scowled hard. She was rinsing the shower wall, and I let my annoyance, my irritation, and, I admit it, my desire for more, carry me across the tile floor. I jerked open the shower door and she shrieked, dropping the wand and putting up both arms, one of her elegant feet coming up completely off the shower floor.

I liked the fear response. Loved as the panic and unknown welled in her brilliant, too-wide, green eyes.

I couldn't let myself go down this road!

I snatched the towel off the bar as she let herself relax in shock. She didn't hide her body from me when she did that, and I couldn't let myself look. I threw the towel at her and she caught it, holding it against her chest, those beautiful, perky tits of hers – the reality was so much better than my imagination.

"Get dressed," I growled. "Meet me in the living room."

It was an effort of will after that to turn away, and stride back the way I came. I wanted to stand there and drink her in with my gaze, go over every fine detail, every freckle, every hair; every soft curve. I wanted to admire her like a fine piece of art– but I couldn't. I was her boss.

I went past the kitchen, between it and the dining room table, to the bar along the window. I plucked a rocks glass from where it rested upside down on its silver, circular platter and set it on its base. I poured a generous measure of whiskey into that glass and downed it in a bid to fortify myself; then I poured at least two fingers more.

Capping the decanter, I moved past her offering of thanks and cookies, pausing slightly, the knife of indecision twisting in my chest. I swallowed hard, and went over to my favorite chair, lowering myself into it to wait.

I heard her before I saw her, my back to the room as it was, the tall wing-backed chair I sat in hiding her from view. I sighed with impatience when I heard her stop and said, "Come here."

Her sneakers tapped lightly across the hardwood and she edged cautiously into view. Her eyes were too wide, her chest rising and falling in rapid breaths beneath her light gray, loose and flowy tank top. The armholes of her top, gaping to her hips, revealed that she wore a black sports bra beneath it. Her legs, encased in black leggings, didn't want to seem to work for her, and she trembled. I glanced over her black low-top Chuck Taylor knock-offs. She was too poor to be able to afford the real thing, and I let out a frustrated breath.

I met her green eyes which were welling up, just short of spilling over. I let no sympathy play over my features. Instead, I moved my gaze from hers to the end of the coffee table directly in front of me. A silent order to sit. I wanted to see if she would follow non-verbal cues as well as she seemed to follow both my written and verbal commands.

She swallowed hard and moved quickly to sit. Her hands gripped the end of the table, knuckles mottling white; her eyes on me; her knee bouncing as she tapped her heel against the floor with sheer nerves.

"Stop that," I said shortly, though I kept my voice even and controlled. I didn't yell, but I did keep my tone stern. She immediately ceased the nervous movement, and it was everything in me to quell the rising erection in my slacks.

"Please, don't fire me," she said quickly, and the tears did spill then, her eyes growing luminous. She went from gorgeous to achingly beautiful then, and I couldn't tell you what that did to me.

I took a fortifying sip of my whiskey and betrayed no emotion. Instead, I plucked my handkerchief out of my suit's breast pocket, shook it out and leaned forward, offering it to her.

"On the contrary," I stated, a decision made – once again against my better judgment. "I have a proposition for you. A rather indecent proposal…"

12

*a*lly…

   Dread coated my insides like tar the entire time I was drying off and getting dressed. My heart pounded against the inside of my ribs, and my face felt hot. My chest squeezed tight as I tied my shoes, and finally, I stood up, as ready as I would ever be to face the music.

Oh, shit… I'm fired. He's going to fire me and I won't be able to pay for Grandma and I don't know what I'm going to do!

I felt sicker and sicker with every step I took up the hallway, and I didn't immediately see him. He was sitting in the wingback chair that faced away from the kitchen and my approach. He swirled some whiskey in a glass and said coldly, "Come here."

Yep. I was fired. Totally. Epically. Fired.

I went around the side of his chair and stopped, equal parts dejected and humiliated. He raked that icy glare over me from head to toe and shifted in his seat, as if unsettled.

He's disgusted with you… I mean, wouldn't you be? I thought.

72

He let out an angry sigh and my gaze bounced from the floor to his, my eyes hot and tight, my vision blurring with unshed tears. He captured my gaze with his and jerked it to the coffee table in front of him in a clear bid for me to sit. I moved quickly to comply, but couldn't hold still. My knee bouncing rapidly as I tried to do something, anything, to keep myself together; to keep myself from bursting into ugly wracking sobs, to stop myself from throwing myself on his mercy and begging him not to let me go.

"Stop that," he snapped, and I forced my leg to immediately still, but lost the battle with my tears. I felt them slick down my face, spilling across my skin in twin heated lines. One of the tears splashing onto the top of my thigh and soaking into my legging.

"Please, don't fire me!" I blurted, and apparently lost the battle when it came to not begging, but I didn't have any pride. The Point Side projects had stripped that from me a long time ago.

His gaze wandered over me, so cold it burned where it touched and he took a nonchalant sip of his drink. When he lowered his glass, he let out a breath and reached into the breast pocket of his suit, shaking out his handkerchief and holding it out to me.

I reached out and took it as he said dryly, "On the contrary. I have a proposition for you. A rather indecent proposal…"

I wiped my eyes and looked up, bewildered. *Did I hear him right? Am I not fired?*

"What?" I asked, still not believing what I heard, waiting for him to repeat it.

He pursed his lips and they twisted slightly with impatience as he searched my face. "You're not fired," he said for my benefit, "I would actually like to increase your pay." I took a breath to speak, and he raised a finger, "No. Hear me out."

I resolutely closed my mouth, half afraid he would ask me to sleep with him. I didn't know if I could do that. If I would do that… not for money. That wasn't the woman my grandmother had raised me to be, at all.

"I would like for you to clean like that all the time. I will double your current rate."

"Wait, what?" I asked, confused and was surprised that I didn't find myself readily denying him. Instead, I asked, "Like, would you be home?"

"No."

I frowned, perplexed, and shook my head, not that I was saying no, but more in that I had no idea where this was coming from and I didn't get it, so I asked him, "If you're not home, how would you know if I did it? Like, how would you know I cleaned naked? The cameras?"

He smiled and shook his head. "No. In fact, I will show you precisely where they all are and how to disable them upon entry into the condo."

I blinked and blurted, "But then how would you know I was doing it?" Somehow I was more concerned with the how and why and what of this scenario than I was with losing my job if I said no.

"First off, let me reiterate, your job is safe, Ally." *Oh, shit.* He was serious. He never called me 'Ally' anymore. It was always 'Ms. Blaylock.' "Second, you may tell absolutely no one about this. What goes on in this house is my business. What goes on between us is our business."

"What other conditions apply?" I asked faintly, still in disbelief but knowing in my heart there had to be more.

"If you say 'no', you still have a job. I will never take that away from you unless you breach my trust."

"Why would I do that?" I demanded, affronted. "I would never do that."

A faint smile graced his lips, and it made my chest ache for an entirely different reason. I swallowed hard and thought about what he was asking. I mean, I would be lying to myself if I said that I hadn't had just the slightest bit of deviant pleasure at being nude in this beautiful man's space. Now, here he was, asking me to do it… trying to pay me more for it…

I did not see this coming, I thought, but I couldn't deny how flushed the idea made me feel. How my body tingled and ached in delicious ways at the prospect of it.

Still, the *why* of it bothered me; why would a man like Damien Parnell want something like this? I mean, he wouldn't even be here to enjoy it… *Well, he isn't here when you get naked and you enjoy it.* Maybe it was the same thing? Just the knowing was enough. *Yeah, but what happens when the just knowing isn't enough anymore?* I asked myself, and was surprised that the delicious ache at the apex of my thighs intensified rather than diminished. I didn't quail at the thought. Not until I thought about the money. I mean, right now I needed that money, but I wouldn't always, would I?

No, don't think about that Ally… you don't want to think about that.

He watched me think it over, his expression neutral as he waited for my answer. I swallowed hard and said, "May I think about it some more?"

"Of course," he said, and I swallowed hard.

"How long do I have?"

"As long as you'd like, but before you walk out that door tonight, I'm afraid I'm going to need an answer."

I pursed my lips and stared at his whiskey glass, at the way the amber liquid coated the side of it as he absently swirled it. I mean, *couldn't he get in far more trouble for this than me?*

I looked back up sharply and said, "I'll do it… but you don't have to pay me extra."

He smiled a secret little smile and said, "Well that would be my pleasure, Ms. Blaylock."

"Show me how to turn off the cameras?" I asked, feeling a little more solid, a little braver.

"Well, now, that would be my pleasure, too." He moved to stand and I stood too, abruptly, the effects of the adrenaline wearing off now. My hands felt slightly shaky, and I honestly felt like I trembled all over. He took me to the security panel and showed me how to turn off the cameras after I disabled the alarm. It was surprisingly easy but required I enter the alarm's code again.

He had me do it twice to be sure that I got it, and took a sip of his drink. We stood there for a moment, in silence and he said, "Look at me." I rolled my lips and did as he asked. He fixed me with those beautiful dark eyes of his and his voice became low and controlled. Words said just between us.

"You're safe here, Ally. No judgment, no recriminations. What you do here, what we do here, is between two consenting adults and you may revoke that consent at any time. You want to stop, it stops. No penalties, no harm, no foul."

"Okay," I whispered and even though I knew that the words sounded too good to be true, that anywhere else, any*one* else delivering them likely didn't mean them. I knew, deep down, that Mr. Parnell did. He wasn't lying to me or bullshitting me. He meant it and I could trust what he said.

The moment hung between us, weighted with promise and he touched gentle fingertips to my chin, his eyes roving my face. He smiled slightly at whatever he saw and said, "Your eyes are red from crying. Go splash some cool water on your face. It will help."

"Yes, sir," I murmured and his breath caught. He nodded at me to go do what I was told and I did. The more I thought about things, the stranger they seemed to me, but I had to deal with them on my own, process them on my own. I couldn't tell anyone. Certainly not my grandmother and as much as I loved her, definitely not Dawnie. They wouldn't understand but this... this whole idea, this whole exchange of power between us, I understood. It tapped into a very basic part of me; it flipped some hidden switch and made me come alive with a tingling rush.

Still, no one could know. Understanding for these kinds of things didn't come easily to regular people. Well, Dawnie might get it. Not only because of the books that we liked to read, but because she was my best friend and knew me sometimes better than I knew myself. It was strange feeling that way about a man, but here I was, and when it came to Mr. Parnell? The same sentiment echoed. The same sort of darkness in him called to some of my own and I loved it, I was definitely attracted to it, but I was still unsure of it. Not because of anything he had done but more of what other people might think. I mean, what would other people think? Probably nothing good and it was best not to find out.

When I returned to the living room, he stood by the door. The whiskey glass was gone and he held my totes and purse out to me.

"Have a good evening, Ms. Blaylock," he said, and I swallowed.

"Thank you; you too, Mr. Parnell."

"I shall enjoy the cookies; thank you for them."

I smiled at that, my heart lightening, and he opened the door and showed me out.

13

Y **ale…**

She had begun making it a habit to text me when she arrived to tell me she was shutting off the cameras. If I was lucky, I would catch her at the panel before she did it. She was always clothed then, of course, but I didn't always get down to the café now that the Reeves case was in full swing when it came to trial. Closing arguments had been given, and the jury was in deliberations. It had been one of the most exhausting cases of my career to date and I wasn't at all sure I was going to win it.

I'm here; I'm turning off the cameras now.

I quickly signed into the app governing my home security system and felt my chest ease when Ally's pretty face came into view. Colorless, of course, due to the cameras, but no less lovely, even if I missed the startling color of her green eyes. The cameras disengaged and the screen went black with the pop-up message asking if I wished to re-engage them. I hit 'no', as good as my word, just as one of the city's paralegals stuck his head into my office.

"Verdict on the Reeve's case is in," he declared, grimly.

"What? Shit! Already?" I stood up quickly and shoveled the folders I'd taken out of my briefcase back in. They hadn't deliberated more than a couple of hours at this point. That typically meant bad news for the prosecution. Very bad.

"Chrissy!" I barked, and she looked up from her desk in the office across from mine, her phone pressed to her ear. She said something into the receiver at the look on my face and dropped it onto the cradle.

"What's wrong?" she called out.

"Reeves verdict is in, let's roll!"

"Wait, what?" she said, alarmed, "Are you kidding me? Please, tell me you're joking right now!"

"I wish I were." I shrugged into my jacket, and we hauled ass down to the street, to the courthouse around the next block. We moved briskly through the other pedestrians on the sidewalk and Chrissy tried to placate me.

"We laid the case out as clear as could be. Even a toddler could follow along. As a matter of law, she's guilty as sin. The jury has to know that," she said, her breathing becoming more labored.

"The defense played to the jury's emotions. Those people saw a scared, barely legal teen on that stand," I snarled.

"Look, Yale, we don't know," she said. "We won't know until we hear the verdict."

"That girl buried that baby alive; they'd better not let her off," I growled.

We took the courthouse steps two at a time and returned to our designated courtroom. The air was thick with tension, the atmosphere crackling with apprehension. My adrenaline raced, my pulse throbbed in my temple. I gripped the back of my chair as the bailiff commanded we all rise.

"The Honorable Judge Angela Marie Bendyk is now presiding."

I liked Judge Bendyk; she was both tough and fair. Also, as far as a lot of the judges went, she was easy on the eyes. She wore her long brown hair pulled into a severe bun, and subtle makeup that didn't look like she wore any at all. Her brown eyes were quick and I liked a woman who could be shrewd, which she was – she didn't let either side get away with bullshit, which in turn usually made my job easier. Very rarely did it make it harder.

I went through the motions, sitting, the jury being led in, listening through all the bullshit legalese we all spent way too much time and money to learn just to hear the fucking verdict which was…

The courtroom held its collective breath; we had shot hard for depraved indifference homicide, and if this little bitch got off, my faith in humanity was going to be irreparably damaged.

Come on, lady, come on, lady, come on, you bastards, do the right thing! My brain chanted at them. The forewoman looked up and said the magic word.

"Guilty–" and the rest of what she said was drowned out by the gallery leaping to their feet and cheering. A sentiment from which Chrissy and I were not immune, we just couldn't show it.

"Oh, my god, I need a drink after that!" Chrissy said, fanning herself as soon as we hit the street.

I hailed a cab, "You and me both."

It was a mistake; I didn't usually make mistakes. Not of that magnitude.

We went to the 10-13 and I had just enough to drink that it was just this side of too much. I was pleasantly buzzed as I pushed back from the bar and declared, "After that shit-show, I think I have earned myself a good night's sleep."

Chrissy giggled, and Youngblood put his arms around her as she said, "Don't worry, I'm sure the next horror show to keep us up at night will be along shortly." The proclamation held the bitter edge of one of the rest of us rank and file, and as a lawyer, I could appreciate that even as a defense attorney in the big firm she'd come from, that she had heard and seen some things to damage the psyche.

"Have a fantastic evening," I told them both. "I am sure you are absolutely correct, but for now, we've earned at least one evening."

"Just one," Chrissy agreed, and raised her wine glass in salute.

I chuckled and picked up my briefcase from the floor beside my barstool, plucked my trench coat from the bar and tossed it over my arm.

"Night, Yale!" they chimed in unison, and I smiled, giving them a wave over my shoulder.

Youngblood whispered something in her ear and she giggled. He was sober, but she was probably just a little bit tipsy. I gave a sharp nod to Skids who was at the other end of the bar talking to a waitress, and he raised a hand in farewell.

I pushed out of the 10-13's front door into the late summer heat, stepping up to the curb and hailing a cab. The ride home was relatively short, I could have walked it, but I was feeling lazy. I should have walked it – because when I keyed my way into the apartment, there was Ally, frozen like a deer and just as graceful, in my kitchen, nude and perfect.

I blinked, long and slow, and let my gaze rove what I could see of her, from her face down to where she was hidden behind the counter.

"My apologies," I said with all sincerity. "I should have texted I was coming home early." Which was the truth. In the furor the early verdict caused, I had completely forgotten she was here. "You may absolutely get dressed if you'd like…"

Her wide green eyes blinked once, and the tension riding her shoulders eased as she glanced me over from head to toe and back again. She swallowed hard and asked, "Why would I do that?" and stepped around the end of the counter so that I could see her better.

I felt my lips curve into an appreciative smile and more tension eased out of how she held herself. I fully blame the alcohol when it came to my lack of control for what I said next…

"Dear god, I want to play with you."

14

———

$\mathcal{A}$lly…

I froze mid-step and cocked my head, searching his face as I drew a breath and asked, "Play with me? I don't think I understand." Okay, that was a lie. I didn't generally like being manipulative, but I *really* wanted to hear him say it and I *really* wanted him to do it. It was hard to be here, in his space, naked all the time, and not be acutely aware of my sexuality.

Everything was different now, everything felt different and held that dangerous edge of sex to it. The simple act of wiping down a counter or dusting a shelf sent my breasts swaying, the cooler air of the air conditioned apartment against my exposed skin sent me into spontaneous shivers that had nothing to do with the cold. When I knelt or bent to pick something up, my sex felt exposed and no matter what I did *I couldn't stop thinking about him.* How could I?

Of course, thinking about him led to fantasizing about him, which led to wanting and wishing and that led me to this near-constant state of low-level arousal that I couldn't always patiently wait until I was home to do something about.

83

"I shouldn't have said that," he said, and I shook my head before he could apologize.

"Genie's out of the bottle... what did you mean?" I swallowed hard, and brought one hand up, wrapping it around the elbow of my other arm. I wasn't hiding from him. If I hid from him, then it would mean I was ashamed, that what we were doing was wrong, and though other people may think that way, I didn't feel that way; not at all.

He set down his briefcase in the entryway and moved to hang up his long coat in the hall closet. That through, he shrugged out of his suit jacket and did the same. He sighed out, unbuttoning the cuffs of his shirt and rolling them back over his forearms. He looked back at me over his shoulder and finally turned, tugging at his tie, unknotting it. I licked my lips and waited for an answer and his jaw tightened. He dragged that sweeping gaze of his from my head to my feet and back up, letting it linger in choice places but not luridly.

"You know what I mean, Ally..."

"You mean sexually," I said, slowly.

He nodded and unbuttoned the top two buttons at his collar. I swallowed hard and he smiled. It held an edge of want, a naked desire I felt in my own heart and I licked my lips again, running the bottom one between my teeth.

"What are the rules?" I asked softly, and it was his turn to freeze and contemplate me the same way I had contemplated him a moment before.

"It stops when you say it stops," he said, and he closed his eyes, the struggle clear on his face.

"And what if I don't want it to stop?" The question was out of my mouth before I even knew I was going to ask it. Something akin to adrenaline surged through my veins the moment the final word was uttered, and I held very still as if any sort of movement would shatter this moment between us. For some reason, the very thought of that made me ache with a sort of grief. I hadn't realized just how attracted I was to my boss, or just how lonely I was… physically among other things.

He bowed his head, a smile curving his lips, but he didn't immediately answer. Finally, it was as if he had come to a decision. He gripped the back of his neck briefly and then dropped his hand to his side. He drew himself up to his full height, and it was as if that commanding presence of his wrapped around him like a cloak. He speared me where I stood with that dark gaze of his, and I was suddenly a rabbit in a trap, heart fluttering wildly in my chest, joining the butterflies taking flight in my stomach.

"Go into my bedroom," he ordered. "In the nightstand to the left of the bed, bottom drawer, there is a roll of black velvet. Bring it to me, and don't look inside."

I swallowed hard and guessed that we were playing. I went and did as I was bid, padding quickly down the hall; the smooth, polished wood of his floors cool beneath my feet, the carpet in his bedroom warm and plush. I crouched in front of the nightstand and smoothly pulled open the bottom drawer. I lifted the bundle he'd requested free and slid it shut. Clutching it to my chest, I returned to the main open living area of his apartment. He stood by the dining room table, his shirt untucked and now open and I froze again.

"Come here," he said calmly and I did. He pulled out one of the chairs and set it aside. I held out the roll of stuff he asked for and he set it aside, at the next place setting. He took a half step toward me and laid a gentle hand on my hip and I jumped at the unexpected, intimate little touch. He cocked his head slightly and drew me towards him, arm curving around my lower back.

I held my breath, as I moved into his personal space, his energy calm, almost frozen, and completely in control. I rested a hand on his muscled chest over his tattoo and let my eyes drift to the ink beneath his skin. The entirety of the right side of his chest and shoulder was done in a beautiful black and white image of some sort of family crest. Surrounding it, in the background and onto his shoulder was Lady Justice, blindfolded and holding her scales before her, a sword upraised as if leading a charge in her other hand.

"Ally," he said softly and I jerked my hand back guilty, his professionally pressed and fitted blue shirt falling forward to cover the shoulder again.

"Sorry," I murmured, blushing hard. He tipped my chin with two gentle fingers and I swallowed hard, meeting his obsidian eyes. Cool and appraising, they held a secret little smile that I couldn't define.

"Sit up on the table," he ordered gently, walking me backward to it. I pressed my palms flat on the highly polished wood surface but paused.

"You really want my ass on your dining room table?" I asked softly, and he smiled at me with patience before saying, "I have a wonderful housekeeper. I'll ask her to clean it for me."

I laughed and some of the ice was broken, some of the nervousness fleeing before his good humor. I think I liked it when he joked. He was so serious all the time; brooding. I hopped up and he brought the chair back over, setting it in front of me. He hitched up his slacks out of habit and sat down, pulling the chair closer and resting his hands on my knees.

He looked up into my eyes, and the somberness he always held was back. I tilted my head and reached up, touching the side of his face. His eyes closed and he turned his face into my hand, brushing the heel of my palm with a light touch of his lips, breathing me in. His hand left my knee and cradled the back of my hand, returning it to the tabletop by my hip.

"What happens now?" I asked, and it came out scarce and breathy. He did that to me. His presence, his touch, and we hadn't even really gone there. I swallowed hard and suddenly wondered if I was in some sort of trouble here. Not with him, or this job, or any of that… but me, my heart.

"Now, we talk. We discuss what you like and what you don't. We discuss what you're willing to try and what you aren't."

I smile and ask him, lightly teasing, "Is this what it takes to play with a lawyer?"

"Explain." Again with that clipped and cultured tone; commanding.

I lost my easy smile, "It's what you sound like," I said. "Like this is some kind of contract negotiation."

"Isn't it?" He raised an eyebrow and pinned me where I sat with his look. I didn't answer, my voice fled. I didn't know what to say that would please him – and I felt like that was worth working for. His smile was so rare, I liked it when I found it and brought it out of him.

He smoothed his hands up and down the tops of my thighs, and I closed my eyes and shivered lightly. I heard him smile. He let out a little hum of appreciation at my reaction and I opened my eyes quickly to see it. It was there but tried to disappear quickly. It was shy, I guess; took some coaxing, like a scared rabbit.

"You like that," he said, and he wasn't asking, but I answered him anyway.

"Yes, I like to be touched."

"What else do you like?" he asked and I licked my lips.

"I, uh…" I felt myself blush and he tipped his head, considering me.

"You're not very experienced," he murmured and his hands stilled on my skin. "You don't know what you like."

I bit my lower lip and shook my head, timidly. It was kind of embarrassing when you stopped to think about it.

"I like that," he said and his hands returned to my knees.

I swallowed hard and asked faintly, "You do?"

"I do; it means I can show you new things, and that there will be a lot of new things."

"That sounds… nice."

"Okay, how about this? We'll go slowly, and afterward, I want you to go home and think about what we did. I want you to write down how you felt, what you liked and what you didn't and I want you to leave it here for me to read the next time you're here."

"You want me to keep a sex diary?" I asked.

"A journal, yes. I also want you to tell me if you don't like something, but I am not fond of the word 'no' so I want you to pick something else."

Oh my god, he wanted me to choose a safeword. This was for real. His expression neutral, searching my face for any unease, but I had always been crap at hiding my feelings, so I was sure that all he saw was the spark of eagerness there.

"Um, I don't know what." I laughed nervously. "There are so many great words, beautiful words…"

He smiled and it was genuine. "What are some of your favorite things?"

"I love flowers, lilies and roses are my favorites but that's because my grandmother grows them."

"So those are probably not something you would want to use." His smile grew and his hands resumed stroking over my skin. I shivered and took a deep breath in through my nose, letting it out slowly. His hands on my skin felt so nice.

"How about the old standbys for now… Green for 'go': you're fine'; yellow for 'slow down': and that you need to process; and red for 'stop': you legitimately can't handle or take anymore and need to stop."

I nodded and murmured, "Okay, I can remember that."

"Is there anything you know you don't like? Like, can't stand the idea of, right off the bat?"

I thought about it for him, and I mean really thought about it and slowly shook my head, "There's nothing I have tried that I didn't like, I mean, not yet…"

"Ah, not true, something just occurred to you," he said and he was right.

"Of course, as soon as I said it, I would think of something," I said, laughing nervously.

"Don't be embarrassed," he said, his voice as hard as the look he gave me. "Honesty before humiliation," he added and I could respect that.

"I, um, I really didn't like it when I, um," I laughed and looked at the ceiling, "Oh, god, I feel so weird sitting on your dining room table naked, talking about this!"

"Don't. It's just you and me, and I happen to like that you're sitting on my dining room table naked… and I could listen to you talk about anything. What didn't you like?"

He was being patient with me, and I could tell this wasn't going to go any further unless I said it and so I bit my lower lip, considered who I was talking to for only half a second and blurted out, "I really didn't like it when my last boyfriend came in my mouth."

He paused, considered me, and said, "Duly noted. Now tell me *why* you didn't like it."

"Seriously?"

He gave me a flat look and I dropped my eyes to where his hands rested on my knees. I rolled my lips together and said, "He wasn't nice about it. I mean, it was one of the reasons I broke up with him. The first time, it scared me, and I asked him not to do it again but he didn't listen. The next time, he grabbed my hair and, um, sort of made me swallow. It was the worst thing... I really didn't like it."

He nodded expression grave, and stood up slowly. He hooked his hand around the back of my neck, cradling my head and dragged my forehead gently, carefully, to his lips. He pressed them to my forehead in a sweet kiss and murmured against my skin, "Good girl, thank you for telling me," and the anxiety and tension that had come with the memory eased out of me, draining from my muscles. It was replaced with a golden little euphoric glow at having pleased him, and I liked that.

"Lay down," he ordered and it seemed the time for negotiation and conversation was over. I lay down, the tabletop cool against my back and he unwrapped the bundle beside me. I went to look and he stopped, raising his eyebrows and saying, "Ah, look away." I licked my lips and turned my face towards the kitchen. Away from whatever it was, he was doing.

My nervousness was back, and I chewed my bottom lip lightly as I heard things subtly click together as he moved things around.

"I would like to try a little bit of everything," he said gently, pulling up his chair and retaking his seat. He grasped one of my ankles and I inhaled sharply. "Relax, I'm not going to hurt you."

I relaxed and he wiggled my ankle back and forth with his hand, signaling I should loosen up and let him move it for me. I complied and he brought my leg up, spreading me, placing my foot on the arm of his dining chair. He did the same to the other leg and nudged my knees apart.

"The last time I was in this position it was a very uncomfortable doctor's visit," I murmured, and he chuckled darkly.

"Yes, but I don't believe your doctor did this," and he kissed the inside of my thigh.

I sucked in a deep breath and said, "No."

"An excellent point you've made, though. Are you on birth control?"

I colored and said, "No, I was hoping you would wear a condom…"

"I had planned to anyway, but are you opposed to birth control?"

"No, I just… I'm not with anyone, not dating; I didn't see the need to put any chemicals or hormones into my body it didn't need."

"Fair enough," he whispered, and his voice was huskier somehow, and I realized he was looking at me, his hands roaming gently along the outsides of my thighs, under my ass, and along my hips, his gaze devouring my pussy like it was a work of art.

It should have felt weird, but it didn't. I felt… beautiful. Desirable and alluring, and that was new to me. New to me, but I definitely liked it.

"I'm going to touch you," he warned and then his fingers were trailing along my inner thighs. I closed my eyes and couldn't escape the wanting moan that escaped me. I jumped slightly when his fingertips grazed my asshole.

"A little bit of everything," he reminded and plunged a digit into my vagina. I arched and cried out a little. That little bit of contact so welcome, the anticipation killing me, the surprise overtaking me. He pumped his fingers in and out of me, and I sucked in a breath, holding it.

"Breathe," he reminded me and I did, and his fingers were suddenly gone, as fast as they had appeared. He touched my backside again, using my wetness to tease at my asshole then pressed something against it. It slid in easily and didn't hurt at all.

I didn't ask what he'd just put inside me, but he said, "Just a little lubricant. Give it time."

I bit my lips together and breathed deep and even, letting out a quick little "Mm-hmm."

Oh, my god, this was exciting. The unknown, having his hands on me, in me, I wanted more, and I waited, I would be lying if I said patiently, for what he was going to do next.

He held up a pair of neon pink silicone balls, a loop on one end, a silicone thread between them, connecting them.

"Do *not* let these fall out," he warned. "I will find a clever punishment if you do."

I blinked, in surprise and he pressed them into me. I was wet, and they slipped in effortlessly. I closed my eyes and sighed at the full feeling they gave me. It was just this side of being any kind of satisfying. I bit my bottom lip, my arousal deepening to levels of insanity. I wanted him. I was desperate to sit up and grab him. I wanted to pull his mouth to mine and devour him… but I didn't. My curiosity at what he would do next ran deeper.

He raised a small little anal plug of the same bright pink, a blue artificial gem at its base. It wasn't very big at all, not intimidating in the slightest and my slight anxiety at what he had planned for my ass abated.

"Not going any bigger than this, not tonight," he breathed and his dark eyes, the way he looked at me, stole my breath. Carnal lust, power, and pleasure played out in their depths as he pressed it to my ass. I squeaked slightly in discomfort but it didn't last more than half a second and the anal plug was in. The full feeling in my pussy with the balls he had placed in it had been nothing as compared to what it was now. I writhed slightly and he smiled carnally, and gave the outside of my thigh a stinging slap.

"Stop moving!" he ordered and I instantly stilled. He grinned then and said, "You need some decoration, I think."

I heard chains rattle and cold metal touched my stomach. I jumped and he laughed, a delighted sound with a slight edge of cruelty to it. The metal dragged across my skin and I shivered at the sensation. I closed my eyes as he circled my left nipple with it first, then dragged it between my breasts to circle the right. My palms were pressed flat into the table top by my hips, fingertips pressing harder into the wood. My chest heaved with breaths as I struggled not to move, to hold still under the tickling sensations he wrought.

He brought up one end of the chain and I realized it had three, each end capped with a metal clamp, thick, shiny black rubber over the pinching tips. He pinched a nipple between finger and thumb and drew it out from my body, settling the clamp around it and easing it on. I hissed, his eyes glued to my face but expression neutral.

"Too much?"

"Yeah, a little."

He turned a screw on the clamp and the intensity eased marginally. He mirrored the action on the other side and I felt myself grow wetter between my thighs, and I was already wet, to begin with. I clenched up tighter, remembering his admonition about keeping his other toys in place. I was determined to not find out what he would consider a 'clever punishment.'

He tugged lightly on the chains attached to my nipples and I cried out, arching slightly.

"Oh!" he tsked. "I told you not to move. I was going to leave this one off, but now…"

He pressed his fingers against my slick pussy lips and rubbed at my clit for a moment. I pressed my lips together, a moan trying to find its way past them, and I squeezed my eyes shut, trying not to move again.

He chuckled, and again, it held that slight edge of cruelty, as he gently pinched my clit and clamped carefully above it, watching my face intently. I bit my lips together and turned my head and he stopped, adjusted the clamp, and tried again. He eased it on and I panted. There was so much going on right now; I wasn't sure I could deal with all of the sensations bombarding me at once.

"Sit up," he demanded, and I slowly and carefully sat up. I pursed my lips – putting my legs together caused the clamp to pinch uncomfortably, so I left them slightly open. "Come on, on your feet, that's it." He helped ease me to the floor and I gasped.

"I want you to clean this table," he said evenly. "Then I want you to pour me two fingers of whiskey and bring it to my chair. Put the rest of the toys on the kitchen counter for now."

"Yes, sir," I murmured, at a loss for what else to say. He closed his eyes and it looked like he was listening to the sweetest music. I stared at him, slack-jawed with the moment. My discomfort, temporarily, was forgotten.

"I don't hear you moving, Ally…"

"Sorry," I moved slowly, the weight of the chains swinging, the stimulation almost too much. I gasped and he pushed the chair he'd been using in and went to his wing-backed chair in the living room. I expected him to swing it around so that he could watch me, but he didn't. Instead, he peeled out of his shirt the rest of the way and let it fall to the floor, with a pointed look at me over his shoulder.

I couldn't help it, I smiled and shook my head. "Oh, don't worry, I'll get that."

He grinned back at me and went and sat down. I bent to pick up the shirt and gasped at the chains dragging on the sensitive points of my body. Taking it to the laundry closet, I slid the doors open and grabbed the furniture polish and a rag, taking it back to the table. I moved the toys and I swear, I grew wetter with every step I took. I was so wet I could feel it slick the inside of my thighs. I clenched hard, scared the damn weight of the balls inside of me would cause them to slip free. I couldn't clench my legs because of the clamp to my pussy and I was so frustrated by that.

This was diabolically clever in its own right; I didn't want to even know what he would come up with if he really put his mind to it. I sprayed the furniture polish onto the table and swiped it across the surface where I had been. The clamps on my nipples had felt good at the start, but the longer they stayed on, the more they began to burn with a sharp ache.

By the time I put the cleaning supplies away and poured his drink I was ready for the whole mess to be off and out. I went to him and held the glass down to him. He looked up at me without taking it and said, "Come stand in front of me."

I did as I was bid and he gestured for me to kneel. I did so, awkwardly, on the plush area rug and he smiled, accepting the glass when I held it up to him. He took an appreciative sip and let his gaze rove over me and my pussy gave a throb that was echoed by my heart.

"So beautiful," he murmured, and cupped my cheek, stroking it with his thumb.

"You are too," I murmured.

He smiled, and it held sadness. "Not on the inside."

"I think so," I murmured back.

"Hush. I'm going to look at you, finish my drink, then I'm going to fuck you on my coffee table."

I gasped, my eyes widening even as my body cried out, *god, yes, please!*

"I would really like that," I whispered, transfixed and unable to look away from those soul-deep dark eyes of his.

"I would really like that..." He said the words slowly, and his voice trailed off. He looked at me expectantly and I swallowed gently, my mouth suddenly dry with how much I wanted what he was offering.

"I would really like that, *sir.*"

"Good girl," he murmured and sipped his drink again.

When the whiskey in his glass was a little more than half gone, he said, "Undo my pants."

I knelt up, staring up his perfect body, rippling with muscle, and gently fed the tongue of his belt through the piece of leather holding it close to his body. I flicked the tongue of metal out of the hole and the leather gave with a little sigh. My excitement spiraled tighter and tighter, my pussy very nearly throbbing in time with my heartbeat.

"I like the way you perfume the air," he closed his eyes and breathed deeply, as I unhooked the decorative piece of fabric from the beltline of his slacks, working the button free. I slowly lowered the zipper and he said, "Bring me out of the front of my boxers and put this on."

He slipped a condom out of his pocket and held it out to me. I swallowed hard and plucked it from his fingers, putting it between my lips so that I could use both hands to bring him out of his pants. He was hard and throbbing, the middle of his cock thick and heavily veined. I stroked him from root to tip, his foreskin peeling back and pre-cum slicking my fingers. He sucked in a deep breath and his eyes closed, his head tipping back to rest on his chair-back.

"Oh, god, that feels good," he murmured. He let me do it for a while before commanding strongly, "Stop." My hand instantly stilled.

I waited, plucking the condom out of my mouth and he looked down at me. "Put that on me, Bright Eyes."

I opened it, my body aching, burning, and needing his still cool touch before I felt like I would go insane. I rolled it onto him awkwardly. I had only put one on a man once or twice before. He was patient with me, watching me with no expression. Once I had the condom rolled to his root, he downed the rest of his glass and held out his hands to me. I held out mine, to place them in his and he helped me up.

I groaned slightly and he asked, "Clamps too much now?"

"Yes, sir."

"Sit on the edge of the coffee table, spread your legs and lean back on your hands. Arch more, that's it. God, that's fucking beautiful."

I followed all of his instructions and I was completely open to him; he roamed my body with his gaze, looking down at me from where he stood, and slid his hands along the tops of my thighs lightly, a ghost of a touch. He went to his knees between my legs and unclipped a nipple. I hissed as the blood rushed back in and he sealed his mouth over it, sucking. The hiss turned into a cry and I threw my head back, my hair trailing on the table, tickling the top of my ass.

He repeated on the other side and I echoed the cry. He repeated his ministrations and I was so close to coming. I had never been so close from any kind of foreplay before. He reached a finger inside of me, teasing through my wetness, seeking and finding the loop on the balls inside me.

"Relax, let them go," he ordered and I relaxed my body. He pulled them out and the anal plug was pushed out with them, dropping to the carpet. I looked at him, alarmed, but he didn't seem to care. Instead, he dropped them with a clatter, trailing his tongue between my breasts, down my stomach and expertly unclamped my pussy lips above my clit and covered the sensitive bundle of nerves with his mouth, sucking on it as he let it loose. I arched harder and cried out in surprise and ecstasy, the cool rush of pleasure flowing completely through my body, my pussy, hot and wet, contracting rhythmically with a light orgasm, a promise of things to come.

He knelt up, capturing my eyes with his own and put his hand on my throat, not squeezing, not hurting, just there, exerting the promise of bad things as he guided his cock to my slick entrance. He thrust into me, his other hand finding the outside of my thigh, my ass, and pressing me further towards the edge of the table, closer to him. I pressed back on my hands and scooted closer, trembling as he filled me and wanting just that little bit more.

15

Y ale…

I watched myself disappear inside of her and was transfixed by the sight, hypnotized by it as I slid in and out of her wet and waiting pussy. She arched beautifully, her breasts pushed out in front of my face, her reactions as pure and sweet as sun-ripened, low-hanging fruit. I wanted to pluck them all, run back into the dark and gorge myself on them.

I had been intense on purpose, hadn't tried to ease her into things slowly and had gone all in because I really wanted her to stop me. I wanted her to deny me and leave, and it was something I was good at; self-sabotage at its finest. But she not only wouldn't be denied, she had kept up so beautifully. Now, I didn't think there would be any saving us from my devious nature. I was a war of emotions over it, too, emotions I resolutely shoved down so that I could let myself enjoy this.

I curved my arms behind her back and she took her hands from the coffee table, which both surprised me and didn't. She was deep in her own headspace and my curiosity led me to see what she would do with it. She slipped off of the edge of the table, into my lap, riding me, and I let out a satisfied, 'ah' when she took me in as deep as I could go.

Her arms twined around my shoulders and she found a rhythm, and I let her take her pleasure. I liked my women to be willing participants in my little games, just as long as they understood I remained in control. I had never guessed Ally would conform so beautifully and again, I was a mix of emotions over it; overjoyed and miserable at the same time, as I tried to find balance or at least tried to fall completely in one direction over the other.

She bit her bottom lip in that way I found sultry and alluring; her bright green eyes, heavy-lidded with her passion and desire, met mine and it was as if I were electrified. I watched her move above me, poetry in motion and half-regretted that we were out here and not in my bed… but honestly, that was for the best. Had I taken her to my bed, it would mean I had designs on keeping her, and I didn't think that possible. Not once she got further down this rabbit-hole with me, and damn me that I wanted to draw her in further.

She touched the side of my face and I refocused on her, her beautiful eyes trapping mine, something passing between us in that undefinable way… Whatever she saw in me made her smile – *smile!* I almost couldn't believe it, but there it was, this sweet little smile painting her so-soft looking lips, tempting me to kiss her and seal my fate, and for a flicker of a moment I wondered who was *really* in control.

"I don't think you're heartless," she murmured dreamily, her fingertips dropping to graze my ribs and the ink under my skin there.

"You don't know me, yet…" I growled, and I turned her to lay her down on the carpet. Her legs wrapped around my hips and I palmed hers, driving into her and pulling her down onto me at the same time. Powerful, driving strokes that made her cry out, those luminous eyes of hers closing, her bottom lip captured between her teeth. I drew it out with my thumb in a light caress and pressed it firmly, but gently past them. She sucked on it like I wanted her to, teasing the pad with her tongue while I drove into her, over, and over, and over again.

I dragged my fingertips over her body, rearing up to look down at her and used my thumb to tease her clitoris gently. She cried out again, arching, *heavenly*. So beautiful, she came around my cock and as she bent beneath me, I fully expected pure white wings to erupt from her back.

She was perfect, she was everything in that moment and more, and if I didn't already think I was a devil, the way she looked at me may have convinced me of an exalted angelic status I didn't possess. Of course, then I might believe myself capable of falling.

Who are you kidding, a voice of betrayal whispered in the back of my mind. *You're falling and you're falling hard for her. She's perfect.*

I placed my lips above her heart and would devour it if she weren't careful. She spasmed around me, jolting in my arms, and I died the little death in tribute to her, filling the condom as pleasure rushed out from my center with the power of a nuclear blast.

She clung to me, her arms around me, her head on my shoulder, lips pressed to the side of my neck as we knelt on my living room's area rug, panting. I didn't want her to let me go. She felt so good, curled in my lap. Like a purring kitten. Adorable.

You can't keep her…

I wanted to, but she deserved better than a depraved bastard like me. I eased her back, holding her firmly by her upper arms and with a shuddering breath she sat up and met my eyes.

"Go turn on the shower. I'll join you, and then I'll drive you home."

She nodded, eyes glazed, body limp and it took a few tries and some assistance on my part to get her to her feet. She stood for a moment, trembling, looking well-fucked, and it gave me such a sense of satisfaction that I could almost feel my ego swell with pride at a job well done.

"Go get in the shower," I ordered again, quietly, and she nodded and moved cautiously in that direction in a trance-like subspace. She would need some aftercare, some time to come back to herself completely, and then I would have to let her go.

I took the few moments I could to clean up out here, dumping the toys in the kitchen sink and disposing of the condom and wrapper in the trash. I probably could have her clean them, but she was beautifully shattered in all of the best ways and I was reluctant to put her back together too quickly. She should enjoy it while it lasted.

I went down the hall, calm and collected, and went into my bathroom. She stood under the gentle rainfall showerhead, face tipped up, eyes closed, and I could picture those missing wings of hers. I wanted to snap a photo and commit this moment to something more permanent than just memory, but I didn't. Instead, I opened the door and stepped in, joining her.

Her eyes opened and she startled when my hand touched her hip and I smiled asking her, "Where did you go?"

"I don't know, but I didn't want to come back… not just yet."

I knew that feeling. I knew I would have to go back to real life soon enough and I wasn't ready to leave this moment, right here, with her. I pulled her arms around my waist and smoothed her hair back from her face. The water collected like a constellation in her long lashes and the way her makeup ran in tracks like tears, was painfully exquisite. It was also painfully provocative. I resisted the urge to put my lips to hers. I didn't wish to lead her on, and for me, a kiss was something far too intimate – yes, even beyond fucking, for me.

"What's wrong?" she asked and her fingertips came up to trace my features. I closed my eyes and let her touch me, enjoying the light and inspired feeling of her hands on me.

"Nothing," I murmured, covering my true thoughts. "A bit tired."

She smiled a little, sympathetically, and murmured, "I can take a cab home."

"I said I would drive you, and I will. The least I can do is see you safely home."

"I don't want to rush this," she confessed, and I smiled.

"That is something for your journal," I said.

"Which you're going to read anyway, aren't you?"

"True, yes."

"So what does it matter if I tell you rather than write it?"

She had a point. Of course, reading things was often times easier than experiencing them firsthand. She took a deep breath and laid her head on my shoulder and I cuddled her close. She sighed out, breath rushing warm over my skin and I fought not to shiver from it. It felt good, standing under the warm shower spray, but all good things must come to an end, even if it is reluctantly so.

"Will I see you again, like that, or was this a one-time thing?" she asked, when I pulled up in front of the project building that she lived in.

We hadn't spoken much between the shower and now, and it had been an entirely too comfortable silence, our energies combining in that perfect way that you only found a handful of times in your time here on earth – or so I liked to think, considering it had happened so infrequently.

"I don't know," I told her truthfully, and caught the flash of disappointed pain in the glass of my passenger door.

"Okay," she murmured without a fight and I felt like scum. *She doesn't know what you can be like...* the voice of reason whispered. Her voice interrupted my thoughts; she cleared her throat and said, her voice even and strong, "Thank you for a lovely evening, Mr. Parnell," and then the door opened and she was gone, striding up the walkway to her building's steps, up into the courtyard beyond the open iron gate.

"Dammit, Parnell," I muttered, and smacked the steering wheel of my Mercedes. I sucked in a breath and let it out in an angry sigh, before pulling smoothly from the curb and back around towards Old Town.

16

*A*lly…

My Monday wasn't going well. I made it to work and Millie needed me to work half the afternoon past my quitting time, the afternoon girl had food poisoning. I agreed because Millie was in a bind, but that meant that I would be late getting to Mr. Parnell's… which meant he would likely be home tonight while I cleaned.

I wouldn't have minded after our last encounter, but I had done what he asked. I had written down everything, how it made me feel, and I had given it to him in a sealed envelope the next morning when he had come in for his coffee, and then… nothing.

It had just been simple, quiet pleasantries and business as usual for the rest of the week. He hadn't come home early, and I did my cleaning – per usual. Cameras off and in the nude the following Monday from our dalliance, but when Friday arrived, I suddenly felt unnerved and had gotten dressed again twenty minutes after I started. I had felt guilty about taking the extra pay and so I hadn't. I'd left a note, telling the truth: that I had begun cleaning but then had gotten dressed and I'd left fifty dollars of my pay behind with it.

The weekend had been spent with Dawnie and my gran and had been good, but Dawnie, damnably perceptive as she could be, had pestered me nonstop with questions I couldn't answer. It had quickly turned stressful and had ended in us fighting. Which then led me to not be as happy as I usually was when I saw Gran, which upset *her,* and it just felt like a domino effect of awful.

I went through my day at the café and if I could have afforded it, I would have begged off going to Mr. Parnell's today, but I couldn't. I needed the money. So instead, with my apologies, I left the café at five instead of my usual two-thirty, begging Millie's forgiveness for not being able to stay longer but she completely understood.

I was on my third bus in the crush of the peak of rush hour when the day just seemed to want to get worse. I had my headphones in, but they weren't on. It was just a thing I did to keep guys from hitting on me. Of course, it was just my luck that not just one, but two of exactly the wrong kind of guys decided that I looked interested despite my intense effort to look anywhere on the packed bus but at them.

"Hey baby, you look *fine…*" one of them said, drawing out the word 'fine' like he was slick or something. I switched hands on the railing and turned my back, hitching my tote bag higher on my shoulder but, unfortunately, that just put me facing his friend.

"Oh! That was cold, girly. Why you gotta be so rude to my friend? Corey here was just trying to give you a compliment."

I pulled one of my earbuds out of my ear, mouth dry and said, "I'm sorry?" as if I hadn't heard either of them.

"Aw, quit playin', baby girl." Corey was entirely too close for comfort, and I hunched in on myself. I was effectively trapped between them, and I didn't like that.

"What's your name?" the one I faced asked.

"Please, I don't want any trouble. I'm really not interested, guys," I tried to be as polite as I could when I said it.

"Come on, baby. We just asking your *name*."

I glanced frantically at the other passengers for help, but no one would even look at me. I got that sinking feeling in the center of my chest and swallowed hard. Fine. If no one was going to help me, I would just stand up for myself.

"I don't want to tell you my name, and I've already told you I'm not interested. Now, if you'd please leave me alone," I said firmly.

"Stuck up little bitch, would you listen to her?" the one in front of me said incredulously.

The one behind me grabbed my ass and I stomped down hard on his foot, just as the bus lurched to a stop at my stop. I shouldered past the one in front of me and checked my hip hard against the little divider by the door getting around it. I leaped over the two steps and started walking briskly up the block towards the corner.

"You little bitch!" I heard behind me, and I didn't look back. I *ran*.

I pelted up the sidewalk and reached the corner and only then did I look back. They were far closer than I liked and I looked between them and the moving traffic, and as one of them reached for me, I stepped off the curb. Tires screeched along the pavement, horns blared and I dodged in front of a taxi, checking my *other* hip on the brush guard on the front bumper. I yelped and ran up onto the other curb and made a sharp right. I pounded up the sidewalk and as soon as he was in sight. I sucked down a hard lungful of air and screamed, "Mr. Clive!"

He turned from the street, eyes wide, and I reached out even though I was still almost a half a block away when one of them crashed into my back. I cried out and went down hard on my knees. I was wearing shorts and a sharp pain went through my knees. I screamed and struggled, and one of them went to punch me in the back of my head but glanced off it and punched the sidewalk instead.

"Ally!" I heard a man's voice bellow, and I looked up, expecting to see Clive, but it was Mr. Parnell getting out of the back of a cab.

"Mr. Parnell, help me!" I shrieked and he was suddenly there. I swear I hadn't even seen him move. I heard a grunt and the man who had me around the ankle let go and the other shoved me down into the sidewalk, pushing off of me by the back of my head. My chin scraped the pavement painfully, and I rolled onto my back and tried to crab-walk away, towards the safety of the dark green canopy in front of the Calvert building.

"Look out!" I screamed, as Damien Parnell leaped back from one of my attackers who now held a knife.

Like some movie martial arts dynamo, he whipped his suit jacket over his head, hands still stuffed in its sleeves and wrapped it around our assailant's forearm. He pulled the man towards him and it was a flurry of activity too confusing to my eyes and so fast I almost didn't trust what I was seeing.

Arms reached under my armpits and I yelped, but it was Mr. Clive, saying "Come on, Miss Ally; come with me, this way now. Police are on their way."

I stood up and went with him, and winced, my knees tight and painful. I moved up the block with him and let him sit me on the bench outside the building's front door.

"It's okay now, you're okay… Here's Mr. Jimmy."

"Is he okay, is he all right?" I tried to look around the corner, but Mr. Clive and Mr. Jimmy were in front of me, fussing over me. A police car coming from the wrong direction screeched up to the curb, and two uniformed officers got out, leaving their doors swinging wide and I sagged with relief. They went pelting up the sidewalk, and I looked up to Mr. Clive and demanded, *"Is he okay?"*

"Ally." My head jerked at the commanding tone and I turned. Mr. Parnell standing there, chest heaving and without his suit jacket, but fine.

I burst into tears of relief, my insides turning to water and my gag reflex working overtime as my stomach rolled. I held up my arms, and he didn't even blink, he came to me and knelt beside the bench and offered what comfort he could in front of all these people.

"I'm sorry," I sobbed brokenly, breath hitching through the words. "I'm so sorry."

"Mr. Jimmy, could you please bring up her things?" Mr. Parnell asked over my head, and I heard the old man agree. His shadow over us disappeared, and before I knew it, I was up off the bench and moving across the parquet floor. The gate on the old fashioned elevator rattled and we boarded and then we were moving. I couldn't even care I was in the deathtrap little box. I just wanted to be as far away from those thugs as possible. Mr. Clive had left his post for me, operating the elevator and then opening the door to Mr. Parnell's apartment for us.

"Thank you," Mr. Parnell murmured. "That will be all for now," and he set me down and punched in the alarm code. I stood, a trembling, shaking mess, knees burning and aching, and he turned to me, pushing aside my hair that was sticking to my tear- and, admittedly, snot-soaked face.

"Are you okay? What happened?" he demanded, and I crumbled. I couldn't make the tears stop; I couldn't make the shaking stop; I couldn't make my racing heart or the fear stop.

He pulled me into his arms and led me over to the kitchen counter and helped me hop up onto the edge. He stood in front of me and pushed all of my hair off my face, murmuring, "You're okay, it's okay now. I wouldn't let anything happen to you. You believe me, don't you Ally?"

His dark eyes were both empathetic and intent, silently demanding an answer. I nodded, not trusting my voice, and he nodded with me, saying, "Good, that's good. More help is on the way; I'm right here, I'm going to get a cool washcloth. You're safe, right? Nothing can hurt you here, right?"

"Right," I echoed carefully, but I still couldn't stop shaking.

17

*Y*ale…

I was scrolling through my phone when the cabbie slammed on his brakes yelling, "What're you doing you crazy bitch!?" and I looked up to see Ally's wide and frightened eyes through the windshield. Of course, by the time it registered that it was *her,* she was gone, and a young man was doing a slide across the hood in pursuit. I scowled as the cab driver threw up his hands and yelled at the man as another streaked by my window.

"Pull *over*! Now!" I bellowed over the cab driver's griping, and he looked in his rearview mirror, startled. I glowered at him and he said, "All right, all right, we're almost there."

He pulled up to the curb and the locks disengaged; I threw open the back door and dropped my briefcase on the sidewalk.

"Ally!" I bellowed and she looked up from where the two men had her pinned to the sidewalk, one holding her down, the other with his hand around her ankle. I ran up the sidewalk and poured every ounce of rage into the kick that I sent over the first assailant's head into the other's face. He let go of her ankle, hands to his face and sat there, stunned on the sidewalk.

The other got up, off of my woman's back, and took a swing at me. I dodged easily, and he brought out a knife with the other hand. I heard Ally scream something, but I was intent on her attacker. I disabled him and when I turned she was gone.

Now I had her in my condo, sitting on my kitchen counter, and she was a bleeding, sobbing mess. I should have 'accidentally' killed them. I soaked a washcloth in the kitchen tap under some cool water and wrung it out, bringing it over to her. She went to take it and I jerked it out of her reach, grumbling, "Stop!" at her like she was a child. She didn't understand, it was *my* place to take care of her, now. My duty, my responsibility.

She put her hands down, gripping the edge of the counter, shaking so badly with the aftereffects of trauma and adrenaline. I smoothed her hair back from her face and gently wiped it off with the washcloth.

"Are you okay?" I asked her again, gentling my tone.

"I… I think so."

A double tap fell on my open condo door, and I said, "Yes?" without taking my eyes off of her.

"Yale, it's me. We got two in custody downstairs; Angel's on the way. Can she give a statement?"

"Yeah, Poe, get in here."

"I don't understand," Ally said helplessly, fixing me with green eyes swimming with unshed tears, "Yale?"

I chuckled and said, "Later, I promise."

Poe came up next to us, his partner lingering just behind him, and asked, "Ma'am?"

Ally looked his way and said, "Blaylock, my name is Allison Blaylock, but you can call me Ally."

"Right, it's nice to meet you, Ally. Can you tell me what happened? Why those men were chasing you?"

Her story was the same as a thousand other girl's statements I'd read. Assault victims, rape victims, it all amounted to the same. Young, idiot, entitled males.

I growled and turned with a hand over my mouth to stop myself from saying something unfortunate. I didn't want to upset Ally any more than she already was.

"Okay, we're going to take some pictures before these guys have a look at you, okay?" said Poe's partner, an officer by the name of Hartnett.

"Oh, okay…" she nodded and he quickly snapped pictures of her knees and her chin.

While he was doing that, Angel sidled up to me and asked, "She okay?"

I glowered at him, "That's what you're here for."

He chuckled and said, "You know what I mean." I glared at him and his face lost its easy smile. He held up his hands, purple gloves in one of them and said, "Sorry. Didn't realize it was that serious."

"It's not," I growled defensively.

"Right, let me get in there." He pulled the purple gloves onto his hands and stepped between Poe and Hartnett.

"Hi, I'm Angel," he said.

"Ally."

"You comfortable if I take a look at you, Ally?"

She nodded, and he pulled out a pen light and shone it into her eyes.

His partner came up and took her blood pressure. I watched with concern as he went through everything, asking what hurt, checking out her chin and her knees.

Poe and Hartnett interviewed me while I watched as Angel cleaned Ally up. She flinched when he applied an antiseptic cloth to her chin and I barked without realizing it, "Be careful!" Angel turned and gave me a scowl.

"I know how to do my job, counselor. You don't see me coming down to the courthouse trying my hand at yours." I bowed my head and pulled on the back of my neck.

"Of course, my apologies." I could admit when I was wrong. I didn't enjoy it, but I could admit it and apologize when it was called for.

Angel shook his head and turned back to Ally who was staring at me, eyes wide, like she'd never seen me before – which made me scowl even harder.

"Dude, Yale, what is the deal with you?" Poe demanded, under his breath. "I thought she was just the maid."

"She's a nice girl, a hard worker, she doesn't deserve this," I answered, but it sounded half-baked even to me.

Poe shook his head, "Whatever, man. It's your business, don't go griping Angel's or my ass for it, though. We didn't do it. We're your brothers, remember?"

"Yeah, sorry, I'm sorry…" I muttered. Ally's eyes were squeezed shut as Angel knelt and cleaned up her legs, patching up her knees with antibiotic ointment and fat, square Band-Aids.

"Yale," Poe said forcefully, and put his hand on my shoulder. I swung my gaze to his. "She's good, man. It's Angel."

I nodded, "You need anything else from me?"

"No, I think we got it. Uniforms are downstairs with the doorman. Perps've already been taken to Oz's tender brand of loving care."

"You should radio ahead, give him a heads-up," I growled and Poe laughed.

"Yeah."

"They from the Point Side?" I asked.

"No, Bitterman projects."

"At least there's that," I said.

"Yeah, she the one from the Point Side that the guys helped move last month?"

"Yeah."

"Shame she lives there seems like a nice girl."

"She is."

Angel came over, stripping off his gloves. He said to me, "Might want to get her something to eat. It'll help with the post-adrenaline shakes."

"Don't have anything around here."

"Take her to the 10-13. It'll give Reflash something to fuss over in the kitchen."

"Yeah, I might just do that; I don't expect she'll want to stick around here."

"Have her take some Advil or something soon, she's all right now, but she's going to be sore in the morning."

"Okay."

"Cool, we're out."

"Have the bill sent to me, and, Angel?" He looked up and back over his shoulder at me from where he was collecting his aid kit. "Thank you, brother." He nodded, dropped his eyes and sighed, hauling the heavy tote up onto his shoulder. Everyone who was not me or Ally piled out my front door. My briefcase and her belongings had been set inside the threshold at some point and were sitting beneath the alarm panel.

Poe gave me a meaningful look and shut the door behind them, and it was suddenly just me and Ally. I turned to her, my hands resting on my hips and the look on her face was enough to thaw even my cold, dead heart.

"Hey, Bright Eyes," I murmured softly, and she hugged herself.

"I am so sorry," she reiterated, and hid those beautiful orbs from me, her eyelids drifting shut.

"Not your fault," I said and went to her, nudging her knees carefully apart so I could stand between them and hug her close. She sniffed but didn't cry, and folded into my arms like she was meant to be there. I stroked her long hair where it lay against her back and asked faintly, "Are you hungry?"

"I could eat," she said, her voice feeble.

"Okay, then. Let me take you out to dinner."

"Okay."

I held her a moment longer and let myself come to grips with how badly seeing her on that sidewalk, two men on top of her, had scared me.

I felt like I narrowly escaped losing her and it troubled me, exactly how many feelings I had about that. However, it would seem, the danger wasn't quite over yet.

"I was afraid you didn't care…"

I let her go, placing my hands on the counter to either side of her hips and stared at her, but she wouldn't raise her eyes from where she clutched her hands in her lap after relinquishing her hold on me. I huffed out a frustrated sigh and told her, "I'm not a mind-reader, Ally. You're going to have to tell me why you would think that."

She looked up sharply and said, "I did what you asked, wrote everything down, then nothing. Nothing at all…"

Ah.

"I see," I said plainly and searched her face. "You know that I am a busy man."

"Yes."

"And that we rarely cross paths here, outside the public eye."

She gave me a flat look, and I pushed back, giving my shoulders a bit of a stretch and bowing my head. She was right, of course, it hadn't been fair or even very clear of me, my expectations. Of course, in my defense, I didn't even know what my expectations were… Which was even more wrong of me, when I stopped to think about it.

"Look, I know that this isn't, like, a relationship or anything…" she said gently, and I sighed again.

"Correct," I grated, and tried to ignore it when she flinched.

She sighed this time and covered her face with her hands. I patiently waited her out and she dropped them back to her lap and said to me, "Do you like me?"

"Of course I do."

"Enough to want to get to know me?" she asked.

I didn't think about it, I didn't even blink, I told her the truth: "I want to know the deepest parts of you, Allison."

"Then could you please *talk to me?* I mean, I can understand that you don't want a relationship, that you don't have time for it, but…" She struggled to find the words and I waited. Finally, she let out a frustrated breath, her eyes sinking shut and her shoulders dropping, but she didn't have to say anything. I already understood.

"You can't handle that level of detachment. You can't just have sex, enjoy the pleasure, without intimacy."

"Yes, that! It takes all of the joy out of it, doesn't it?"

"No… at least not for me," I said even as my mind said, *liar. It's not as good and you know it.* "But I can understand and respect that it's that way for you. Of course, I care, Ally. If I didn't care, I wouldn't have come to the rescue, would I?"

"I don't know," she whispered. "You're a very confusing man, Mr. Parnell. You have 'heartless' tattooed on your body like it's some kind of badge of honor yet you've helped me so much. You've admitted you're attracted to me, have had sex with me, yet you won't kiss me…" She looked hurt, and I rubbed a hand over my mouth, trying to figure out what I should tell her when it came to that.

To me, you didn't kiss your toys. You kissed your lover, your partner, but not someone you had no intention of going further with. I wasn't ready to give little innocent Allison Blaylock more of me. To do so would be corrupting her absolutely. I wasn't prepared to be the instrument of her fall.

"You need more from me than I am prepared to give you," I said finally and she surprised me. She nodded, and while hurt clouded her clear green eyes, there was understanding there, too.

"You make me feel good," she whispered. "You make me feel pretty and desirable. I've never felt it like the way I feel it with you. It's not like those two men. They saw something pretty and wanted to hit it and quit it, you know? You… I don't know. It's like when you look at me, you see past the window dressing and it's like you go soul deep." She drew a shuddering breath, and her raw honesty made me still. I watched her waiting and praying silently for more.

"It scares me, but I like that about you… you make me feel dirty, but you make me feel clean at the same time."

Her choice of words was both fascinating and haunting. I cupped her face in my hands and met her eyes with mine.

"You've been such a brave and beautiful girl," I said and I meant so much more than just the way she had kept cool and collected during her attack earlier. I kissed her forehead and her eyes drifted shut, her breath leaving her in a sigh. I swallowed hard and murmured against her warm skin, "Such bravery should be rewarded."

Before I could change my mind, or talk myself out of making the mistake, I lowered my lips to hers and I kissed her.

18

*A*lly…

I met the unexpected kiss with a mixture of excitement and confusion which melted into a sweet, calming, bliss. His lips were warm and soft against mine, his beard lightly tickling my face. He plunged his tongue into my mouth possessively, and I melted even more. I loved how it made me feel. How I didn't feel so much *owned* as I did *safe*. Protected in a way that made me feel nigh on invincible.

I felt my chest loosen, the tension draining out of me, off the countertop, to pool on the floor, forgotten, as I gave myself over to him completely. To the feel of his mouth on mine, the feel of his hands at my throat and in my hair. He pulled back and his dark eyes were liquid and deep and I felt like I could topple down them and fall, fall, fall, forever and never get tired of the sensation.

"I'm going to take you to dinner, and then I am going to take you home, but first I'm going to change. Do you feel up to playing?"

I nodded mutely, everything about me crying silently: *Yes! I'll do whatever you want, whatever you say…*

"Stay here," he ordered, and he disappeared up the hallway to his bedroom. I swallowed, hands shaking for a completely different reason this time. He was just so overwhelming, so magnetic, so gorgeous and confusing. I think that was part of the appeal… He wasn't shallow. Far from it, he was something complex. Made me wonder, kept me wondering, and the attraction I felt was overwhelming in all the right ways.

I waited impatiently, trying not to fidget, wondering just what he had in store for me, and the elation that brought was nice. It was a pleasant sort of excitement, as opposed to the upset of earlier. If he were trying to make up for the unpleasantness, he was off to a fantastic start.

My heart leapt at the heavy tread of his booted step returning up the hall and promptly fainted and plummeted into a barrel roll when he came into view. He'd gone from gorgeous to ruggedly handsome with a simple change of clothes. I don't remember a time I had ever seen him dressed casually and truthfully, even dressed as he was, it was still in a refined sort of way.

He wore scuffed motorcycle boots and light jeans the way they were supposed to be worn by a man (with his gorgeous ass in the seat of them and not with the seat around his knees.) Tucked into those belted jeans was a form-fitting, faded black tee shirt, comfortable and soft looking. Something he had owned for years but couldn't part with was my first thought, but as faded and broken-in as it looked, it had no holes or parted seams.

In his hands, he held a small bundle, like the one he'd had me bring to him from his nightstand last time and I felt a lump develop in my throat. He came to me and stepped between my knees, his eyes boring into mine.

"What's in the bundle?" I asked breathlessly.

"Wait and find out," he shot back, setting it aside, his fingers going to the button and zipper in the front of my shorts. I had put together an adorable outfit for today. It was hot out, the height of summer, and I had paired my short olive-drab shorts with a white tank top under a cropped, matching olive-drab denim sort of jacket. Both the shorts and the jacket had been Good Will find's a couple of summers apart, but paired with low ankle socks and my black Chuck Taylor knockoffs, it had become one of my favorite heatwave outfits.

Now he was tugging insistently on the shorts and I put my hands flat on the counter, raising my ass so he could skim them down my legs and off. He repeated the motion with my white cotton thong panties and, careful of the bandages on my scraped knees, pushed my legs apart.

"Scoot closer," he demanded. "Head back and stare at the ceiling."

I did as I was bid and he went to his knees, hands smoothing up and down the outsides of my thighs, tongue flicking against my pussy lightly, fingers pressing against my opening. I closed my eyes and gave myself over to the sensation.

Too soon he stood back up and I could hear it in his voice, his smile when he said: "Keep your eyes closed." I kept them closed and jumped slightly when the velvety smooth texture of a silicone toy pressed against my opening. He worked it gently inside me, and I had the same hot, full feeling as I had with the balls. Just enough of a presence to press against my walls. I swallowed hard and he said, "I'm going to put your clothes back on and you're going to keep that in. Right?"

"Yes, sir," I breathed.

"Open your eyes, Ally. Look at me when you say that, please." The request was delivered softly, much more gently than he'd asked me for anything before and I wanted to see the expression that went with the change. His gaze was something else. Deeper, darker, but much more vulnerable somehow. It was a fleeting glimpse, but it was enough.

"Yes, sir…" I repeated, and his expression grew grim, closing down but not in a bad way – just like he was hiding again and I didn't understand what had just happened. *He can be so confusing…* I thought, but then he was helping me to stand, helping me step back into my panties as I held the foreign object inside of me, growing wet with arousal and anticipation.

He brought my shorts up my legs, so careful of the front of my knees, which stung mercilessly and burned with a fierce, throbbing ache. He fastened them for me, taking care like I was his little china doll or something, and I liked the feeling. It was sweet and kind. He let his hands linger on my hips and asked me, "Are you ready?"

I swallowed hard and nodded gently, and he smiled and it was that rakish debonair smile, as my grandmother would have called it. I loved it. It made the butterflies take flight in my stomach and made me feel special, mostly because, I realized he seemed to reserve that smile just for me, the more and more we went along; the more I saw him.

"You ever ride a motorcycle?" he asked casually, stepping over to the hall closet and opening it. He brought down his leather jacket with the vest over it. The one with all of the patches on it, and how I knew that the men who had come to my apartment to move me had been sent by him.

Apparently, we were past pretending that he didn't know them, and I was glad for that. It was hard enough keeping secrets from Dawnie and my grandmother.

"No," I told him truthfully, "but I've always wanted to try."

"It's a good night for a ride; traffic is busy, so we'll be going pretty slow… do you trust me enough to ride with me?"

I chewed my bottom lip; I really wanted to go but…

"Can I tell my best friend?" I asked, and he cocked his head and gave me a long, slow blink.

"What have you told her about us?" he asked.

"Nothing… nothing at all and that's the problem. She's my best friend and you asked me not to and it's causing fights. I don't want to tell her anything about…" I faltered and I knew that he knew what I meant: the sex. I blushed furiously and waved my hands, saying, "Well, you know," and I found it positively wicked, the way he smiled at me, the dark light of desire lighting his already deep and dark eyes. I rushed on with, "I like this, but I would like to tell her about some things… like how you stopped those men," I couldn't help but smile, "and my first motorcycle ride, if I take one."

He drew nearer and his arm went around my waist. He pulled me closer and asked, "You really haven't told her anything at all, have you?"

"No," I whispered, and he nodded slowly.

"I can trust you to carefully edit the…" he cleared his throat, "little details?" he asked, his hand sliding to my ass and giving it a firm squeeze and I smiled, happy.

"I really like that it's just between us, I've never had a real secret worth protecting. I understand you're a private man and I feel… honored … that you let me in like you have."

His eyes searched my face, his expression stony, but finally he nodded gravely and my heart nearly exploded with joy.

"You may tell her anything that occurs outside that door or inside in the presence of others," he said and I nodded.

"I understand," I murmured.

"Come on," he said, "I'm starving."

His fingers wrapped around mine and he led me gently to the front door. He set the alarm and we stepped out into the hall. He didn't retake my hand again until we were safely in the elevator and on our way down.

We stepped off in a basement that was similar to the one below the Point Side, open with support pillars, reinforced here due to the extreme age of the building. I followed Mr. Parnell around the bank of elevators to the right as we stepped off and found a heavy fire door set into the basement wall. He pressed on the crash bar in it and held it open for me to pass through into a musty garage below the building that was behind the Calvert building.

The first time we'd been down here, the first time he had taken me home, he had explained: "We have a floor or two for our cars. A contract with the company who owns the garage." The Calvert building was from the 1920's and didn't have the capability of having a garage of its own. In a fascinating little history lesson, he'd told me about how they had converted an old Prohibition-era tunnel entrance into a back door of sorts for the Calvert building to access the garage.

Like before, we took the painted crosswalk from that door to the next bank of more modern elevators which whisked us down even lower. I hated that part. I hated elevators with a passion. I would always take the stairs if I could. I couldn't get off the thing fast enough when we reached the floor of the garage where Mr. Parnell had three parking spaces. One was for the sleek, silver Mercedes he'd taken me home in the first time. Another for a big black Cadillac Escalade SUV, and finally, one with a metal locker against the back wall, a motorcycle hidden by a taupe protective cover in front of it.

He went to the locker and opened it, and pulled out a couple of helmets. He passed one to me, a flat black affair that was one of those half styles, like a bicycle helmet, only affording more protection. I put it on obediently and hitched my tote higher on my shoulder while he removed the cover from the bike and stuffed it away in the locker. He put a helmet with a full facemask on the seat while he put everything away and locked up.

"Come here," he ordered and had me sit on the back seat. "Feet go here and keep them there. The pipes get hot, and I don't want you to get burned. When I lean, you lean, don't stiffen up. You could throw the balance of the bike off, and that would be bad."

"Okay," I murmured, and he got on in front of me. He put his helmet on with the mask up and said: "Most importantly, hang onto me and enjoy the ride." I smiled bravely; the idea had sounded fun upstairs but now that he was firing up the machine, my heart was in my throat and I was suddenly as nervous as I could get. I settled and put my arms around him obediently and he grabbed the handlebars. We lurched gently into motion and my mouth went dry.

I did everything he asked as we took the sweeps and curves of the garage upwards. By the time we reached the street, I was excited. I wanted to feel the dying sun and the breeze on my face. Maybe catch the smell of the bay, taste the tang of salt on the wind. It was one of my favorite things about living in Indigo City, being so close to the water.

The ride was disappointingly short before we were pulling off a one-way into a brick paved side alley, beside an old building that wasn't quite as old as the Calvert building – or maybe it could have been older. I didn't know enough about the city's history or architecture to know for certain.

He tapped the outside of my thigh, and mindful of the exhaust pipes, like he'd told me to be, I got down carefully. Although, embarrassingly, he'd had to signal me more than once for me to get the picture. I carefully worked the chin strap loose from its two metal D-rings while he backed his motorcycle into a line of them against the wall before the dumpsters started further down the alley.

He shut off the bike and took his own helmet off much more efficiently, peeking into one of the rear view mirrors and raking a hand through his hair to settle it from sticking up at strange angles. I smiled and held mine out to his outstretched hand. He hung it from the handlebars and left his on the seat and I frowned.

"Aren't you afraid someone will take them?" he smiled and pointed out the obvious security camera.

"Plus, just about the whole city knows, this is a cop's bar."

"It is?" I queried.

"As I said," he winked, "Just about the whole city knows."

"I guess I'm the exception to the rule," I murmured, blushing a faint pink.

He laughed and got off the bike, palming his keys and putting them in his jacket pocket. His other hand he put against my lower back and with a gentle pressure, ushered me around the corner to the restaurant's front door.

"I thought this place was called the 10-13," I said, pointing at the shingle depicting the place's name as *The Cormorant*.

"It's the address and a police call-sign among radio cars."

"Oh. What does it mean? The call-sign, I mean."

"Officer in need of assistance. Which, I think someone familiar to you might provide by way of alcohol." He dipped his chin purposefully in that direction and I followed his gaze.

I broke out into a smile as Skids, the leader of the trio and most personable of the three men, lifted his chin over at the bar and called across to us, "Hey, will you look at what the cat dragged in! Step right up, little lady. Let's have a look at you."

I glanced back to Mr. Parnell and he smiled, a warm thing, and said, "Go ahead."

I went up to the bar and Skids frowned, asking, "What happened to your face?"

"Ally has had a rough day," Mr. Parnell murmured, taking the seat beside mine.

"Yale!" someone called behind us and we turned. There were a couple more guys in the same motorcycle vest as Mr. Parnell's. One, a big man, tall and broad-shouldered, with curious hazel eyes had his eyes fixed on me. He had a woman, slender, tall and beautiful with tattoos on her arms, under one of his. She swept her long black hair over one shoulder and raked me with unfriendly, flat black eyes that glittered with calculation. She leaned into the bigger man and murmured something and he frowned down at her like he didn't like or understand what she had to say.

I took an almost instant disliking to her, but kept quiet, to see how she would continue to treat me. He came around the long table they were standing at and she reluctantly went along with him. Otherwise, she would have had to let him go. I smiled as they approached and looked to the man they left behind where they were playing darts.

"Oh! Hi, how'd you get here?" I asked, and the paramedic raised his eyebrows.

"Sorry?" he asked, and looked amused.

"Ally, that's Golden. You met Angel back at my place." I blinked and looked over to Mr. Parnell who was smiling.

"What?"

"My twin's working," the other man, Golden, said. "Why'd she have a reason to meet him? And at your place, no less."

"Like I was telling Skids, Ally's had a rough day."

I blushed faintly and rolled my lips together, suddenly self-conscious with being the center of attention. The woman raked her dark eyes over me, but the way she did it, the expression she wore while she did it, left me feeling almost dirty everywhere her look touched.

"Yeah, what the hell happened to you?" she asked and smirked.

"I, um, I was attacked coming off of the bus," I said faintly.

The men's expressions all crushed down into frowns, but the woman's eyebrows went up. "No shit? Where at?"

"Torrid, cut the kid some slack," the bigger man said, and gave his girlfriend a little shake.

"What? She's here, she's with Yale of all people, and she's obviously fine."

The big man made a frustrated sigh and gave me an apologetic look. I tried a smile on him and the woman rolled her eyes. *What a bitch...* I thought. I also didn't think it was me. At least, not given the way she shot Mr. Parnell a dirty look.

"Ally cleans my place a couple of times a week. She was on her way into work when it happened," Mr. Parnell supplied.

"Cleans… oh, yeah?" She eyed me, and I felt myself blush under her suddenly heavy scrutiny.

"What happened?" Golden demanded, bulldozing all of the innuendo and uncomfortable double entendre completely, although his irritation with the woman was pretty clear by the way he stood next to her with his shoulder turned, almost giving her his back while he focused on me.

"Just a couple of guys on the bus that didn't want to take no for an answer," I said, and wanted to fade into obscurity.

"They catch 'em?" Golden asked.

"I made sure of it. Poe and his partner responded," Mr. Parnell said flatly.

"Well, I think the little lady could use a bit of liquid courage. You *are* 21, aren't you?" Skids asked me with a wink.

I smiled, "Yes."

"Show me some ID and I'll get right on whatever you'd like."

I bit my bottom lip to keep my smile from growing into something ridiculous and reached into my little purse at my hip. I handed over my license and he nodded, handing it back.

"What d'you like?"

"I honestly have no idea," I said laughing.

"Whatever it is, should be put in a sippy cup," the woman snarked under her breath.

"Backdraft, would you like to have a talk with Tori, or shall I?" Mr. Parnell asked, coolly.

I swallowed hard at the awkward and tense silence left in their wake as the man hauled her over by the front door. He bowed his light-brown head, so light it was almost blond, in her direction and said some low and intense words. She snapped back at him, eyes blazing, and Mr. Parnell sighed.

"Don't worry about it," Golden said to me. "She's just pissed because Yale put bros before hos."

"Golden," Mr. Parnell's voice dripped with caution.

"What? Bitch had it coming," Golden remarked and took a slug from his beer.

I stared from one to the other of them wide-eyed, and Skids set down a drink at my elbow, on the bar behind me. I swiveled in my seat and looked down at the glass. A cone shape, sitting on a pedestal of a blob of glass. If it'd had a stem, I would almost call it a Martini glass, but I liked this version better. Seemed more real, less pretentious.

"What is it?" I asked curiously, staring at the sunny yellow liquid inside.

"Lemon drop; that's sugar on the rim. Taste it."

I took a sip and it was sweet, surprisingly sweet, and like candied lemonade. I smiled and nodded. "Thank you!"

He chuckled and moved off to help someone else for a moment. Golden remarking, "For a guy who's completely dry, he knows his booze and people."

I smiled at him and found Mr. Parnell roving my face as if gauging my discomfort. I was shy to begin with, around new people. It took some warming up. I think that was a byproduct of where I grew up, though. In the Point Side projects, you had to be careful.

"Let me get us a couple of menus," he murmured, and suddenly it was just me and Golden. I turned and looked out the front window to where Backdraft and his unpleasant girlfriend were now arguing on the sidewalk.

"I don't like her much," I said and then covered my mouth with my hand. Golden laughed.

"You're in good company. None of us do. She cheated on him with one of his firehouse bros but the first time there was smoke was when she was drunk and hitting on Yale. Yale let Backdraft know right off and they've been at it ever since. Don't even know why he's trying so hard with her."

I looked over my shoulder where he was gesticulating hard, his demeanor calm but upset, while she practically screamed in his face. "Because he's a good man even if she's not a good woman?" I speculated softly.

I turned back and Golden eyed me up like I'd done something interesting. He nodded slowly and said, "What about you? Diddling your boss or what?" he grinned at me and I burst out laughing, all the while on the inside I quailed. *Oh if only you knew how close to the truth you were...* I thought, but Mr. Parnell saved me by getting back up on his stool, a couple of menus in hand.

"Hey! What's goin' on out here?" a voice called and I looked up.

"Yale brought his cleaning girl in for some dinner, a 'sorry you got attacked outside my place' consolation prize," Golden stated dryly.

"Golden!" Mr. Parnell barked, and something occurred to me.

"Wait, all of your law degrees in your home office say Columbia on them... why do they keep calling you 'Yale?'" I asked. He closed his eyes as if pained and Golden and the man who'd come from the kitchen laughed.

"Because they're assholes," Mr. Parnell said and I laughed, not getting the joke. It must have shown on my face because he smiled a little wanly at me and said, "I'll explain later."

I took another sip of the sweet, yummy drink and smiled behind the rim of my glass. The man from the kitchen was looking me up and down. Slightly portly and affable, he was Hispanic, like Golden, but older – maybe fifties? He eyed me up and down and said decisively, "Put those down. I think this calls for a special kind of dinner."

Mr. Parnell gave a secret little smile and called at the man's retreating back, "Thanks, Reflash!"

"Oh, ho, ho! I'll be right back," Golden said and we followed his gaze to where Backdraft was rubbing his cheek and Torrid was full-on screaming at him now. My heart broke for him but lifted when Golden went out and hauled her over to a parked car and backed her up to it. Whatever he was saying was both pissing her off and cooling her down, and I felt my heart grow all the sadder.

Why couldn't people treat each other better?

I jumped startled as the toy inside me buzzed to life, eyes going wide with shock as I looked at Mr. Parnell. His expression was as closed down as I had ever seen it, peaceful and neutral even as I swallowed hard and licked suddenly dry lips. I didn't ask what he thought he was doing. If there was one thing I saw in his dark eyes, it was that he knew precisely what he was doing, and it so wasn't fair.

A cruel little smile curved his lips, and he leaned forward. I moved as drawn by strings, meeting him across the short distance half-way, and he murmured in my ear, "I said I wanted to play, and I have a question for you..." The buzzing in my pussy intensified and I nearly fell off my seat. "Are you sure they won't be able to hear it?"

He leaned back and all I could think as I clamped my thighs together tightly was *oh, you bastard!* Because I couldn't be sure. Because the buzzing was awfully loud in my ears. I gave a panicked glance out the front window to watch Golden stuff Tori, who was crying, in the back of a cab. Her makeup, slicked down her face in a Rorschach display of how ugly she was on the inside, left me feeling no sympathy. Usually, the sight of anyone crying tugged at least one heartstring of mine, but for some reason, I couldn't muster one iota of pity for her. I could, however, muster a whole lot of cover for the surge of panic I felt as the guys came back into the bar and headed our direction.

I turned an alarmed look to Mr. Parnell who simply smiled and kicked the vibrator inside of me up another notch. *Oh. My. God.*

I writhed on my seat a little and tried to make it look as though I was just trying to get comfortable. The tall man, Backdraft, palmed the back of his neck, the red welt of her palmprint fading on his lightly-tanned skin.

"Sorry y'all had to see that," he said, and I gave him a sympathetic look, pressing my thighs tight, clenching my pussy hard around the vibrating egg. I was nearly dying with how hard I was trying to pretend nothing was wrong.

"It's not your fault," I rushed out on a sigh. "If it's one thing I learned living in this city, the only behavior you have control over is your own." I polished off the lemon drop drink Skids had given me and he drifted by, setting down a big glass of water in its place. I smiled and mouthed 'thank you' and he winked at me.

Oh God! My mind swirled with what-if's, *what if that wasn't him just being nice? What if he knows?* I watched him go and calmed down… *No, it wasn't that. Oh. My. God. What is Mr. Parnell doing to me?*

The excitement, the rush, was real. Casting furtive glances, hiding from his amused looks, how humiliating would it be if we were caught? I took a big drink of water and he raised an eyebrow at me. The look was unmistakable. *You might want to slow down.*

I blushed faintly and wondered what I was supposed to do if I did have to use the bathroom. I really didn't think I was ready to find out, not with that wicked gleam in his eyes.

"Here we go!" Reflash, the man from the kitchen, set a plate with a giant slice of decadent chocolate cake in front of me.

"For dinner!?" I asked, laughing.

"Best thing for you after a shit day," he declared. "I'll pack you up some real food to take home, but for tonight?"

"Chocolate cake," he and the rest of the men around me declared and they were brooking no argument. I laughed and looked to Mr. Parnell who was smiling so genuinely, so freely, I think I lost my heart. At least for a minute.

"Is this why you brought me here?" I whispered, and he nodded.

I smiled and took a bite of cake, but didn't say anything as the rich and decadent chocolate flavor swirled across my tongue. It was good, but what was even better was the open smile he gave me when *I* smiled. That more than made up for the absolute crap day I'd had.

Laughter tempered by secret thrills, smiles that made my heart race, the evening wound down perfectly and all too soon we were standing in the alley. It was late, and I needed to go home. I had work at the café in the morning.

"Get on," he ordered lightly, and I stood there, thighs pressed together in the cooling evening and asked, "Aren't you going to turn it off?"

"Nope, now get on."

I got on behind him, the vibrator pulsing pleasantly inside me and he fired up the bike. The thrum was an amazing counterpoint to the little egg pulsing away and I moaned. He chuckled, I could feel it, as he reminded, "Hold on to me."

The ride was amazing, but I swore I was going to go completely insane. I was so close, right on the edge, and I wanted to come so badly, but it just wasn't enough to get me there. When he cut the engine in front of my building I whimpered. I got off the back of his bike reluctantly and handed him my helmet. He held out the little remote and, with a sexy smirk, said, "You can have this."

"Come inside with me," I murmured, and he shook his head, his own helmet cradled against his hip so I could see him.

"Not tonight, Bright Eyes," he said softly and I had to admit, I loved the little pet name he'd given me.

"Please," I begged, and he stroked a thumb along my cheek.

"Here are the rules," he stated. "You aren't allowed to touch yourself. You aren't allowed to come until I make you. Do you understand?"

"That is so not fair!" I hissed, and he smiled darkly.

"Life isn't fair, Ally. I'm not either. Far from it, in fact."

I swallowed hard and he said, "I'll see you Friday. Break the rules and I'll know. Break the rules, and I'll punish you. Clear?"

"Crystal," I said miserably and swallowed hard. I wanted him. I didn't know what a punishment would entail, but I knew I didn't want it so I would most definitely not be getting off. *Holy shit that's going to be hard...* I thought.

"Good night, Ms. Blaylock," he said, and I stepped up on the curb and felt my lips twist in a wry grin. Playtime was over and back to reality.

"Good night, Mr. Parnell," I whispered, and he started up his motorcycle, though he didn't pull away until I was safely inside.

19

*Y*ale…

If only she knew what it had cost me to leave her there, and not follow through. I wanted her, badly. I was so hard it was to the point of pain, and when I arrived home and shucked out of my jeans, there was a spot of pre-cum the size of a damn half-dollar coin on my boxers. The difference between Ally and me, however, was that I was under no imposition to be hands-off.

Finally stripped nude, my clothing in the hamper by the bathroom door, I flopped onto my back on one side of my bed. I reached up and clicked on the bedside lamp, reaching for the thick, tri-folded sheets of homemade paper resting below, in the pool of golden light.

I unfurled them and smiled at the first line…

Dear sex diary…

Okay, I'm sorry, I just had to get that out there. I've never penned anything like this before and I'm not sure what to do or really even what to say. It's embarrassing almost – but not at the same time. I don't think they have a name for what I'm feeling right now. I guess if I had to come close it would be 'anxiety' or 'apprehension' but those don't quite cover it either, do they?

I pictured her pausing here, and I wrapped my hand around my shaft. I'd been hard for a while, and the head of my cock was super sensitive, and I wasn't quite ready to get off so quickly. I wasn't to the best part of her letter yet.

I'm stalling, aren't I? Okay. You asked me to tell you what and how I felt while we played. I guess the first and most important thing is that I felt safe. That's not a luxury I get afforded very often here. Like now, I hear yelling above me. It's two men so I should probably go into the bathroom. If a bullet is going to come through the ceiling, it's most likely going to happen in the living room.

I'm not writing any of that for sympathy; I'm just trying to explain myself, I guess. It's not just being in your apartment that I'm talking about when I say I feel safe. It's guys and men in general. You think you're safe with them but are you really? How do you really know? My grandmother raised me to be super cautious, to always spend the time figuring out what they want and their ulterior motive... that they always have one.

With you, I don't have to do that. Do I think you have them?

I pictured her biting that lush bottom lip of hers and closed my eyes as I swept my palm up my shaft and over my head, slicking through the pre-cum and back down. Electricity flowing down from it and sweeping through my body in that pleasing first rush. I opened my eyes and picked up where I left off, that first rush echoed by her next words…

Yes. But I have them too, and for now, I think they align and it's something... magical.

Standing there, in your kitchen, nude... I wanted you to see me. I wanted you to want me and it felt powerful and so good that you did, but I have a confession to make. It felt even better that I could just switch off for a time and not have to make any decisions. That was the best part. I like it when you get bossy. It's like a relief like a weight lifted off my shoulders. I feel like this whole adulting thing is hard and even though I'm making it? I feel like I am on the edge of failure daily and you give me that back. That sense of purpose, like I am good at something like I do something right and I love that.

It's the thing I cherish the most out of our encounters, the pleasure I get from pleasing you is almost like a drug... and I know that should scare me, but it doesn't. It feels too right.

I'm sorry, I'm babbling and probably procrastinating again because honestly who writes a detailed report of their sexual encounter with their boss for review? But I'm liking this, too... It's dirty in all the right ways. Hot and erotic and I'd be lying to you if I said I wasn't turned on.

Fuck, yes. I moved my hand up and concentrated more on the head, swirling fingers and palm around it, the energy from her words galvanizing me, turning things up a notch, I was close. Really damn close, so I rushed to read the best part...

I can't stop thinking about you. Your hands on my body, your mouth on my body, the feel of you inside me... I want it again. I want more of it, and I know that's probably not the best thing but it's true. I want more of you –

"Oh, god yes!" The pressure built, and I sucked in a breath as the first weak spurt painted the backs of my knuckles, the second and third pulse of my orgasm bringing more cum hot and sticky against my hand but immediately cooling against my skin. My balls tightening, my asshole pulsing along with it as I shuddered and lay still completely spent and satisfied.

Still, I wouldn't waste a single one of her precious words... even if I knew them all by heart by now.

– and I'll take what you're willing for as long as you're willing to give

it. I can't explain it, but what we do feels right. It feels good in a way that I've never experienced before, and I enjoy that exploration of that part of myself. I would be lying if I said that I wasn't scared of what you're going to think of all of this. Of what this means, or if this will drive you away, but you asked for the truth and so here it is.

I wish the best for us, whatever that may be,

Ally

I set the three pages aside, safe from the mess and just lay still staring at the ceiling for long minutes. Every time I read her words, I pictured her. Nude and perfect, riding me. Bright green eyes heavy-lidded with passion, lips gently parted, begging me, her hair wild around her face in a golden halo.

We were on the same page and I liked that, but everyone had their limits. I needed to find hers and push them, mostly because that was the kind of bastard that I was. I pushed up and, containing my mess with my hands, padded into the bathroom and started the shower. I stood under the spray and let out a gusty sigh, another scene playing out behind my closed eyelids. This one of her green eyes clouded with hurt as she asked me if I even liked her…

Yes, too much. The traitorous voice in my mind whispered.

I thrust my face into the spray and held my breath until colored spots went off in the dark of my vision. I came up for air and sucked in a deep and deeper breath and resisted the urge to punch something. I lost and took some skin from my knuckles against the shower wall.

Ally was sweet. She was a pure and innocent girl despite coming from the Point Side. She may have been street savvy enough, sure, but sexually her inexperience was clear. Clear and tempting. Completely alluring and a fucking siren's call.

I knew, even young, I was different. That what I liked wasn't *normal.* Let's fucking face it; when you're a rich kid going to a fucking prep school, there were all sorts of illicit and deviant wonders to behold. My introduction into the lifestyle I had become accustomed to, sexually speaking, had come by way of Veronica Pratchett.

She'd introduced me slowly, at first by begging me to hold her down while we made out. Pretty soon she was topping from the bottom – which I hadn't known it at the time, but that evolved pretty quickly. I'd gotten a taste for the *control* and I'd liked it.

Right up until my mother walked in on me with another girl, Marion Becknell, tied to my headboard with a pair of my neck ties as I'd shoved myself in her with such a punishing force she'd cried. She'd cried… but she'd fully admitted that she loved it. It worked for her. Gave her some kind of catharsis… but my mother? Controlling, conniving cunt that she was, she'd gone ballistic. Sent me off to an all-male boarding school in Connecticut and hadn't looked back.

Never hesitated to remind me or demand if I were still engaged in my 'disgusting deviant behavior' anytime we encountered one another, even to this day. I'd been fifteen when she'd caught me with Marion and I'd been eighteen when I'd graduated with full honors but still, nothing was good enough for her. Nothing would make up for me being a grade-A pervert in her eyes. So, it had become a battle of wills. I'd gone to Columbia instead of Yale; I'd become a city-paid prosecuting attorney rather than a high-priced defense lawyer, or, what she'd really wanted me to do, which was to go into finances like my father. My father, who had secretly—practically begged me to do anything *but* go into finance.

And now the cardinal sin, you're letting yourself fall in love with a girl from the fucking projects. Mother is going to have a conniption if she finds out.

I pushed back from my shower wall and swallowed hard, images and vignettes of Ally Blaylock flickering past my mind's eye. Walking away from my building with her blind friend, looking back and up at me… Green eyes filled with tears on my countertop… Perfect body on display on my coffee table as I entered her… Nude and wonderful in my shower, eyes wide with shock and fear... A shy smile playing across her lips at the 10-13 as Golden had talked with her...

She was beautiful. The perfect amalgamation of sweet, shy, and, behind closed doors, bold, adventurous, and yet still submissive. I'd been resisting, I still needed to resist but those worried and sad green eyes, so full of hurt filtered back into my vision as she'd asked me tremulously, intrepidly... *Do you even like me?*

Communication, negotiation, consent. These were some of the top tenets to make playtime between adults, both sexual and otherwise, safe and fulfilling, and I had been neglectful of the first. I had demanded clear communication from her and yet had been giving her non-committal vagaries in return.

I shut off the shower and dried off, wrapping the towel loosely around my hips. I marched purposefully to my home office and pulled the cord on the banker's lamp on my desk, flooding its top with illumination. I dropped into the seat and opened a drawer, extracting the fountain pen my father had given me upon my graduation. I pulled a blank note card from another drawer and sat staring at its crisp white interior for an age...

Shit. I wasn't good at this part. It was damn near social suicide to confide the truth about yourself to anyone in white-collar high society. I took a deep breath and put pen to paper.

20

*A*lly…

He glanced at Millie behind the till, and satisfied she was distracted, slipped me a small rectangular white envelope. I quickly put it in my apron pocket and tried to interpret the resigned look in his eyes as he took his coffee in silence and went to the register with it. My heart beat in a rapid tattoo against the inside of my ribs, and I felt light and almost faint with excitement.

I had to wait, slogging through orders and trying to get through the day as much as I could on no sleep. I had gone to bed, burning with a deep desiring ache and unable to sleep, staring at the ceiling until my alarm had gone off. I had already canceled my plans with my grandmother. I'd called her room first thing, knowing she would be up, and telling her I would see her tomorrow instead, begging off due to not feeling well, and feeling incredibly guilty as I'd done it.

As soon as my shift ended at the café, I boarded the bus to go home, Mr. Parnell's note tucked between my hands. I sat and stared at the round gold sticker holding the envelope closed for a long time, and finally unstuck it so I could slip out the card, a white stock with an embossed family crest on the front. The same as was tattooed on his chest.

I opened it and focused on the flowing script from what looked like a fountain pen, the writing too smooth to be ballpoint.

Ally,

I do indeed like you, perhaps a little too much. When I am with you I feel blessed to be in your presence. You improve my quality of life in many ways. I am grateful for your friendship. On Friday, please arrive no later than five pm. I would like to take you somewhere. A new adventure.

Yours,

D.

There were points in his missive where he had paused a little too long, at the end of "feel" and again at the end of "blessed", the ink bleeding into the page a little more and I sighed, my eyes sweeping the letters and soaking up the sentiment until my stop came. I was still aroused and was beginning to wonder if I would be in a permanent state of it until whatever he had planned on Friday. I guessed I would have to wait and see.

I walked the rest of the way into the Point Side, and up the flights of stairs to the hall my little apartment resided on. Keying my way in, I shut out the outside world and threw all of the locks and chains to keep it out. Except, Mr. Parnell, *Damien…* Him, I brought in here with me. Him, I thought of while I undressed and got between the sheets. I picked up the beautiful notecard from beside my pillow and sighed. I was looking it over when my phone chimed. I traded them and smiled softly at the text message waiting.

You didn't look like you'd slept at all this morning.

I tapped out a return message.

I didn't. I couldn't. I'm home now, and in bed.

I waited for a return and was very nearly asleep when it came.

Sleep. Will I see you on Friday?

Of course, he would…

Yes.

Again I had nearly drifted off when the phone chimed. I sighed, a little exasperated, and checked.

Good. Keep your hands to yourself. That hasn't changed.

I smirked.

Yes, Sir.

I didn't get a response. I went out like a light and woke up later that night. Super late… like I had less than two hours before my alarm went off and I needed to head to work. I sat up and waited to see if whatever had woken me would do it again but nothing. I picked up my phone to the low battery warning and plugged it in, smiling at the last text message that was displayed, waiting for me.

Minx… To be clear, Friday is not to be talked about.

Excitement fluttered through me and resolute that I would *not* be falling back asleep, I got up and showered. Taking off the Band-Aids on my knees, I decided to let them breathe but put a little ointment on them. A check in the mirror and I put a little ointment on my chin, too, likewise letting it have some air. I twisted my lips and sighed heavily. It was already Wednesday and Friday would be here before I knew it. I wondered if they would be healed up in time for wherever he wanted us to go.

I dressed in mind for the weather. It was supposed to be another scorcher out there, and so I went with a light, breezy silk wrap skirt that fell just above the knee and a white cotton tank top. As I was slipping on my sandals, a knock fell at my front door. I went and checked and saw Dawnie on the other side.

I'd forgotten, she was supposed to come to work with me and listen to one of her books. We were supposed to hang out today after I got off work and I was excited because for once, I had something I could tell her.

"Woah, you're all fresh and ready to go," she said when I opened the door. She came inside and I locked everything.

"I didn't go see Gran yesterday," I said guiltily. "I came straight home and went to bed."

"Why?" she asked suspiciously, still tapping her cane around my new apartment, trying to get the lay of the land. She reached out and touched the frame on my daybed and smiled, feeling her way along so she could sit.

"Have I got a story for you…" I said and she perked up.

"Really?"

"Yeah, really."

I flopped down next to her and told her the ballad of the Mondayest Monday ever and she sat still, soaking it all up with rapt attention.

"You should have seen him; he kicked those two guys' asses before the police even had a chance to get there."

"Then what happened?"

"They called the paramedics and they cleaned me up in his kitchen and Mr. Parnell felt so bad, he took me to dinner… on his motorcycle."

"Shut the fuck up!" Dawnie cried and clapped a hand over her mouth, giggling.

"Oh, shoot, we have to go!" I declared catching sight of the time.

"Well hurry up then! You have to tell me *everything.*"

I got my things together and we left, locking up the apartment and her hand on my shoulder, traipsed down the hall.

"Stairs," I warned and she let her cane unfold and we took them down; she had the handrail and after the first couple of steps fell into an easy rhythm.

"So what was *that* like? The motorcycle ride?" she asked and I smiled.

"Way fun. It's so different! Like instead of watching the scenery, you feel like a part of it. You know?"

She let out a dreamy sigh and said, "I love living vicariously through you. What else?"

Laughing, we caught the bus to work and it was the best time I had spent with my best friend in a long time.

I keyed my way into his apartment and was met with soft music rather than the alarm on Friday. I had worked an extra hour or two at the café which had suited his timeline and ensured I would makeup, at least just a little, how much I would be missing out on for having not cleaned this week. I had been carefully saving any extra, though, and would be okay.

A white box was resting on the dining table and there was another note card leaned against it, my name on the front of the envelope. I set my things down by the door and went and picked up the card, unsticking the seal and sliding it free from the envelope.

Ally –

Get yourself ready. Use what I have provided and my bathroom. You have one hour.

-D.

I looked up and around and saw him sitting behind his desk. He wore a black dress shirt and crimson tie, his elbows resting on the arms of his chair, fingers steepled in front of him. His dark eyes swept over me and all of the arousal and desire from earlier this week came flooding back anew.

I nodded once and took the large garment box up; it was heavier than it looked, and went down the hall to his room, closing the door and setting it on the bed. I opened it and shivered at what was inside.

Unrelieved black. A fine material met my eyes and I didn't know what to make of it. I pulled it free and laid it out and sighed, a bit intimidated. It was a little black dress, a fitted sheath with a tank-top-like neckline to it, simple and more elegant than anything else I had ever owned. With it was a garter, crotchless panties with a matching bra and a pair of very high heels... the kind with the red bottoms.

What's more, there was makeup. Like, everything I would need for a full face, the lipstick likewise a red, only deep and rich, an almost-burgundy which would do magically with my fair skin tone. I quickly went and showered, dried and styled my hair and did my makeup in front of the bathroom mirror before I stepped into the dress and slid my arms into the straps.

A light tap fell at the door and I went to get it. He'd added a jacket over the shirt and wore the suit well. He pursed his lips, expression grave and said, "Turn."

I turned around, and he drew the zipper up my back so slowly it made me shiver. I'd never had anyone affect me in such a way dressing me before.

I went over and stepped into the heels and we were nearly even for height now. He nodded, and despite a lack of change in his rigid expression, I could tell that he was pleased. He went to the final article in the bottom of the garment box and held it out for me. I turned and he slipped the red satin interior of the black velvet cloak onto my shoulders. I turned again and he fastened the brooch at my throat and drew the hood up over my hair.

"Perfect," he breathed. "Come on; we're going to be late."

"Where are we going?" I asked.

"Someplace special, to test your limits."

That sounded ominous, but I trusted him and the slow burn of excitement was worth finding out what he had in store for me. We went down to the garage and he opened the door to his Mercedes for me and held it. I slipped onto the expensive leather seat and he closed it, coming around to his side and getting in.

"When we get out of the car, keep your hood up and your head bowed until you are taken inside. Am I understood?"

"Yes."

"Good girl," he murmured, and that golden glow of pride that I'd done something well suffused me… even though I hadn't really done anything at all. At least not yet. He pulled down an alley, brick buildings rising to either side and stopped in front of an unmarked door. A man in a dark suit stepped out of the shadows and opened the door for me. I looked to Mr. Parnell who nodded and went to his own door, leaving his car running. He came around the Mercedes and put a hand on my waist, guiding me down the few steps and through a door which another man, also in a dark suit, held open for us.

Once the door was firmly shut behind us, we were in a sort of antechamber, curtained with a podium, a man behind it standing straight and tall, hands behind his back – and faceless. A white mask, blank and featureless, covered his face.

Track lighting fell on a wall where more masks, the pretty kind, were pinned and waiting. Mr. Parnell went to the wall and perused them. Finally, he turned to me and lowered my hood.

"Turn around. No one will be let in until we are masked and inside. Let's not keep them waiting."

I gave him my back and he lowered a tatted lace mask over my head, pulling it over my eyes and securing it in the back.

"Turn," he murmured and he adjusted it and guided me over to a mirror to look. I blinked, the black lace complimenting my dress, tiny white rhinestones scattered across it at the apex where bits branched out and connected. It was something beautiful and elegant and framed my eyes making them seem larger than life, yet did surprisingly well at concealing my identity.

I turned back to Mr. Parnell and he had donned a black leather mask, one that went straight across his forehead and over his nose, twin peaks of leather stabbing down over his cheeks, bracketing his mouth. The forehead was molded into a permanent scowl. I smiled and said lightly, "It suits you."

He smiled and unclasped my cloak, handing it to the man behind the pedestal. He took it and gave Mr. Parnell a ticket back. Tucking it into his pocket, he took my hand and tucked it into the crook of his arm, an old-fashioned and gentlemanly gesture. He led me down a curtained hall and spoke as we walked.

"There are no real names, here. You will call me 'sir, ' and you will do as I say. If you must call me anything other than sir, call me Mr. Silver. Your safeword works, it *always* works. The masks stay on and never come off." He stopped us at the end of the hall and made me look at him, "Don't take it off, Bright Eyes, not for anything. You don't want these other people recognizing you on the street."

"Okay," I murmured and swallowed hard. He was beginning to frighten me.

"You're safe with me; you're here *with me.* No one else will touch you."

"Where *is* here?" I murmured softly.

"Indigo Nights… it's a sex club."

I gasped and squeaked out, *"What?"*

He chuckled darkly and muttered, "Limits, beautiful. I said we would be testing your limits… I want to know, how far are you willing to go to please me? How much do you trust me?"

It was a good question… I guess we were about to find out.

21

$\mathcal{Y}$ale…

She was beautiful – her green eyes wide and framed in black lace, her blonde hair falling around her shoulders artfully. Her crimson lips, parted in surprise, begged me to slide my cock between them but that was for my eyes only, at least when it came to our first time for that. We stepped into the locker area and I turned her to face me, cupping the side of her neck with my fingers, smoothing my thumb along her jaw.

She had no way of knowing this entire evening had been bought and paid for by me. That the other patrons here were all well aware of my plans and the boundaries I had set in place. She was not to be touched. No one was to speak to her without my express invitation. The protocols typically abided by in these circles did not apply to her by my design.

For this scene she was natural, innocent, and pure, and no one would hold her or I to task for any gaffes real or imagined. I had certainly paid them all enough to ensure it. These moments were for her and me, real, raw, and genuine for her to experience with none of the guilt that could be imposed. Of course, she knew nothing of the nature of my game. That was for my knowledge alone. I guess I hadn't completely left the manipulations of the rich behind, but I did sometimes miss the games, just never the cruel intentions behind them. It was nice to put some of those machinations to use for good rather than ill.

"Turn around so I can unzip your dress."

She searched my face, and even through the masks I could see the apprehension in her clear green eyes. She reluctantly turned around, and I moved her long hair over her shoulder, out of my way. I reached out and parted the material, drawing the zipper down, revealing her silky smooth skin. She'd been so brave to this point, and I rewarded her and myself with a light touch of my lips at the base of her graceful neck, where it met her shoulders, right over the center of her spine.

Her breath caught and my prick stirred but I wanted them to see her. I wanted them all to see that I'd caught an angel and I wanted to defile her in all of the best ways in front of them all, and ride the high of their jealousy because, agreements and money aside, I *knew* they would be jealous.

I turned her around and slid my jacket off, putting it around her shoulders and murmured, "You can have this for now until you're used to it… but then I will be taking it away. As the night goes on, I intend to take you in front of them."

I watched the effect my words had on her, her breath catching, her lips parting in surprise. There, though… her eyes wide, pupils dilating slightly with desire. Oh yeah, she was game, she just needed to feel secure. She needed to feel safe and ease into things, get over her natural shyness, her inherent mistrust. I could help her with those things.

I tucked her dress away, folding it neatly in a locker, and pocketed the key. She let me guide her in front of me down another long hall and into the parlor of the club. She stopped to take things in, and I drew up next to her, my confidence increasing as she took in the room. Men and women alike were scattered about; in some couples the men were clothed like me, in others it was the woman elegantly dressed and their men sitting at their feet. A few couples were same sex, mostly men, but at least two lesbian couples were in the mix.

It had been a while since I had come to Indigo Nights, and there were a lot of fresh new faces behind varying Venetian masks.

"We are going to find a seat, then I will send you to the bar for me. There's a two-drink limit, so there is no concern about anyone here being intoxicated."

"Okay," she breathed and I turned and pinned her with a withering look. She blushed prettily in the blue-white light and amended, "Sir."

I led her into the room and over across the bar to a seating area. I indicated she should sit on a silk cushion on the plush area rug and she lowered herself onto it, her legs curled beneath her like a cat and I sank onto the end of the deep blue velveteen settee edged in rich dark wood. I held her hand on my knee and she looked around us, soaking it all in.

I watched her, stroking her long hair, down her back and wishing it weren't against my suit jacket. She peered around the room, taking it all in and her wonder pleased me. What pleased me more was that the more I watched her think, the less tense she became. She was wonderfully accepting, and it was a quality that I could appreciate even if her judgment seemed like it was merely suspended or reserved.

"Tell me what you're thinking..." I murmured and she looked up at me.

She swallowed hard and captured that bottom lip with her teeth, making me glad I had chosen the permanent, matte, everlasting lip paint, or whatever it was. She glanced behind her at the others in the room, dressed well and displaying their class within society with their suits and evening dresses.

"I'm the only one in my underwear," she whispered, and I felt my lips curve into a smile.

"Of course you are, it's what I wanted."

"I don't understand…"

I chuckled darkly, "There's a certain power in flaunting what you have that they can't," I murmured and let my gaze slide through the room. "While it's not something I would do when it came to money or cars out in the general population – here, among the elite? There are plenty of beautiful women I can have on my arm, but everyone here knows that you're something special. Likewise, I'm something of a commodity. Plenty of women here would kill to be where you are now but none of them hold my interest. Social climbers, gold diggers, the lot of them…"

"I don't care about your money," she breathed and fixed her gaze downward, her cheeks painted in fire and shame. We both knew that wasn't entirely true. We both knew that she depended very much on what I paid her, but I also knew that if she didn't… that if her job at the café had been enough, that she would still be here with me regardless. I touched her face and brought it up with gentle fingertips and said as much.

She swallowed hard and said, "The lines are so blurred now…"

I couldn't disagree. Perhaps it was time for a new negotiation? It was of no consequence now. Right now, I wanted to indulge in my fantasies and indulge in her.

"Go to the bar, order two glasses of champagne and charge it to Mr. Silver's tab," I told her. She nodded and I held out my hands and helped her to her feet. Before she could turn to do as I'd bid, I said, "Leave my jacket."

She froze and pursed her lips, her nervousness apparent, yet she was brave. She slipped the dark material from her shoulders and held it out to me, dangling from two fingertips, brazenly meeting my eyes. I smiled and let my pride in her fill my eyes even as eyes from around the room were drawn to her.

She stepped carefully across the room to the bar, the heels I'd bought her putting a sexy little sway into her hips, and I felt that deep, pleasurable and warm tingle of arousal stir my cock. She returned to me and knelt, offering up one of the glasses to me, and I took it. I clicked the rim of my flute against hers and said, "To exploring our darker sides and indulging our passions."

"Cheers," she murmured and she tentatively sipped with me.

"Tell me what you're feeling," I said again, and swept her face with my gaze.

"Uncomfortable, nervous, a bit... not embarrassed, but something... I don't know the word for it."

"Vulnerable?" I supplied and she nodded.

"Exposed..." she whispered and I smiled.

"You're beautiful," I assured her and she laughed nervously.

"I don't know if I can do this–" she stopped herself and said "Sir," catching herself before she used my name.

"Drink your champagne," I ordered and she sipped some more from her glass. I took a drink of my own and studied her, hoping against hope that she would follow through for me. I was worried I may have pushed her a touch too far, too quickly, bringing her out into the world like this, into *my* world.

"I would never let anything happen to you; you know that don't you?"

"I don't..."

I sighed and smiled, knowing it held an edge of bitterness. I stroked her cheek and stared through my mask, through hers, into those green orbs I could never seem to get enough of looking at.

"I am actually quite fond of you, Bright Eyes. To the point, I wish that this could be something more sometimes..." I shut my mouth. It wasn't a thought I could follow through on.

She deserved better than a twisted deviant fuck like me and something must have read on my face because she took another, fortifying sip from her glass and swallowed before saying, "I don't think you're bad at all. Quite the opposite actually. You've only ever been kind to me. Gone out of your way to help me and even had your friends help me… which is why this cold affectation is so confusing to me. It's like you do these things that show you are a good man but then you're so…" she struggled to find the words, and I think she was actually afraid of hurting my feelings. I can't tell you how much that amused me. "Distant… you're so cold."

"That's not you. That's me." I told her and she looked apprehensive.

"I wish you would just be *you* with me," she said softly. "But it's like you're behind these walls, almost high up in a tower." She closed her eyes and sighed a defeated sound.

"That's the way it needs to be," I said gently after downing at least half of the remaining champagne in my own glass in one swallow.

"I wish it didn't have to be. I'd like more for you."

Ah, but I saw it in her eyes, she wanted more for herself, too… I just couldn't give it to her. Not the way she wanted. I felt it would just bring more misery than joy to her and that wouldn't be fair. I already knew our sordid affair was taxing her personal life and relationships with her closest friend and only family. Guilt prickled across my awareness, but I batted it away. I could hear any number of my brothers from the MC in the back of my mind saying the cold hard truth of the matter, *you either need to shit or get off the pot, man.*

I either needed to take her, claim her as my own and stop toying with her heart, or I needed to man up and let her go. However, for tonight…

"Finish your champagne," I said softly but not sternly. She nodded and swallowed some and I followed the movement it made down her gorgeous throat. I polished off my own and set the glass aside on the little marble side table and watched her. My jacket was gone, I laid a hand on her shoulder, where it swept up into her neck as she faced out into the room and swept my thumb lightly back and forth on the back of her neck. I applied gentle pressure, not enough to call it a massage, but neither was it light enough to be considered nothing.

Her eyes fluttered shut and I brought my other hand to the other side and murmured, "Kneel in front of me, face the room." She adjusted herself accordingly, slipping from the cushion next to me to the plush black area rug between my knees, back to me as I'd ordered. I rubbed her shoulders and neck, and she let out a shuddering sigh, relaxing beneath the touch.

"Finish your champagne," I reminded her, and she did, the last third of the glass of liquid disappearing between her lush burgundy lips. I took the glass from her and set it aside and returned to my ministrations, a plan beginning to develop as to how I would accomplish getting her nude and on the stage beyond the next set of curtains.

Just the thought of it excited me, bringing my cock from half-mast to fully erect. I put my lips to her ear and whispered just for her, "Do you know how erotic I find the idea of making love to you in front of all of these people?"

I buried my nose behind that same ear and breathed her in, even as she gasped and whispered back, "No…"

"Hmm, I don't think there are words," I murmured and placed my lips in a gentle caress against the side of her neck. Her sharp intake of breath told me I was on the right track. I pulled back and placed them slightly lower, leaning forward, my hands sliding against her body, sweeping against her silky skin as I marched my lips down the side of her throat in a quest to find *that* spot.

"I think it's better if I just show you." I breathed over it as I spoke and she let go of a breath I didn't think she'd realized she'd been holding. I kissed her there, open-mouthed, nipping lightly at the spot, capturing it between my teeth just enough to draw it into my mouth, licking across it until she shuddered in my arms.

I smoothed one hand along her ribs while I continued to ravish her neck with my kiss, trailing the backs of my fingertips along her spine, ever upwards, along the nape of her neck. I buried that hand in her hair, gripping it, knuckles close to her scalp, locking it in. Her breath whooshed out and carried with it a deep, satisfying moan, her body falling limp against mine in perfect submission.

I used my hold in her hair to bring her back to my opposite shoulder so that I could give the other side of her neck the same attention as the first. I loved her reactions, her small cries, her shuddering against me, her rapid breaths, the gasps, and oh, my god, how she bit that bottom lip. I watched us in the mirror across from us and it was a beautiful sight: her body captured against mine, pale flesh framed in all that black, eyes closed behind the delicate lace mask.

"Up," I demanded in her ear, my voice harsh with my own breathlessness that her sheer beauty had stolen away.

She rose with me, my hand in her hair controlling her, tightly wound in her tresses in the way that would allow me to control her without hurting her. There was a distinct art to pulling hair correctly, and it was one of the first tools I perfected when it came to controlling a woman, right after the first tool I used which was always to get her consent.

I walked us past the bar and through more curtains beyond into another room. A stage was set up, a half-circle sweeping out from the wall and lit from hidden lights above, in blue-white spotlights. Illuminated in the center of the black stage was a single black chair; wood, like something that should be at someone's kitchen table.

I loosened my grip in her hair and swept my hand down her back, curving it around to rest on her hips. I stood with her in front of me and let her take in the scene. No one was in here with us yet. It was just us.

She let her eyes sweep the empty chairs staggered in rows around the stage, and her mind calculate through the haze I'd started in her. She turned to me at her side and asked, "You really want this, don't you?"

"Yes."

"Would it make you happy?"

"It would please me, yes…"

She turned to face me and traced the edge of my mask where it lay over my cheek and nodded slowly. I took her hands in mine and returned her to the front of me, putting myself between her and those who would be joining us in the room.

"It's just us for now," I told her evenly. "Just you and I, and nobody even knows your name."

"You do," she whispered and it sounded like that was important to her.

"I do," I agreed.

She looked a touch sad when she said, "But you don't know me… at least, not really."

I chuckled darkly and pulled her against my chest, my hands sweeping over her skin, down over the supple curve of her ass, where I rested them on the lace of her panties.

"I know more than you think, Ally," I whispered it carefully in her ear and her fingers dug slightly into my biceps. I smiled and pressed a light kiss to the front of her shoulder. She sighed out and her hands smoothed over the fabric of my shirt. Soft, light, timid as if unsure it was okay for her to touch me like that.

"Tonight you're my lover, not my conquest, not my maid, do you understand?"

"I think so," she whispered, and I felt my lips curve up once again.

"Show me," I ordered, and her hands smoothed around my shoulders, along my triceps as she drew herself closer to me. Her hands continued their upward sweep along my collar before lightly resting to either side of my neck, her mouth moving hungrily to mine. I let her have it, I let her kiss me, but once she did I lost some measure of my control. I kissed her back just as fervently as she kissed me, and it was pure nirvana.

I brought my hands up in a firm caress and unhooked the back of her bra, turning her away from the empty chairs, having her face me and the wall at the back of the stage. I was slightly vexed by the fact her touch and kiss had become a sort of kryptonite for me and so I made a decision. I looked up and sure enough, it was there, and within easy reach. I stepped back from her, where she shook with the after-effects of our passionate exchange, and I pulled at my tie, sliding it through the knot. I would need it for this.

With my other hand, I swept her bra off her chest and down her arms, casually tossing it onto the back of the nearby chair. As luck would have it, it landed perfectly, artfully hanging from the back as if I had planned for it to do so.

"Put your hands together, like you're praying and hold them there," I said, and I let my tone brook no argument from her. She did as I commanded and I swept my red tie off the rest of the way. I wound the silk around her wrists and between them, making sure the binding was loose enough to allow for her circulation.

The seats in the gallery were slowly beginning to fill with voyeuristic onlookers but Ally was focused on me, on what I was doing. I knotted the tie and held her wrists in my hands, looking at her over her bound hands.

"You know your safeword," I whispered, and she took a tremulous breath.

"Yes, Sir."

"What is it?"

"The color red."

"Good."

I raised her hands high above her head and set the bindings over the hook dangling from the industrial chain in the beam of the ceiling. She gasped and I stooped, cupping the heel of one of her stilettos with one hand, wrapping the ankle gently with my fingers. I eased first one, then the other, shoe off and set them neatly by one leg of the chair.

I let her hang, helplessly. If she stayed flat-footed on the floor, her arms would stretch. Even if she stood on tiptoe, without the aid of the shoes she could never unhook herself to bring her arms down.

"You're safe," I reminded her, as I unbuttoned my shirt. "You're with me." The slight panic in her green eyes eased immediately, and she swallowed hard... nervously. Nerves that change quickly from anxiety to anticipation, the more of myself I revealed by way of unbuttoning my shirt.

I cocked my head and swept her with my gaze, taking my time, deciding just what I wanted to do with her, now that I had her trapped firmly in my web...

22

*A*lly…

I jerked, pulling at my wrists, but they were held fast by the binding of his tie. I looked at him and felt a sort of fear for the first time. I think this was it. This was him with all pretenses stripped away. This was what he enjoyed, what he liked, and I didn't know how to feel about it now that I was in it. This wasn't at all what it was like in the storybooks, you know?

He looked me over, hanging there like a piece of meat and I swallowed hard as he slowly unbuttoned his shirt. Whatever was on my face must have told him something, even beneath the masks we wore because he smiled slightly and said, "You're safe," and reminded me that even though we were in unfamiliar surroundings that I was with him.

I closed my eyes and the panic subsided. I was with him, and he had never, *ever* done anything to hurt me. If anything, he had gone way out of his way to help me. This was no different. He was pushing me to expand my horizons, so to speak, but he was taking it slow. There was no one in here but him and me, and I could appreciate that.

160

I could also appreciate how his muscles moved beneath his skin as he pulled his shirt open and back off of his shoulders. *God,* he was magnificent. My eyes trailed down his ribs at the lettering there, large gothic script proclaiming 'heart' vertically until it reached his hip at which point the letters tumbled into 'less' as they dove into his pants, ending near his cock, which was tenting the dark material.

My eyes flicked up to his which held a cold heat to them as they devoured every line and curve of my body. I could feel it, like a very real physical caress, even as his hands reached for me, cascading down my flanks to come to rest on my hips which were clad in the black lace underwear and garter he had provided. He moved closer to me, hovering his lips over my own and I closed my eyes waiting for him to close that last little gap, wishing he would.

I would gladly die to experience his kiss and he so rarely let me have it. He denied me now, instead placing his lips under my jaw working his mouth down my neck once more. Where he had worried that place that made my knees weak before, he barely paid attention to it now. Instead, nipping his way along my skin, to my breast where he sucked the sensitive stiff peak of my nipple into his mouth.

I felt my voice escape me but I didn't hear it. I definitely felt the fireworks scatter through my body at the intimate touch of his mouth, the sensation bright and flaring from my chest, in an explosion of sparks that fell through my body and settled in my pussy causing it to give one, long, slow, throbbing ache of want.

It was no less intense when he moved to the other breast, and the way his arms twined around me, gripping me against his hard body, bringing me off my feet and to his mouth. I loved that sensation. Loved that I felt so small and frail, loved that I indeed did trust him and the knowledge that he wouldn't hurt me combined with the pleasure he was giving me made me go liquid with relief.

I let go, let him have me, and shivered at the satisfied growl that he let loose against my flesh. I opened my eyes when he left me, dangling there, but it was a short-lived thing. He fetched the chair and set it down in front of me, taking the seat. He looked up at me, eyes somehow deeper and even darker than usual through the black leather mask as he smoothed his hands over my nylon-covered legs in a warm, worshipping caress.

The intensity in his gaze caused the last of my nerves to ease and I watched him, looking down from where I hung, as he hooked his fingers in the waistband of my panties and swept them down to my knees. His hands went to my ass and brought me closer to his mouth which he used to kiss my stomach, and I felt my breath rush out as his intentions became clear.

His kiss fell on my mound next and his tongue, hot and wet, delved between the folds of my labia, looking for that tiny kernel of nerves that would drive me absolutely mad with pleasure.

I tugged on my restrained hands, the tie digging into my wrists. I wanted so badly to touch him, to reciprocate, but I was held fast, stretched tautly, and at his mercy. I gazed down my body at the light reflecting off his deep brown hair and bit my bottom lip. He tipped his head back carefully, dark eyes staring into my own as his mouth worked my body and I could see it buried deep in his gaze. *He owned me.* Maybe not permanently, but for right now, he did. Completely and utterly, and I cannot tell you how much that excited me. How much I ached and twisted and wanted it to be true. Not just for now, but for always, as long as he could make me feel like this.

I let my head fall back, my eyes shut, and a wild cry escaped me even as I felt my legs wouldn't hold me. I felt him slide a finger inside me and I couldn't... I couldn't stop it; I couldn't control it. With another desperate cry, I came, shuddering, the pleasure pulsing up through my body in time with my wildly beating heart. My knees gave out and the chain above me jerked and chimed as I lost my footing.

He stood, arms going around me, and held me up until I could get my feet under me though the haze of pleasure from the orgasm made it hard to think.

"Good girl, Bright Eyes," he whispered in my ear and then he turned me around, to face our audience.

I balked, silently, eyes widening at the full gallery of chairs as men and women, elegantly dressed and masked as we were, sat and watched us. I tried to look away, but his hand was at my chin, gripping it firmly, but not painfully, the heel of his hand resting at my throat, his skin warm against my back as he pressed into me, drawing me back into him as he worked his belt with his free hand against my ass.

"Look at them look at you," he growled into my ear, and oh god, I was looking, he didn't give me any other choice.

"Those women want to be you," he breathed, and I felt the head of his cock hotly brush my thigh at the crease of my ass. He let me go, and I heard a packet tear open as he rolled a condom onto himself. His hand returned to my chin and my throat, the other to my hip, pulling back on it even as he guided me forward with his hand at my throat. He positioned me, and his lips returned to my ear.

"Those men want to be inside of you," he told me, and he pressed his cock into my opening, easing his way in. "But you're mine tonight, baby. All mine and all they get to do is watch."

He shoved deep into my body and I cried out, forcing my hips back to meet him. I wanted him, I wanted this, and I couldn't believe how turned on I was meeting the audience's collective hungry gaze.

He didn't give me time to think about it, stroking in and out of my pussy in long and controlled rolling movements of his hips that left me breathless and stoked the embers of my last orgasm back to life. Fire licked low from within my body and leaped, flitting along my veins, desire fanning them into a wildfire that ate through me and rose quickly. I gripped the tie binding my wrists together with my hands and held on, bowing my body, presenting my ass to him, making it easy for him to fuck me in front of these people, these strangers.

I did what he told me, too. I looked, I saw the women, the heat in their eyes past their bejeweled harlequin masks, their parted lips, their gently rising and falling chests, breaths deepening with desire. I watched the men, gripping the arms of their chairs with mottled fingers, likewise leaning forward in their seats as if they could take one of my nipples into their mouths. And the effect was astonishing.

A low, desperate moan escaped my throat and I could feel the tension and jealous desire rise. I was choking on it, drowning in the power our sexual energy unleashed into the room and I swear to you... I grew drunk on it. I succumbed to it completely and I when I let go? *I let go.*

This orgasm was different from the first. It was longer in coming, and when it did, rather than spilling through me as if through a crack in a dam, it welled up as if a cup being slowly filled had finally run over. It filled me just as surely and spilled over the crown of my head, running in rivulets over my skin in a tingling wash of pleasure that made me whimper and go limp against the chain holding me up.

It was as if he couldn't get deep enough, I mean, I had come, but it wasn't satisfying. It wasn't quite enough. I needed more. I needed harder and deeper and I found myself begging him with my hips thrusting back into his, writhing against my bonds.

I heard him chuckle darkly and there was a whirring sound, as machinery kicked on and suddenly the tension holding my arms high above my head slacked off. He unhooked me and pulled from my body, gently lowering me to my knees on the floor. He stayed behind me and I parted my knees and arched low to the floor, putting my palms flat to the stage, raising my ass in offering to him, and he wasted no time in filling me once more. The change in angle was perfect, allowed him to press into my wetness that much deeper, touching that secret place that had been begging for it just a moment before and I felt another whimpering, begging, little moan escape me.

He drove me wild, stroking deep with a satisfying grunt before grinding against my body a few times. Oh, when he did that, though, I thought there was some truth to the French calling orgasm 'the little death', because when he plunged deep like that and worked me on his cock, I died a little more each time, blissfully so. It only took a half a dozen or so of these strokes and I was coming apart again, bowing low to the floor, a thin wail of pleasure escaping my body as the firestorm swept through me and over me.

I panted, spent, against the stage, and his hand swept along my stomach, pressing between my breasts to bring me up to my knees. He walked around me on his own knees and turned me to face him, taking the bonds from around my wrists. We were turned, profile to the audience when he locked his mouth over mine, tongue plunging past my teeth and sweeping possessively into my mouth. I melted a little more, wilting into his embrace even as he palmed the outside of my thigh and encouraged me to ride him. The same as I had the first time, in his living room after I'd slipped from his coffee table into his lap.

I climbed him like a damn tree. I couldn't get enough of his hard body against mine… *in* mine, and I wanted him desperately. I needed him desperately. It was as if he were the one thing I had been missing my entire life to this point. That feeling of safety, of being precious to someone. That a man cared enough to want me the way that he did. Not as an ornament or possession… no, this went deeper than that. Much deeper… and, oh, as he slid up inside of me, that felt much deeper, too.

I rested my hands on his taut, muscular shoulders and rode him, staring into his eyes and finding a match for my desire there. Something undefinable passed between us, a deep emotion that I had no name for. His arms were around my waist, one hand pressing between my shoulders to keep me upright, his other hand buried in the back of my hair, like before, locking into place, turning my insides into liquid as he exerted his control and brought my mouth to his. He kissed me like he would devour me from the mouth down and all else fell away – the room, the stage, the people in it watching us and their arousal. All of it faded into the background as the world, the very universe, narrowed down to the man beneath me and inside of me.

I kissed him back, fingertips from one hand touching his bearded cheek where the mask didn't cover, feeling the muscles of his jaw work beneath his skin as he ate at my mouth, taking everything I offered him sweetly and willingly. I wanted to give him everything. I wanted him to have all of me. It was, after all, the only thing a poor girl like me had to give.

He moaned into my mouth and thrust up to meet my downward strokes and I could tell, he was close. We both were, riding that sharp and silvered edge at the end of the very universe where everything was just one divide, light and dark, spinning so fast that when we fell, it would be a near thing on which we would fall into.

I closed my eyes and concentrated on him, the feel of him, the sound, the taste, the heat and light touch, the pleasure and the wonder. It rose in me like flood waters and with a cry, we both plunged off the edge of the world and fell and I still couldn't tell if I were swallowed by the light or the dark.

23

*Y*ale…

Flawless.

She rested, panting against me, face turned from the standing ovation we received from the crowd as the curtains whisked along their automated tracks, concealing us from view. I held her, our breaths mingling, sweat cooling on our skins as we drifted slowly back to earth from the unearthly heights of our passions.

"Look at me," I whispered, smoothing her hair back from her face. She sat up slowly, using my shoulders to aid her, her green eyes glassy and distant, unable to focus just yet.

"How do you feel?" I asked softly, pushing her hair back from her face.

"Good, really good," she murmured vaguely, her voice so very far away. I smiled to myself, riding the high of power, fully entrenched in my top-space even as she floated along, deep in her sub-space.

"Does anything hurt?" I asked her, running my hands along the indentations in her wrists from my tie, massaging the marks gently.

"No, I feel good. Really good." Her voice held that far-off and dreamy quality and I didn't wish to ruin it for her. Instead, I held her close, pulling my shirt over to us and wrapping it around her shoulders until she was ready to move. I was perfectly content to wait for such a time. There was no rush.

"Mr. Silver?" I looked up at the quiet male voice, and the masked attendant held up my suit jacket and set it at the edge of the stage. I nodded and told him quietly, so as not to disturb Ally, "Locker 118, I can't get to the key."

"Very good, sir. Leave it upon the chair."

I nodded, and rocked Ally in my lap, pressing her head to my shoulder as she curled against me, motionless and still, riding out the afterglow in peace.

The attendant returned and set her dress and cloak neatly at the edge of the stage, and with a slight salute, backed through the curtain and left. On top of her clothing were the keys to my car. As part of the arrangements, I had requested that it be parked at the back entrance to the club so that I could take her home away from any prying eyes. The show was over, there was no need, in my estimation, to mingle with the guests. I had gotten what I had come for and was beyond pleased with the outcome.

"Come on, baby," I murmured into her hair and immediately bit the inside of my cheek at the too-familiar term of endearment. She sat up reluctantly at my urging, and I helped her to stand, moving her over to the chair. She sat obediently while I gathered my pants from around my ankles and fastened them around my hips. I redressed first, taking my shirt back from her gently and replacing it with the cloak I had bought her. It was far more rich and luxurious against her skin than my shirt and she deserved that. She had exceeded my expectations beyond my wildest dreams, tonight.

Once I was dressed, my ruined tie in my pocket, I knelt in front of her.

She looked down through her lace mask, her eyes clear and bright and I smiled.

"Still feel good?"

"A little shocked, actually." I tilted my head, a silent command for her to go on, and she smiled faintly. "I mean, was that really me?" she asked.

"It was," I said with a light laugh and she laughed too. I looked her over, where she was huddled on the chair, holding the cloak to her chin like a blanket and I said to her, "Let me help you."

She let me take the heavy velvet material and I helped her back into her clothing a piece at a time starting with her bra, and then her dress. I pocketed her panties, crotchless as they were, I couldn't remember why I had taken them off rather than just fucked her with them on. I wrapped an arm around her waist once her dress was on and hauled her up hard against my body. She took a sharp intake of breath, her hands going to my chest, half in surprise, half to make me stop. I raised both eyebrows and despite the mask, she took my meaning, her hands relaxing, her touch softening as she yielded to me.

I swept a hand between her thighs and pressed it against her bald pussy beneath her skirt.

"While I appreciate the effort, you need to at least grow a landing strip of hair or something. I like to make love to women, not little girls. Understood?"

"Yes, sir," tumbled so beautifully from her lips I rewarded her with a kiss, pressing my fingertips to her clit and rubbing it in slow circles, I swallowed the surprised cry she emitted into my mouth like the sweet piece of candy that it was.

I broke the kiss and swept my hands down her skirt, smoothing her dress into place, holding her steady as she stepped into her heels, a happy pink blush across her cheeks.

I fastened her cloak at her throat for her, and murmured, "Keep the mask as a memento, don't take it off until we are in the car."

"Of course, Mr. Silver," she said and the wicked little curve to her burgundy lips brought an answering one to my own.

I let myself have a moment to wonder if it was her corruption that was just beginning or if it were, in fact, the opposite and that the levity I felt in my soul was the start of my own redemption. I didn't dwell on it, leading her off the edge of the stage and along the back hall to the side door. I pulled up her hood and held the door open for her to step into a different sort of indigo night, a warm and sultry late-summer one.

She held onto me as we went up the cement steps into the lot at the back of the building and I unlocked my waiting Mercedes with my key fob. I opened her door and tossed my suit jacket, which was over my arm, into the back seat.

I helped her into her seat, sweeping the remaining material of her cloak, which was trying to spill out of the door, into her lap and onto the passenger floorboard and making certain she was secure, her seatbelt going into place, I shut her safely inside the car. I got behind the wheel and started it, putting on my own seatbelt and taking off my mask, which I carelessly went to toss behind me, but Ally plucked it from my fingers, placing it on her lap.

"You want it?" I asked and she nodded softly. I nodded and let her have it. It cost me nothing, and I had no further use for it.

The drive to the Point Side went by in comfortable silence. Ally stared out the window after pulling her own mask free, her eyes wide with wonder as if seeing the city beyond the window glass for the first time. I remembered the feeling. When I had first found myself, what I liked, and that I could have it all? I'd almost felt like a real life superhero with a secret identity. I still felt that way sometimes. Like now, when I reveled in her self-discovery, in the feeling of accomplishment and power that rested on her slim shoulders like the cloak I'd purchased for her.

I turned down her street and rolled to a stop at the curb in front of her building. She turned to me and I tucked some of her hair behind her ear. She smiled a little sadly and whispered, "Thank you."

I felt my smile grow and said, "You're very welcome, and thank *you*."

"Of course."

"Wait," I said as she stepped out of the car and straightened. I dipped my hand into the pocket in my door and retrieved the envelope of pay I usually left on the dining room table for her. She may not have cleaned this week, however, I felt a deep desire to take care of her, nevertheless.

She bowed and looked inside the open door, and her eyes fell on the envelope, her face contorting, stricken and... horrified. She straightened, took a moment or two and bowed again, her eyes alight with rage.

"I'm not your whore, Damien!" she hissed, and before I could open my mouth, she had slammed the door to my car and was striding up the walk. I rolled down the passenger side window. I was angry at the accusation but that didn't absolve me in any way of ensuring to her care and safety post such an intense scene.

"Ally!" I called and she froze mid-step and refused to turn around. That pissed me off too, but wouldn't stop me from saying what I had to say. "Take some ibuprofen before you go to sleep and take a hot bath tomorrow," I ordered. "It will help with the soreness."

She turned her head slightly but then her posture stiffened and she marched resolutely away from me. I scowled, my anger bubbling even closer to the surface that she would so blatantly defy me. I tossed the envelope onto the seat, shifted gears and pulled away from the curb with an angry squeal of tires.

24

*A*lly…

I spent the weekend going back and forth between hurt and angry tears. When I had keyed my way into my apartment, I had been angry. When I had gone to bed, staring at his mask, lying forlornly on my small sewing table next to my machine, I had hurt. The empty eye holes and furrowed brow in the leather seemingly mocking me.

I hadn't done what he'd told me. I hadn't taken anything before bed and the next morning I certainly had regretted it. I'd woken up stiff, my shoulders and back killing me. I'd grudgingly taken some of the anti-inflammatories that morning and schlepped myself into the bathroom and put myself under a hot shower's spray. I didn't have a bathtub.

The rest of my Saturday had been spent alone, doing my laundry, begging off from seeing Dawnie with a lame excuse of not feeling well, even though the pills and hot water had done some magic. I'd then tried to find my happy place by throwing myself into my favorite hobby. My grandmother had been a seamstress and she had taught me a love of all things sewing. Most of my clothing was actually repurposed thrift store finds.

In fact, I made most of mine and Dawnie's clothes. Right now, I was working on a broomstick style skirt for Dawnie using strips of different textured material in complementary colors. I had been hoarding for a while to make it happen. This one was in different greens and golds to complement her long auburn hair. I used pieces of corduroy from jackets and pants, bits of velvet from evening dresses and scarfs, even some burned-velvet patterns from a scarf or two. Some heavy Asian silk and jersey knit material also went into the making of it, and I was determined to have it done before fall.

She couldn't see, so I did my best to make things to excite her other senses, like this. It was the least that I could do for her. Well, that, and choose and sort yarn with her. She had taught herself to crochet to pass the time and she made some of the most beautiful things by touch. It was a secret dream of ours that one day we would win the lottery or that we would be discovered through our little online shop and we'd be able to open a boutique someday.

Sunday, I had made dessert and gone to see my grandmother. She had, once again, noticed my lackluster appetite and my strained smile. I had lied to her again, not wishing to worry her. Told her that I was just tired and that everything was fine while I wrestled with my feelings over what I had done with Damien Parnell.

I don't know what had made me do it, other than it felt right for me to get it out somehow, some way, but I had written another letter, fulfilling his wish that I write about our sexual escapades afterward.

I was less than kind when it came to my feelings this time. Harsh. Angry. My bitterness at how the night had ended bleeding onto the page. I'd shredded it. I wouldn't dare dream of giving it to him. He didn't deserve to know anything more about me. Not unless he gave me something of him. I couldn't anymore. I just couldn't… but neither could I afford to stop working for him. At least not until I found another job.

I had been squirreling any extra away, and it was enough to cover the missing money from the last week, but now as I ground the beans and packed the portafilter and made overpriced coffee for under appreciative people, I was just tired. Emotionally drained. My anger fled with time and left me facing a chasm of deep and awful aching hurt.

"Allison Blaylock?" someone asked and I looked up and over to the register. Millie was staring wide-eyed at the delivery person, and the huge bouquet of bright red roses he clutched in a heavy glass vase, her finger pointed in my direction. I blinked and said, "I'm Ally."

"These are for you," the young man said, holding them out to me. I went around the counter and took them from him. He smiled, flashing a dimple in the side of his cheek and it was a nice smile, but it didn't affect me the same way as when Mr. Parnell smiled at me.

I gave him a weak smile back, and he tipped his ball cap at me and rushed out the door. He didn't even wait for a tip. I took the roses to the back counter, their heavenly scent perfuming the air even over and above the permanent rich smell of coffee. Millie didn't even ask. She simply took up my place behind the espresso machine and pulled double duty so that I could read the card.

I plucked the familiar white envelope from the plastic fork thingy holding it in among the roses and turned it over to the familiar sticker seal holding the triangular flap closed. I sighed and with some trepidation, worked a nail under it and freed it so I could liberate the card inside.

Ally-

You're my lover, <u>not</u> my whore. I simply want to take care of you...

Please, arrive on time today. We need to talk.

-Damien

The word 'not' was underlined twice, savagely, and I swallowed hard. He was angry, and I was pretty sure I was fired, but... I looked up at the tight roses that had yet to fully bloom and frowned slightly, counting. There were twenty-four. Two dozen roses, for me? Two dozen red roses. I read and reread the note wishing there was more, wishing there was some sort of indication as to what to expect when I arrived at Damien's for work.

I sighed and rubbed my eyes; the hand with the note dropped to my side helplessly. He was magnetic. I couldn't believe I had already decided I would be meeting him, but I couldn't help it. All of these mixed signals were driving me a little crazy. I swallowed hard and slipped the card into my apron, having a hard time dragging my eyes away from the riot of color on the counter.

No one had ever bought me flowers before. A boy had brought me a handful of marigolds that he had ripped out of my grandmother's garden once, but he was seven and I'd been more than a little dismayed, so I hardly thought that counted.

I went back to work, ducking and avoiding Millie's looks of curiosity and teasing smile for the rest of the afternoon. When it was finally time for me to go I stared at the flowers, my bottom lip between my teeth. I didn't know whether to take them with me or if it was all right to leave them here.

"You work for Mr. Parnell today, right?" Millie asked and I nodded faintly.

"Yes. I'm not sure I want to take these on three buses and then on three more to get them home," I said honestly.

"Say no more. Leave them there, you can take them home tomorrow and I sure don't mind! They brighten up the place."

I smiled weakly, and said, "Thanks, Millie."

"Don't mention it," she said, and then her curiosity won out. "Who is he?"

"I'd rather not say," I told her. "I don't think it's going anywhere."

She laughed, clear and bright like it was the funniest thing I had ever said. When she got herself together, she said to me, wiping a tear from her eye, "Two dozen red roses says that it is *definitely* going somewhere, Ally Cat. Whoever he is, I think it's safe to say he loves you." She winked at me and I quickly plastered a smile onto my face over my blush and ducked out the front door.

I was glad, at least, that there had been a pocket inside the cape he'd had me wear and that I was able to keep my wallet and keys in it. I could only imagine the questions I would have had to answer if I had had to knock on Mr. Comey's door in the middle of the night to have him let me into my apartment. Frustratingly, the rest of my things, my tote bag and purse, were still at Damien Parnell's.

I hopped the buses that would take me to his apartment and got off at the last stop with a heavy heart. I didn't know what waited for me inside his apartment. If he would be there, or if he expected me to wait until he came home. I walked up the block and crossed the street, turning down in front of the Calvert building and making my way to the familiar green canopy and carpet trimmed in gold. I smiled for Mr. Clive's benefit.

"Hey, Ms. Ally!" he greeted me brightly and swung open the door for me.

"Hi, Mr. Clive," I greeted him back, and slipped through into the dim-but-opulent lobby of the building. It never failed to take my breath away, not even today, when I felt a heavy leaden weight of dread in the pit of my stomach as I took the healthier option and ascended the stairs.

I paused outside his door, key in hand, and let out a breath before shoving it into the lock. I knew as soon as the door swung inward he was home; the alarm failed to keen at me, wanting me to feed its code to it to shut it off. I stepped inside and turned, shutting the door behind me and when I turned back to the wide open living space, he was there, standing just a few paces away.

He had no tie, his top two buttons at his collar undone, his sleeves rolled back over his muscular forearms, his jaw clenched, his dark eyes raking over me, his expression unreadable. God, he did that so well, too well, the neutrality thing and I hated it. I hated that I was never immediately able to see what he was thinking or feeling unless he wanted me to.

"Hi," he said simply, extracting his hands from his expensive slacks' pockets.

"Hey," I murmured and sighed.

He smiled faintly, and it reached his dark eyes, and I realized what I was seeing in them was a careful caution. One that I think I echoed in my own frozen stance.

He took a breath, braver than I, and started speaking, "One of the things about me, about what I do with you…" he swallowed hard, gathering his thoughts, but quickly frowned as he tried to choose his words carefully. I just wanted him to speak. I wanted to listen to his warm, soft, yet strong and intense voice because I think I parsed out one more thing in his eyes when he looked at me… *hurt.*

"I didn't mean for it to come out that way," he said finally. "Giving you the money wasn't for anything we did Friday night. It wasn't even about you cleaning or working for me, or any of that."

"Then what was it?" I asked, frowning in confusion.

"Taking care of you," he said simply. "It's about taking care of you. I want to." He stuffed his hands back into his pockets and tipped his head back with a giant heaving sigh to stare at the ceiling. He stared at it for a handful of seconds and I realized this, what he was doing, was opening up to me and it was hard for him. Very hard.

I licked my lips and clutched the strap of the little bohemian bag I had stitched together to make myself a new purse, a project I had completed along with half of Dawnie's new skirt on Saturday.

"So what happens now?" I asked, carefully.

"I don't know, Bright Eyes. That's up to you. All I know is that I don't want to lose you over some dumb misunderstanding, and I think it's time we renegotiate the terms of this relationship."

I huffed an incredulous laugh and rolled my eyes a bit and said, "Okay, I get that, but did you really have to sound like such a damn lawyer right then?"

He chuckled lightly and pulled his hands from his pockets again, holding his arms out in an invitation for me to fill them with my body. I hesitated, but only for a half a second while it hit me just how much I wanted that. How much I ached to curl up against his chest and just live there. I so fiercely wanted him to love me because I was certain that, if I hadn't already, that I was well into falling in love with him, myself.

Still, the relief that flooded me after living with the hurt of his action, trying to hand me that envelope after our dalliance at the club, it was still fresh and still there. When his arms closed around me, though; when his hand pressed into the back of my head, stroking my hair and his lips met the top of my head, I let it go. I had to but not without doing what I promised first.

"It hurt so much when you tried to pay me after…" I couldn't bring myself to say it, because the whole experience had been so incredibly and exquisitely beautiful for me, and then for him to cheapen it that way…

"I imagine that it hurt as much as your accusation did me." He rushed out the rest before I could finish drawing breath to protest, his arms tightening around me. "Even if it wasn't unwarranted. I understand how it looked, how it felt, even though I swear to you, that's not how I meant it. I screwed up. I didn't communicate, and that's on me, and for *that,* I apologize."

"I'm sorry, too," I whimpered and the first few tears choked me up as they squeezed their way out despite my best efforts. He leaned back and fixed his eyes on mine, wiping away my tears with a gentle hand, his other on my waist, holding me near him so I wouldn't try to get away, not that I even wanted to. I loved it when he held me like this.

"I want to protect you from everything," he whispered and smoothed the moisture off my other cheek. "I just don't know how to protect you from myself."

His confession broke my heart and I didn't know what to say, I shook my head and whispered, "You don't have to. I don't want you to. I…" I almost let it slip out. I almost told him the truth, but I was afraid. I rolled my lips together and said the only thing I could think to say that would put his mind at ease. The only language he'd given me that was just *us*; just between us two.

"Green."

His mouth engulfed mine in a kiss so fiery, so passionate; it welded my cracked heart back together so seamlessly and so flawlessly, I don't think that even I would ever be able to tell that he'd nearly broken it.

25

*Y*ale…

I held her tight, unable to deny that I was past wanting to keep her; that I had to admit I needed someone like her in my life. Her gracious beauty unmatched in only one arena, her integrity. That turned me on beyond anything and I had been looking for a woman like her for so long. The perfect amalgamation of pretty, smart, innocent, and with such an honest purity.

She was beyond corruption, but what's more, she was some sort of an angel, lifting me out of my brooding and misery. She gave me something to look forward to, allowing me to hope and even dream for myself for a change.

I let my hand drift to the back of her hair, gripping it tightly in my fist to control her head. Tearing my mouth from hers I marched my lips down the side of her neck, exploiting all her most sensitive places with them, adding my teeth as necessary. She gasped, sighing out in a rush of breath, her body leaning limply with submission into mine. The tingle in my cock grew as I rose swiftly from half-mast to full and I wanted inside her elegant body so badly. I was done tiptoeing around with her, though. I would be taking her to the bedroom for this.

I wanted her in my bed, needed her there, a symbolic thing with heavy importance to me. I only took women to my bed, in my space, who I wanted to keep, and I wanted to keep Ally. I wanted to claim not just her body, but her heart and soul as well, and I would go to any limit, beyond any limit to do so.

So involved in her rushing, moaning, whimpering breaths was I, I almost missed her nimble fingers making quick work of my shirt until she was drawing it from my waistband to reach the last few buttons.

"You naughty girl," I said, smiling by her ear, and jerked back on her hair carefully. Her reaction was beautiful: a sharp, surprised cry, back bowing, going to her very tippy-toes before putting her feet flat on the floor. I turned her away from me, and brought her back against my chest, turning us both toward the hall. I plunged my free hand down the front of her little shorts and pressed my fingertips past her plump pussy lips, seeking her opening, pleased to find her growing wet. I slicked the moisture up and over her clitoris and massaged it firmly, teasing it into a hard kernel as she writhed and tried to get away from my hand.

"Not going to happen," I murmured and kissed the shell of her ear. "Now march. End of the hall, into the bedroom."

"Yes, sir," she gasped, shuddering. I propelled her forward and she went, obediently and I loved that. I loved everything about how she sweetly obeyed, even though she struggled slightly against my hand at her front.

"Take your shorts and panties down," I commanded when I had her facing the foot of my bed. Her hands immediately went to the button and zipper at the front of the denim and she quickly unfastened them, giving her hips a sexy little shimmy as she forced them down. They slid to pool around her ankles and I smiled.

"Good girl." I thrust her forward, throwing her down on her stomach onto the bed. She yelped with surprise and turned onto her back, but I was already pulling my shirt back off of my shoulders, devouring her with my gaze. She leaned up to watch me, hands pressed flat to the comforter, pushing herself up when I went for her shoes and to pull her bottoms the rest of the way off.

"Play with your pussy, I want to watch you," I told her, and with a shy smile that held a wicked edge, her fingertips drifted over her body, from her throat, over the many fashionable necklaces she wore, between her breasts, encased in the charcoal-gray tank top she wore beneath her little denim jacket, over her stomach, drifting over the mound of her pussy until she pressed light fingertips into the top of her sex in rapid teasing circles.

She arched, and cried out lightly, her breath coming in even, long, slow gasps as she writhed and played with herself for my eyes while I worked my pants open and went for a condom in the bedside table. I tore open the packet while she watched me, eyes heavy-lidded with desire, and I could tell that watching me put it on myself was as alluring to her as watching her play with her little pink pussy making herself ready for me, was to me.

I wrapped my arms around her thighs and yanked, hauling her bodily across the mattress closer to me. She shrieked with delight, laughing, which quickly turned into a sultry moan as I introduced my body to hers in the most intimate way possible. I took it slowly, easing my cock into her until I was buried to the root. She felt so good, amazingly hot and wet, her walls pressing around me gently. I stroked out of her, then back in once, and closed my eyes, bowing my head and savoring the sensation.

"Did I tell you to stop?" I demanded and her fingertips, which were still pressed against her clit, resumed their motion as I set an accompanying rhythm.

"Oh, god," she moaned and arched again, her back coming up off the bed, forcing herself down on me tighter, and it felt so good but wasn't quite enough for me. This was going to be a quick fuck as compared to what we'd done before, but it was right and had its place.

"Tighten up for me, Bright Eyes," I urged, and she gripped me like a second skin, her tight little pussy fisting my cock to such a fucking perfection I couldn't hold back. I drove into her a final time and fucking exploded, starbursts of white fucking light going off behind my tightly closed eyelids, even as I heard her cry out beneath me. Oh, god, she milked me fucking dry with her own orgasm as she fought not to writhe too much beneath me.

I collapsed over her and pressed my mouth to hers, smoothing her hair away from those gorgeous green eyes of hers as they stared into my soul, sightlessly seeing everything and nothing at all.

"God damn, I love you," I whispered, and her arms came up and went around me, her legs following suit as she gave me a massive full-body hug, twining around me like ivy.

I'd never felt as complete as a man until right then.

26

$\mathcal{A}$lly…

    I woke suddenly in an unfamiliar but luxurious bed, the sound of clattering dishes and the dishwasher door shutting wresting me from my nap.

More like blissed out coma, my inner voice corrected me and I smiled. I stretched, deliciously sore as I twisted from my stomach and sat up. I blinked in surprise as Damien, sexy as hell in just a pair of black cotton lounge pants came through the door bearing a tray.

"Welcome back," he said with a devilish smile and I felt an echoing one curve my lips.

"I'm sorry, I didn't mean to fall asleep."

He shook his head, "Don't worry about it, you needed it and you weren't out long. An hour, maybe two." He lifted his chin to indicate I should get comfortable. I pushed my hands flat against the mattress and dragged myself up and back against the headboard. He set the tray across my lap and sat down by my hip. I felt my mouth drop open in surprise.

A petite cut of steak, roasted vegetables, and a small salad graced the plate. A glass of sparkling water and a single rose in a fluted vase finished the tray but then I froze when I spotted the simple white business envelope. Precisely like the one that had nearly torn us apart with its presence.

I opened my mouth but he stopped me with an, "Ah before you say anything, this one is different… it's not like the rest. Just open it."

The food momentarily forgotten, I picked up the envelope, and he was right. It was thicker somehow, fuller than any that had come before. With some trepidation, I tore off one end carefully and slid a sheaf of paperwork out of it, unfolding it so I could read.

I blinked and looked up at him in shock, dropping my eyes back down to the page and reading and rereading it in disbelief. It was paperwork from my grandmother's care facility. The open balance had been paid, what's more? The forwarding balance for the next *year* had been paid as well.

I felt tears brim my eyes and I looked up at him. He didn't know my grandmother. Why would he do this?

He smiled a little sadly, and I realized I must have voiced the question. He reached out and cupped my cheek gently, stroking a thumb along my skin in a light, reverent touch.

"I didn't do it for your grandmother, Bright Eyes. I did it for you." He sighed and looked reluctant for a moment, slightly wistful when he went on to say, "I'm afraid there's some bad news that comes along with it," he said. "You might not want to thank me just yet."

I felt my heart seize in my chest and asked, "What?"

"You're fired, Ally. I can't be caught dating one of my employees and if I'm going to take you out for real…" he watched me gravely, letting the thought trail off, his eyes guarded and his expression stone.

I covered my mouth with my hand in an attempt to catch my laughing sob, and careful of the tray in my lap, held my arms open, begging him to hold me. He laughed too, and put his arms around me, holding me tightly. He drew back and tucked my hair behind my ear and said, "It was the only thing I could think of to fix this, to make it right between us and clear the air."

"I've never been so happy to be fired in my life," I said and we shared excited happy grins.

"I was hoping you wouldn't be too broken up about it," he confessed.

"I can't believe you would do this for me," I said with wonder and I let my eyes rove the paperwork one more time.

"Eat your dinner, Bright Eyes. I told you, I take care of what's mine." He kissed my forehead, and drew back saying gravely, "You're mine, aren't you?"

I nodded, knowing precisely what he meant and it didn't feel creepy or overbearing at all. If anything, it felt *safe*. Damien Parnell knew the meaning of consent, and we had had a long talk before I had drifted off to sleep, listening to his voice as he explained some of the world he had come from.

To be from his family, you would think it was a real life *Cruel Intentions*. I had said as much and he had chuckled without mirth, a bitter, angry sound and said, "They had to get the idea for the movie somewhere. East coast high society was certainly it." I'd kissed him then, trying to dispel the dispassionate tone, abolish the mantle of discord that had settled over him so suddenly and completely.

I was beginning to understand precisely *why* he was so guarded and it broke my heart. There were entirely too many sets of circumstances in which to grow up and become hardened and callous in today's world. It made my heart hurt. The fact that Damien had grown up under such circumstances, yet still remained able to be so tender with me... I do believe in miracles. I see small ones in this city, at the projects, every year.

"Try the steak, before it gets cold," he urged. I smiled and cut into it.

"Medium rare, how did you guess?"

"I didn't," he said chuckling. "I just fixed it how I liked, figuring I could always cook it more thoroughly if I needed to."

"Where is yours?" I asked and he chuckled.

"Was starving, I ate already, but you needed the sleep. Eat up, it's a school night. I'll drive you home. What were your plans for Friday?" he asked.

"Well, you see, I thought my boyfriend might take me on a date somewhere."

"Smart man," he said smiling. "I certainly wouldn't waste a Friday night with you. Dress casually; we're going to the 10-13 to hang with some of the guys."

"Sounds nice," I said softly, the fact he wanted to take me back there, introduce me as his, causing butterflies in my stomach. I didn't think I would ever get tired of the sensation. Nor did I think he would ever not cause them. They took flight now, just by the way he was looking at me.

"I plan on taking this slow, Ally. Treating you right…" he said gently.

I nodded and chewed carefully, "I like the sound of that," I confessed.

"Good girl," he whispered and kissed my forehead reverently. I completely loved when he did that. It was just *everything*.

I finished my meal which was one of the best I think I had *ever* had and took my time getting dressed. Damien threw on a hoodie over his bare chest and shrugged his feet into some sneakers.

"I want you to keep the keys and the code," he told me when he handed me my things that had been left behind. I nodded and he said, "Come whenever you want, whenever you need. Okay?" I nodded again.

"Let's get you home, as much as it kills me to say that," and he pulled me close for another one of those amazing forehead kisses that made my eyes drift shut and the whole world fall into perfect place.

He drove me home in his big Escalade and when he pulled up to the curb, he sighed, frowning at the Point Side.

"Text me when you're in your apartment with the doors locked. I need to know you're safe."

I smiled gently and agreed, "Okay, but I've lived here my whole life. They know me, and I know them. I'll be fine."

"I know, but it's the Point Side, Bright Eyes. I'll never be comfortable with letting you go in there as long as you're mine."

"I know, but it's fine, really. It's where I live," I said firmly.

"Right."

He leaned over the center console and kissed me and I was reluctant to have it end and to go. He drew back and I smiled, though it felt brittle.

"I'll see you soon," I promised, and he sighed.

"Just have to get through the work week hustle," he agreed and didn't sound at all happy about it.

I slid out of the SUV and looked back, murmuring, "In case you didn't know, I love you too," before I shut the door behind me and took the walkway quickly before I lost the nerve to leave his side completely.

I am a strong, confident, modern woman. I reminded myself. *Now, forward march, Ally.*

Still didn't stop me from turning back to look before I had to round my grandmother's fountain garden to go through the doors into the building. He was watching me, the dome light dimming and going out until I couldn't see him anymore. I went inside and quickly to my apartment. As soon as the locks were in place, I texted obediently.

I'm inside, safe & sound.

He texted me back a heartbeat later with **Good girl. Sleep well.**

I smiled and sighed happily answering, **I will, you too.**

Sleep came surprisingly quickly that night and I was on a high for the rest of the week, even though it seemed to drag abominably slow. On Friday, Damien came into the café and when I handed him his coffee said, "Come over to my office after work, I drove today. I'll take us where we need to go. I don't like the idea of you taking the bus."

"Okay," I murmured and blushed faintly when Millie fixed me with an impressed gaze and smile. I hadn't planned on that. Didn't realize that he wanted me around where he *worked*. Also, I had planned on going home and changing, but that wasn't nearly as big of a deal. I had some money set aside for a thrift store run and might be able to come up with something cute there that I could quickly wash and dry at his place before we went out.

I blushed harder the more Millie wouldn't stop looking at me, and as soon as the café was mostly clear, she came over to me, wiping her hands on her apron with an eyebrow raised. I blushed *again* even harder and wouldn't meet her eyes when I mumbled, "He fired me first, okay?"

She laughed derisively and said, "Seriously? He fired you so you could see him?"

I looked at her and said, "I want to see him too, so it's not even like that."

"Oh, honey, I didn't mean to upset you," she reached out and put a hand on my arm and I swallowed nervously.

"I really like him, and I know he likes me, too. I guess I just didn't think that the suspicion and that would start so soon…"

"I'm sorry," she said dismayed and sighed. "He's just a very powerful man in this city and –"

"I'm just a poor girl from the Point Side. Yeah, I know." I put my hands to my face and pressed my fingertips into my eyes, stress washing over me and through me. We'd both been afraid of how it would look since the beginning, had managed to fool one another into believing that it wouldn't be so bad, but apparently, our initial assessment of people's reactions was on point. Frustrating. Especially that it was coming from Millie.

"I didn't mean it like that, Ally." She had the grace to look embarrassed, but we both knew that wasn't exactly true. Still, it was Millie, and I knew her heart was in the right place. Her judgment came from a place of concern, not malice.

"I'm going to make us some coffee and then you are going to tell me all of the good things, like how this came to be. I believe some perspective, specifically *yours* is in order," she said with a smile.

"Basic white girl special?" I asked.

"One pumpkin spice white mocha coming your way," she agreed and I smiled.

I took one of the two person tables by the front window within easy reach of the register and espresso machine while Millie whipped up our drinks. She brought them over and took a seat across from me while I carefully edited some things in my mind. I wasn't about to give away any of Damien and mine's secrets. Some things were best left private, and privacy was something that, despite our extreme differences in demographic backgrounds, we could both appreciate.

I told my *other* boss, and honestly, Millie was like a second best friend next to Dawnie, who was already caught up by this point. Except where Millie got the edited version, Dawnie not so much. Of course, I didn't tell either of them anything that Damien wasn't okay with me sharing. I'd discussed things with him and he had been reluctant on a few points but ultimately he had sighed on the other end of the line and asked me if I trusted Dawnie and when I'd told him absolutely, he'd acquiesced.

I understood. Again, despite the differences in our backgrounds, much remained the same. Whether it be high society or the slums of the Point Side there was one universal truth to both of them. Be careful who you told what. It could and would be used against you to another person's gain. Also, it didn't necessarily have to be true, either. We were determined to keep it short and simple. As far as the world at large needed to know, Mr. Parnell had been charmed with and fallen for the girl who made his coffee in the morning. The other details weren't relevant, but if they came to light, it could be potentially damaging to him professionally.

People loved gossip, especially if that juicy bit of gossip involved a sex scandal surrounding a prominent public figure such as the city's star ADA.

Millie looked at me across the small table where we'd spoken in hushed tones after I laid all of this out and her shoulders dropped. She shook her head in wonder and said, "Ally Cat, I love you, my dear girl, and sometimes you break my heart with how wise beyond your years you've needed to be."

"Thanks, I think," I murmured and took a sip of my drink.

She chuckled and patted the back of my hand. "Most definitely that was meant as a compliment. You've been handed a very poor hand in so many ways, yet you've borne it all with such grace. You wear the weight of the world on your shoulders like a set of wings, dear girl."

I stared at her for a moment, a little wide-eyed. Her final compliment catching me off guard, my eyes misting from it. It was quite possibly one of the nicest, most beautiful things anyone had ever said to me.

"Oh no! Don't cry!" she came around the table and hugged me and I told her how I felt. She smiled and pulled back and said, "And that's what ultimately matters, that you're *happy*."

I *was* happy. Happier than I could remember being not just in a long time, but ever.

27

*Y*ale…

A light tap at my door. I kept my eyes on the report in my hand and did what I usually did and said, "Yeah, what is it?"

"Um, hi…" her lyrical voice trailed off into an uneasy laugh and I looked up. It never ceased to amaze me how hearing her voice made my heart lift in the center of my chest, soaring to great heights until we had to part again.

She stood nervously in the doorway to my office and it did things to me. It was both strange and wonderful having her here in this space and it was telling to me how much I wanted to integrate her into every part of my life. Once I was in, I was all in, and Ally was no exception to that rule. I dropped the police report in my hand and let it fall, momentarily forgotten to my desktop.

"You're late," I said gently, with a devious smile. I'd told her to meet me "after work", meaning when *she* got off work, but she hadn't been incorrect in coming here when she knew it was time for me to get off. I just wanted to punish her for the sake of it. I wanted to hear her whimper and moan.

"Um, I figured I had a little time before you were off, so I went to the thrift store a couple of streets over. I thought I would need something to wear tonight."

"Don't you need to wash things before you wear them?" I asked, amused.

"Yes," she said slowly, coming into the room to meet me in front of my desk. "But I thought I could wash them at your place. Maybe while I made us some dinner?"

"Ah, maybe." I pulled her closer to me, an arm around her waist, "I was planning on taking you to dinner. Besides that," I kissed her gently and loved how she melted into me, "I like my dessert first," I whispered against her mouth.

"Oh," she breathed and I could tell, she was as turned on as I was at the possibilities.

Another thing I loved about Allison Blaylock was her ability to keep up with my sexual appetites. I smiled at her and she smiled up at me but our moment was shattered by another interruption.

"Yale, do you have the Gerard case file in here, I could have sworn I had it in my office but I can't seem to find –"

I cleared my throat and Chrissy looked up from the legal pad she was jotting notes onto against her other arm. She looked up through those naughty librarian glasses of hers and froze mid-step.

"I'm sorry, I didn't know you had a visitor."

"Quite all right, Chrissy; you know my girlfriend, Ally, right?"

She looked dumbfounded and I tried not to laugh at her expression. Ally was blushing in a riot of soft pink across her nose and cheeks as she stammered out, "Hello Ms. Franco."

"Hi," Chrissy said, finally recovering. "Good to see you again, it's been forever," she joked and Ally laughed. I raised an eyebrow and Ally let me down gently.

"She came into the café for lunch earlier."

"Ah," I smiled.

"Gerard case file is in the pile," I said and thrust my chin at my overflowing filing cabinet.

"Right." Chrissy went over, and, as she rummaged, asked, "Are you both going to the 10-13 tonight, then?"

"That was the plan," I responded.

"Good, I guess I'll see you there," she smiled tightly and I had a moment of rue. She was going to tell Youngblood, and by default, the rest of the guys will know I was holding out and the ribbing would likely be brutal as a result.

"What just happened?" Ally asked, confused, and I laughed.

"I believe my temporary downfall with the rest of the Knights over holding out about you."

"Oh, fun," she said dubiously and laughed. I laughed too, and it felt good.

"Speaking of the 10-13, it awaits. I figured we'd go back to my place and I could grab a change of clothes. You," I held her out slightly in front of me and swept her with my gaze, "You're beautiful no matter what you wear." It was true. She had a knack for being fashionable in this bohemian-chic, city girl sort of way.

"Thanks," she said softly. "Especially considering I make most of mine and Dawnie's clothes."

I jerked back, frowning slightly and said, "How did I not know that?"

She shrugged, lightly and I nodded. "Now I'm curious."

"Tell you all about it on the ride?" she asked.

"Sounds like a plan; let me wrap up a couple of things and we'll get out of here."

"I like the sound of that," she said softly and I gestured for her to take a seat in the chair across my desk. She sat down and we made small conversation as I shifted things around, organizing it for the following Monday. I wasn't oblivious to the curious and wide-eyed staring going on outside my office door; I simply didn't care. The jealousy in some of those stares was a palpable thing, and *that* I did care about, but I would have to address it as situations with more merit than a simple dirty look came up.

"Ready to go?" I asked finally, and Ally smiled gently.

"When you are," she said and I gave her my arm as we went out and I locked things up.

"Good night, *Mr. Parnell*," Chrissy called and I gave her a tight-lipped grin. She shot me a look full of barely-suppressed laughter that pretty much guaranteed the ribbing I would receive at the hands of my brothers. I was fairly certain she owed it to me. Working under me as a prosecutor and as my second chair wasn't always an easy thing.

I led Ally to the garage, held her hand and opened her door for her. The drive back to my place was light on the talking and we *did* have a couple of hours to kill before we needed to head out. She took the time to strip and put her clothes and that which she'd procured from the second-hand store into the wash. I took the opportunity to ambush her from behind as soon as the washing machine started.

"Shower with me," I ordered, and she giggled lightly, turning in my arms and looking at me with those luminous eyes of her.

"I'd love to," she said, and it was the perfect blend of soft and seductive to my ears.

She led *me* to the master bathroom and opened up the shower door.

With a sultry look over her shoulder, she turned on the rain feature shower head and crooked her finger in my direction. Amused, I undressed, eyes locked on her as she stood under the shower fall, tipping her head back and letting the water soak her hair.

God, she was beautiful, and I couldn't wait to join her, have her body warm and close. She thawed something in me. My cold and frozen soul felt like springtime had finally arrived anytime I was in her presence and it was a miraculous feeling. Even when I forced her to her knees in front of me. Of course, not that it was much of a struggle.

I peered down my body at her, jaw clenched, and with a look, told her exactly what I expected of her. A piece of my darkness was echoed in her eyes as she looked up to me and took me into her lush mouth for the first time.

I groaned bowing my head and closing my eyes, just concentrating on the feel of her hot wet mouth on me. The way her velvet tongue teased the ridge under my head. How it felt to stroke into her, over that tongue, touching the back of her throat. She choked, and I backed off, working with her on relaxing her throat, guiding myself to her limit, testing her gag reflex and finding the right cadence.

It took her a while to time her breathing, and I loved the edge of fear in her eyes when I held her on my dick just a touch too long for her comfort. It was an aphrodisiac all on its own. She let me know when it was too much with a light series of taps against my hip with her fingers and I could tell, this wasn't exactly her favorite thing, but she did it because it pleased me.

As a reward, I didn't come in her mouth but rather in my hand, letting the falling water wash it away and bringing her up to kiss her.

"Thank you," I murmured against her hair, holding her close and I felt her lips curve into a wan smile against my shoulder.

"You're welcome," she said and her voice was brittle. I drew her back and smoothed her hair back from her face, searching it, cocking my head.

"Talk to me," I said. "What didn't you like?"

She blushed and I waited her out. We wouldn't be getting out of this shower until she told me. I didn't like how rattled she seemed, I was afraid she had let me push her a little too far past her limits in order to please me and while I was proud of her for pushing her limits, I was also unhappy that she let me go too far. That was unacceptable to me. I didn't want to hurt her. Push her, yes, damage her, no.

"I really didn't like not being able to breathe. Um, I don't know, I trusted you not to actually hurt me but it was scary. Like *really* scary."

"Okay," I murmured and cradled her close, smoothing my hands over her comfortingly, "Okay, I'm sorry. I didn't realize it was bothering you that much."

"I don't think I did either," she said honestly, and I understood that. First time trying something and all, sometimes it took a little longer to decide on if that something was just uncomfortable, or a strong dislike.

"I'll be making this up to you," I whispered against her hair and she nodded against my shoulder, hunkered against me, almost huddled miserably as she mulled things.

I gave her the time to fully process those thoughts and feelings, washing her hair for her, lovingly slathering my hands over her skin with soap, caressing every dip and curve of her physique while she calmed. My touch was intended to soothe and it did. I was pleased with how responsive she was to my attentions and to my moods, it strengthened my resolve that she was the one for me. No mistakes, no going back. *God, why would I ever want to go back?*

She shivered a little as I wrapped a towel around my hips and handed her one for her long hair. She bowed, wrapping it up into one of those turbans girls were so fond of before trying to take the towel I had for her body. I wouldn't let her have it. Instead, I rubbed her briskly through the terrycloth and told her, "Get under the covers and get warm. I'm going to start your clothes in the dryer and then I'm having my dessert first."

I gave her a playful slap on the ass and she jumped, yipping in surprise. She went to the bed, suddenly all happy and glowing and I loved that.

Her clothes drying, I went back to my room and spent the next twenty or thirty minutes making her howl. It was a good way to start the night, one I wouldn't mind repeating every Friday night from here on out, but I didn't want to get too ahead of myself. I needed to make sure for myself and for her that this was good for us both. Healthy in a way that no other relationship I had before, was. I was fairly certain of it, however. Especially considering that *everything* about what was blossoming between Ally and me felt different from anything that had come before.

I watched her, in the mirror beside mine as she put the finishing touches on her makeup. She had found some sort of over-large women's country blouse, a plaid pattern in salmon, yellows, purple, and white. By itself, it was crazy to think she could do anything with it, but she had also found a slim, brown leather belt and a pair of sandals that matched. She rolled the sleeves to her elbows and used the little straps on the inside of them to hold them back.

I leaned against the vanity and crossed my arms over my simple tee shirt and jeans ensemble and watched her as she applied a shimmery peachy-gloss to her sensual lips and turned to me, asking, "What do you think?"

"I think you're going to lose the panties and I think that it will do for tonight because you're fucking gorgeous, but at the same time, this is the last time you get on the back of my bike dressed for the ride and not for the slide."

She swallowed hard and asked, "What does that mean?"

"It's a late summer out there," I said with a shrug. "Hot, so you won't be cold and you're probably going to enjoy the ride – but if something were to happen? If I laid the bike with you dressed like that?" I shook my head.

"So lend me a pair of jeans. I'll put my sneakers back on and when we get there, two minutes in the bathroom and I'll be back to this."

I smiled, "Love the practicality…" I pulled her close and kissed her forehead so I wouldn't ruin her lips she'd just put on. "I mean it about the panties, though. They're gone."

"Yes, sir," she murmured, breathy.

Accommodations made to her outfit, we headed out for the 10-13. She held onto me, and smiled the whole ride, letting the wind wash over her. She was a different woman than a week or two ago. Lighter somehow, the veil of somberness lifted from her. Her burdens less. I was pleased that I could do that for her, and relieved of my own heavy weight at the same time. She did that for me, simply by trusting and accepting me. For loving me the way I was, without caveats or condition.

I honestly hadn't thought I would ever have that.

I knew I was in for it the moment we walked through the door at the 10-13, but I was in far too good of a mood to let it bother me when Pasquale, Chrissy's drag queen, nurse, friend barked in my direction, "Mm-mmm, motherfucker! No! I cannot believe you held out on me, crushing a sister's hopes and dreams!" I laughed slightly. He was somewhere between man and woman tonight, his short dark hair slicked back tight to his skull, makeup done to the nines. His brown eyes were lined in dark kohl in a perfect cat's-eye and magenta shadow graced all the way to his brow bone.

His outfit was something else. Torn skinny jeans and a Lisa Frank white kitten tee shirt hanging off one shoulder.

"Who is that?" Ally asked me softly, her arms wrapped around my one.

"Who am I? *Who* am *I*?" Pasquale tossed back his head and snapped out a fan, waving it at himself in full airs-and-graces. I laughed. Everyone was lightly laughing and chuckling. It just was who he was and he didn't pay us any mind about it either. A born entertainer, that one.

"Restroom is back that way on the other side of the restaurant. Do your thing and hurry back here. What do you want to drink?" I asked Ally.

"Something girly, something fruity," she said blushing faintly, trying to read Pasquale, to see if she had actually offended him.

"On it," I murmured and kissed her lips, lightly, mine coming away tacky with gloss. She could fix it.

"Okay, Yale. Who is miss Little Bo Peep? Who, on god's green earth, could steal one of my most handsome men away from me?"

More laughter, a bunch of the Knights hanging their heads and fighting off semi-uncomfortable blushes at Pasquale's penchant for collecting us all like fucking Pokémon or something.

"Seriously, short dark and handsome, dish. I have *got* to know." Pasquale fixed me with a look that said he would *not* be denied, and laughing, I stepped up to the table.

"She is beauty, she is grace, now put that in your fucking face," I said with a wink. "Seriously, talk to her yourself and figure it out. She's a fantastic girl and I couldn't do her justice to explain it, nor do I need to talk behind her back."

"All right, all right, rich boy. I'll put the claws away… for now."

"Man you need to be quittin' with those hormones you been takin' or some shit," Oz muttered, and Pasquale rounded on him, shoulders back, hand poised, eyebrow raised.

"Oh, the drag queen make you uncomfortable, Milk Chocolate?" he asked and Oz started cracking up.

"Hey, he's Mexican chocolate, man. Get it right," Golden declared. "Got some cinnamon in there."

"I know *that's* right," Oz declared. "This chocolate goes into milk, not the other way around, homeboy."

Oz reached out and clapped hands with Golden and they laughed while Blaze shook his head and said, "You racist, homophobic, motherfuckers."

Oz made a tsking sound, "Man how many times I gotta tell you? I ain't racist; I got a color TV at home same as you."

"Okay, what the fuck?" Pasquale asked as the whole table busted up laughing around him.

"I notice you ain't deny the homophobia," Backdraft said taking a sip of his beer.

"It's in a man's nature to fear what he can't understand," Oz said philosophically, adding, "I'm tryin' to, though."

"Well *I*, for one, am not offended by any of y'all and am happy to call you friends," Pasquale said raising his glass.

"I'll drink to that," Youngblood declared, and glasses rang all around as Ally returned, smoothly tucking herself under my arm and into my side.

"What are we toasting to?" she asked.

"To comfort in friendship and not being offended by every-motherfucking-thing," Pasquale interjected before anyone else could say anything. "Except," he declared, "The fact you stole my favorite fuckin' man, now why you gotta destroy my hopes and dreams like that, sugar? You seem like such a nice girl and I really hate to have to hate you!"

Ally laughed and looked at me, "I don't know," she said softly, "We just sort of… fit."

"D'awwwww!" Golden declared, and there was more laughter and cutting up around the table.

I had slid up onto one of the stools and Ally leaned back against me, fitting easily between my knees, her head against my sternum thanks to the changes in height. No one either noticed or cared when my hand slipped inside the neckline of her shirt-dress to cup one of her breasts. Of course, there were so many broad shoulders and backs between us and the rest of the restaurant I somehow doubted anyone *would* notice.

"So, what do you do?" Blaze asked her and she smiled.

"Ally works at the café Yale and I get our coffee at across from the DA's office," Chrissy said and Ally nodded.

"Nice, how long you been doing that?"

I listened to my brothers in the club make small talk with my girl and watched, making my small remarks here and there. I know I probably seemed aloof and removed, but I wanted to see how things would go and if they would accept her. So far, so good, but I needn't worry about it. Not really. Ally was an exceptional woman in that she was both sweet and personable. She laughed easily and cuddled back into me as we sipped drinks and waited for our food.

"Dude, are you even listening to me?" Golden's sharp accusation caused Ally and I to turn at the same time where the Hispanic brother was frowning at Backdraft. We followed Backdraft's gaze with interest to a nearby two-person booth, but I couldn't make out what was being said. Golden scowled and asked the firefighter, "Did that dude just say what I think he said?"

"Uh-oh, looks like Backdraft's putting out a different sort of fire," Pasquale remarked and suddenly became very interested in the bottom of his glass.

"What is it?" I asked Ally when she shifted in my grasp.

"I could *swear* I know that woman from somewhere," she said.

"The table Backdraft is at?"

"Yeah. I recognize her, I just don't know where from, and it won't come to me."

"Hmm," I murmured, but then our food arrived, and we turned to rejoin the smattering of other conversation and to eat.

"Yo, Backdraft! Seriously?" Golden held out his hands and I looked over. He was standing at the table the couple had been seated at, the woman behind him and the man, looking irritated, in front of him. The woman's fingers were laced with Backdraft's and he was about to follow her to the front door.

"Later!" Backdraft barked and he gave her hand a light tug in the direction of the door, indicating she should precede him out.

The man she'd been with pulled a money clip out of his pocket and hurriedly peeled off some bills, leaving them on the table. I swept my gaze ahead of him and out the door while he scrambled to get out there with his girlfriend. Ally was watching the exchange just as intently as I was.

"I feel so bad for her," she said, cuddling back into me as we watched the girl and Backdraft stalk around the corner, the guy she'd been with trailing after them like a lost puppy. I knew he wouldn't do something so drastic without just cause so I wasn't worried about the why of it. However, I was concerned for his safety. How many domestic disturbance cases had I prosecuted in this city where bystanders with good intentions had tried to help? Where those same bystanders had been injured because of it? Too many, but this was Backdraft, and though he wasn't law enforcement, he trained with the rest of us.

Hell, I may be law enforcement but I wasn't front lines by any means. I could handle myself and Backdraft was a hell of a lot more imposing that I would ever be. He was physically fit and intimidating to an extreme.

"I wouldn't worry," I told Ally. "Backdraft can handle himself."

"I still swear I know her from somewhere," she said and I could tell it was bothering her.

"The café?" I asked, and she frowned.

"No. Someplace else. I seriously can't place it and it's driving me nuts." I chuckled and kissed her behind her ear to the music of her contented sigh.

"It will come to you eventually, Bright Eyes."

"I hope so. I hate it when this happens."

I smiled, we finished our food, we talked and played darts and I was rather taken by how seamlessly she fit with everyone. Even though, to hear him say it, she crushed Pasquale's hopes and dreams and irreparably broke his heart, by the end of the evening even he admitted he liked her and I should keep her.

"Stay with me tonight," I growled into her ear as things were winding down and the lot of us were beginning to go our separate ways.

She sighed unhappily and turned, putting her arms around my neck, looking into my eyes with regret clouding her own. Disappointment flared in my chest before she even had the chance to say 'no.'

"I wish I could, but I promised Dawnie I would take her to the library for the blind and I have to make my grandmother and me dessert for our Sunday dinner."

"I understand," I said gently and though the disappointment was there, I *did* get it. I stroked a thumb along her cheek and she smiled at the little touch.

"I really wish I could, and I would invite you to stay with me but everyone knows who you are and I don't know that it would be a good idea – for you or for me."

"It's a valid concern, Bright Eyes, and a pretty well-founded one." I kissed her forehead. "I'll drop you off and maybe we can plan for sometime next week?"

"I like the sound of that," she said softly.

"Oh, puh-leeze! I am going to take it back that I like you, sweetheart, if you're gonna rub it in like this."

Ally smiled and turned to Pasquale and said, "My deepest apologies, but you know, I might be willing to share…"

"Oh, Lord…" Oz muttered, and I echoed the sentiment. I shot a wink in his direction and he grinned back. None of us minded playing along with Pasquale's feigned infatuation. It was, after all, all in good fun.

28

a lly…

The late summer heat blurred into temperate fall days and by mid-September, it was all about jeans, boots, and my-very-favorite-sweater weather. Today was no exception. The sky was leaden out there, the clouds pregnant with rain that just refused to fall and it was humid in the café as a result. Steam gathered against the windows in drifts, and it just made the shop cozier.

I swept out front of the counter while Dawnie sat at one of the window tables soaking up light she couldn't see, crocheting on a project she could only feel. Meanwhile, Millie was behind the counter, wiping things down. We were all in a light mood, the café empty for now, between the morning and afternoon rushes, the conversation loose and flowing from one topic to another, but inevitably drifting back to their favorite, mostly because of how it made me blush and stammer.

"So, how are things going with Damien Parnell?" Millie asked.

"Don't bother," Dawnie said, looping yarn over her hook and pulling it through. "If she won't share any of the good stuff with me, she won't share with anyone else." Her smile beneath her round hippie sunglasses took any sting out of what she said, as did her light tone. I *had* shared a few details. Just enough to keep her happy and so she'd understand why Damien and I were so private about our relationship. With a little explanation of our point of view, she'd understood just how misunderstood we could be, how damaging it could be to Damien's career if it ever got out.

"Hey, not fair!" I declared in Dawnie's direction anyway. To Millie, I said, "Really well. We're taking things slowly and carefully." My phone buzzed in my apron pocket, ringing. I checked it, didn't recognize the number, so I declined the call. They could speak to my voicemail, and I would get back to them as long as they weren't selling anything or trying to collect a bill I had no money for.

"He's always been such a mysterious sort," Millie commented lightly. "What's he *really* like?"

I smiled and dragged the broom across the tiny blue and white octagonal tiles of the café's floor. Sighing lightly, I said, "Well, he can be bossy, but in a good way. He's kind, very intent on my safety." I rolled my eyes at that last one. If anything he could be a little *too* over-protective, but nothing I couldn't fend off with a gentle reminder that I had taken care of myself thus far.

Millie made a happy, dreamy sort of noise and leaned on the counter, "If I were twenty years younger…" she said wistfully.

"Millie!" Dawnie cried. "That's her *boyfriend.*"

"What? I'm getting older, I'm not dead!" she declared, and we laughed. My phone began buzzing in my pocket, the same number, but seeing as they hadn't left a voicemail after the first call, I hit ignore again. I was working; I could call it back on my break.

"You're making it hard to live vicariously through you, Ally Cat," Millie said, and Dawnie laughed, a mocking bray.

"Oh, ho, ho! Don't I know it?" she asked, and I rolled my eyes.

"What on earth could I tell you, to assuage your curiosity?" I asked, and that was a mistake. There was a deep, pregnant pause between the three of us, and Millie and Dawnie burst out laughing while I blushed deeply and said, "Um, no… pick something else; *anything* else." My sex life with Damien was –so– not up for discussion in the café.

Millie gave a mock long-suffering sigh and said, "Fine, what did you guys do last weekend?"

"Oh, we didn't do much," I said, carefully. "Stayed in on Friday night and watched a movie. On Saturday, he went thrift shopping with me."

"He willingly went shopping with you? That's a keeper," Millie declared, and I smiled.

"What movie?" Dawnie asked, innocently, ferreting out my small white lie.

I didn't bother glaring at her because she wouldn't see it but I was sure she picked up on my displeasure all the same, by way of my frosty tone when I said, "Some action thing, I fell asleep so I don't really remember." Of course, that was even more of a lie. I had spent my last Friday evening tied to Damien's bed, blindfolded, while he'd spent hours titillating me with a variety of sensations. Hot, cold, sharp, and soft. His lips against my skin, his fingertips trailing along my body as he used it as his own personal playground. I had to press my thighs tighter together just thinking about it.

My daydreaming about it was interrupted by my phone buzzing in my apron pocket again. Dawnie tilted her chin down and one ear up, cocking her head to the side, which was basically her version of rolling her eyes.

"You might as well answer that," she said, and Millie sat up straighter from where she was leaning heavily on the counter.

"Answer what?" my boss asked.

"Her phone. Whoever it is, isn't going to stop calling. That's like the third time in five minutes."

"It is?" Millie seemed bewildered and I smiled, holding up my phone, the screen lit with an incoming call.

"It is," I assured her.

"I'm blind," Dawnie said, with a self-deprecating little shrug. "Over the years my hearing's got better. Ask Ally; I can hear bats." She stuck out her tongue and made a face. I laughed and answered the phone just before it could go over to voice mail.

"Ms. Blaylock?" A woman said through the line, before I could even say 'hello'.

"Yes?" I said, immediately picking up on the concern straining her voice.

"My name is Melinda Montgomery, do you have a minute?"

I felt my stomach knot in dread at her sympathetic tone.

"Yes, what is it?"

29

Y ale...

"Miss! Miss, you can't go in there, he's on a call!"

My office door swung open and Dawnie, Ally's best friend, thrust it in until it swung back and hit the wall. "Yeah, that's the nice thing about being blind, sister. Not like you're gonna tackle me."

"I'm sorry," I said into the phone. "I'm going to have to call you right back."

I hung up on the opposing counsel before he could say anything. It wasn't like I was willing to parley with him, anyway. His client was up on second-degree murder charges in the beating death of his sister's infant son. Shook the baby boy until his neck broke. There was no deal on the table for that kind of callous disregard for human life.

"Okay, I know you're in here, lover boy. Speak, so I can find you," Dawnie said, her hand outstretched and her cane lightly tapping the floor as she came into the room.

"What is this?" I demanded, scowling, and came around my desk. She reached me, a light hand against my chest as I tried to fight down my utter irritation with her.

She wrapped her fingers around my tie giving it an insistent tug and said, "Come on, we gotta go. Ally got a call and left out of the café like a bat out of hell, crying. Millie and I couldn't get her to talk to us. She hailed a cab and split. It has to be her grandma. I don't know where the place is to even get a cab of my own, so you were my next best bet. You gotta help me."

"Let go of my tie, and I will," I said, and she made an exasperated sound.

"Sorry, my dad helps me around that way sometimes. Leaves him hands-free. Come on, you gotta hurry, though. That's my best friend and might as well be *my* grandma. I'm scared for them."

I didn't pause. I just shoveled the briefs I would need into my briefcase and picked up my phone, punching in the code that would give me reception.

"Yes, hold my calls and reschedule my meetings for the rest of the day, I need to leave for a family emergency."

"Of course, Mr. Parnell. Will everything be all right?" Darcy asked.

"Yes, thank you," I said shortly and dropped the phone back into the cradle. My cell phone, I slipped into my inside jacket pocket.

"You're lucky I drove today," I said "Come on."

She reached out and found my arm, feeling her way up to my shoulder and placed herself around a half- step behind me.

"Let's move it, just try not to run me into anything," she said and I nodded once, realized my stupidity and the futility of the motion and ground out, "Of course."

We made our way out of my office and across the floor of prosecutors at their desks, all staring wide-eyed at our brisk pace from the office.

While I was sure that I would be the subject of rumor and speculation, I was equally certain I didn't care. My woman was out there somewhere, emotionally wounded beyond compare, and I needed to reach her. I didn't think there was anything I could do to fix whatever had gone wrong, but we would just have to wait and see.

I'd driven the Mercedes today, and I helped Dawnie into the passenger seat saying, "It's low, watch your head," protecting her auburn head with a guiding hand.

"Smells expensive, what I can get through your cologne, which is nice, by the way," she remarked. "Way too expensive to be a cop car."

"Mercedes," I told her, shutting her into the car.

By the time I got around and in, she was trying to feel the two seat belt halves together. I clicked it home, and she frowned at me from behind her round hippie glasses.

"I'm blind, not completely helpless. Worry about your own."

"Wasn't a mark against your capabilities; more of a self-serving move on my part. I want to get there. Untwist your panties."

"Whatever, Romeo. Just get us there already. What are you waiting for?"

I had paused to slip my phone free and clip it to the dash so that I might use the navigation to find the place. I had only been there once in the last few weeks with Ally, and she had directed me via the bus routes. I plugged the address into the GPS feature of my phone and said, "We can't go anywhere that I don't know where we're going. I'm pulling up the GPS."

"Well, your phone is slow as shit."

"Noted," I said and though I loved Ally, her friend was grating on my nerves. I did have to hand it to her in one regard, however. She was far more emotionally invested in Sylvia Blaylock than I was. I was mostly concerned with Ally's well-being.

Traffic was a nightmare. An accident caused us to re-route and, of course, that sent the GPS into a fit. Dawnie very nearly hummed with nervous energy and irritation at the delays as she sat rigid beside me. Her mouth set into a grim line, face turned towards the window and the rushing scenery outside. It was a peculiar thing, the way she carried herself and with the glasses, you could almost fool yourself into believing that she was watching things go by.

"What's taking so long, now?" she asked, desperation and impatience shading her tone as I pulled up to the curb in the loading zone in front of the care facility.

"Nothing, we're here."

"Thank God!" She reached for her door handle, smoothing fingertips over things as I hit the catch on her seatbelt for her.

"It's not where you're reaching, just wait, I'm coming around to get you."

"Ally might listen to you, but I'm a different bag of bricks," she said defiantly, and I rolled my eyes.

The two girls might as well be exact opposites, and I was seriously on the fence as to whether I liked Dawnie or not. She seemed suspicious of me, and was more than a little standoffish, even before today, for all that I'd only met her once before in the intervening weeks since Ally and I had become an official item to my inner circle of friends.

Dawnie held onto my elbow as we made our way into the building, her cane swishing carefully back and forth in front of her as she tried to feel her way around. I noticed she didn't use the cane with Ally so much. Another sign that Dawnie didn't trust me herself, not as much as Ally did. It made Ally's trust all the more precious to me, for some reason.

"Going to ask reception?" Dawnie asked, softly.

"No. Going to her grandmother's floor. Just going to find her."

"Okay, now I'm starting to like you," she said, and I felt myself smile.

The elevator pinged and we stepped on board. I pressed the button and Dawnie made to turn around. I said, "No need. The second set of doors, they'll open in front of us."

"Thanks," she said. "Ally usually takes the stairs. Kills me, but I guess it's good exercise."

"That's what treadmills, exercise bikes, and stairmasters are for," I remarked, not liking the idea of Ally in stairwells – outside the reach of cameras – where she could easily be attacked.

"She doesn't like elevators. When we were kids, the elevator in the Point Side got stuck between floors with us in it. Her, her grandmother, and I were trapped for close to fourteen hours. It's one of my best memories, but it scared the hell out of Ally. She avoids them every chance she gets."

I hadn't heard the story before. It was something I hadn't known. It definitely put things into a sharper focus where Ally was concerned. Like why she liked my large shower so much. She said she loved how spacious it was, and was completely enamored with the fact, mentioning it every time she or I used it. I'd found it peculiar but hadn't assumed that there might be a darker root cause behind her notions about it.

The elevator pinged and bounced to a stop; Dawnie's hand tightened around my elbow and said, "Woah, rough stop. Yeah, she definitely wouldn't like that."

We stepped off onto her grandmother's floor in front of the nurse's station and I caught one of the aides' eye. She straightened and smiled somberly at us and in a low tone said, "Ally's in Ms. Sylvia's room."

"What happened?" I asked, and Dawnie was very still beside me.

"Ms. Sylvia passed in her sleep; we don't know much beyond that. It just happens sometimes."

Dawnie crumbled a little, but found some sort of well of inner strength, straightening almost immediately. She shook my arm slightly in a bid for me to get on with it, and I led us up the hall towards Ally's grandmother's room.

I stopped in the doorway, struck by how beautiful she was. She stood crying softly, at the wall beside Sylvia's empty bed, her shaking fingers reaching out and plucking one of the magazine cut-outs of their flower garden from the industrial wallpaper. I placed Dawnie's hand on the door frame to give her reference and stepped into the room gently. I didn't want to startle Ally, but it seems the best-laid plans of mice and men…

She turned and jumped, tears staining her cheeks and breath hitching, but she didn't make a thing about my scaring her, instead, it was as if whatever resolve she had managed to dredge up failed, now that I was here. She crumbled on the outside as well as the inside, her knees failing her as she backed against the wall to support herself, so she wouldn't collapse completely.

"They don't know what happened," she said through fresh sobs. "I don't know what to do…"

I went to her and pulled her against my chest, arms around her, pressing her face to my shoulder and the side of my neck. I gave her a place to shelter against me and I told her, "You don't have to do anything but grieve. I'm here now."

I couldn't fix it, but I could at least give her that.

30

*A*lly…

  I couldn't hold back the tempest anymore. I broke down, choking on sobs, hauling in a tortured breath and letting out a pitiful wail that I muffled against the shoulder of his suit jacket. I hadn't called him; I had simply forgotten to. It was my grandmother, and it had just been her and I for so long, I had completely forgotten that I had anyone else that I could lean on. Still, somehow he'd known, and now he was here.

I jumped when a light touch that wasn't him fell on my waist and I looked over to Dawnie, her expression weak and trembling, like mine, around her glasses. I opened my arm on that side and dragged her against me, too, and the three of us stood there together while two of us cried. Damien was amazing and held us both up. Giving us strength in a continual stream that neither of us could seem to hold onto. Standing in the face of our onslaught of heartache and withstanding it all. Remaining cool and level headed in the face of our grief until we were both simply all cried out and numb for the time being.

Damien let me go slowly, his hands drifting from my back, trailing along my shoulders, to cup my face, his thumbs smoothing through my devastated tears, his eyes, for once, warm instead of cold. The compassion and support I needed radiated from them as he searched my face.

"What do you need?" he asked softly and I sniffed, wiping my nose ungracefully with the back of my hand and looking around the room.

"They said I needed to pick up her things. That they need the room for somebody else. That I had to take it all down if I wanted to keep it," I said helplessly.

"Dawnie, can you fold her grandmother's clothes and box them up?"

"Might not be pretty, but I can get the job done. Just lead me to it," my best friend said grimly. Damien guided her to the bureau that held my grandmother's things and lightly put her hands on the empty box on its surface.

"Do what you can," he told her. "I'm going to help Ally with the walls."

"Okay," she said and began feeling her way around the drawers, getting the lay of the land.

He drifted back over to me and kissed my forehead in that way that always made me swoon. I closed my eyes and he let his lips linger on my skin, murmuring, "I'm here now, just tell me what you need."

I sniffed, faltering, more of the endless tears springing to my eyes. I just couldn't seem to completely shut off the tap. I got a grip, and when I could trust myself to speak, I said, "You, I think. I just need you."

"Right here, Bright Eyes. I'm not going anywhere. What else?"

"Um, I need to take all these down. I'm trying not to rip them. I want to keep them. I don't know what for yet, I just..." I scrunched down, curling in on myself and he held me through another round of tears, murmuring, but not telling me not to cry. No, he told me the exact opposite.

"Just let it out; let it all out."

It only took an hour, maybe an hour and fifteen minutes, for the three of us to pack up my grandmother's life in here. That was even more depressing to think about, but honestly, I was too numb to speak, or to really feel anything at all. I just wanted to go home.

Damien drove us to the Point Side. It'd only taken one trip for the three of us to get everything of my grandmother's to the car. I'd asked about the money he'd paid. I mean, he'd paid for a whole *year* for my grandmother to be there, but he just shook his head and said, "I'll make arrangements for it to go to another patient. It was already spent with no intention of a refund. Let it help someone else in Sylvia's name."

"Big ups for that one," Dawnie said, before ducking with my help and sliding into the back seat of Damien's Mercedes. I tried to let her take the front seat, but she wouldn't hear of it.

She helped me and Damien carry the boxes to my apartment and sighed, handing hers off to him and holding her arms open and out in my general direction. I hugged her tightly, and we both got weepy again. She sniffed and said, "I'll tell Mr. Comey and my parents."

"Thank you," I said, relieved of that burden, at least.

"I suppose you should go," I said, turning to Damien, as Dawnie went up the hallway, hand trailing along the wall, cane tapping in front of her.

"I'm not leaving you like this."

"But your car…"

"Is parked and insured."

"Look, I'll be okay. At least take it home."

"Come with me." He searched my face and I turned, looking at my pitiful space. It was the first time he'd ever been in it and I liked it. It was cozy somehow. Made me feel less alone.

He shut my front door and started flipping locks and chains. I shook my head and he silenced what I was about to say with a hard look.

"Not tonight, Bright Eyes," he said, and took off his jacket, hanging it off the back of the chair at my sewing table.

"Go wash your face and get ready for bed. I want you to use everything that is your favorite. Understand me?"

"My favorite pajamas are in the top of the laundry basket," I said.

"They have one more wear in them. Go get them." His tone brooked no argument. I did what he said, moving through the small space and into the bathroom where I stared at my makeup-streaked face in the mirror. I washed it and felt detached while I did it. Like I wasn't really there. I was just going through the motions with nothing, nothing at all left to feel.

I changed and went back out and found Damien tucked against the metal rails of my day bed. He held the blankets up for me to get in and I did, mutely, the twin bed nowhere near big enough for the both of us, but he made it work, mostly by virtue of draping me across his chest, hauling one leg over both of his.

I cuddled into his warmth, snug against the side of his body, and closed my eyes. He kissed the top of my head and smoothed a hand over my skin where it was exposed by my short sleep-shorts and cami, and I melted even further. The exhaustion swept over me and I don't remember anything after that.

I startled awake; I don't know how long it was later. I stirred and tried to figure out what was different and realized there was someone carefully moving around in the dark of my apartment. I sat up abruptly, and Damien shushed me, sitting down on the edge of the bed. I put my hand to my chest and willed my heart back in it.

"I need to run home, get cleaned up for work. I already called Millie. Unfortunately, the prosecutor's office won't give me time off for your grandmother. Only if she was my own. Plus, I have court in the Neely case today."

"Okay," I said, huffing out a miserable breath and sliding back down into my warm nest of blankets.

"Pack a bag for a few days and come stay with me…" he urged and I swallowed hard and thought about it.

"There's a bunch of stuff I have to do in a packet," I said.

"What packet?" he asked.

"In my tote, from yesterday."

He went over to it on the floor, by the chair where his briefcase sat, and looked inside. He slid the fat nine-by-twelve envelope from the funeral home out of it and said, "I'm a lawyer. Let me look over this and we'll do it together, tonight."

"Okay," I said, softly.

"I'll pick you up here. I'll call you and let you know what time."

"Okay."

He came over and kissed me, and my heart gave a pitiful, aching throb in my chest. He stood up reluctantly and murmured, "Go back to sleep."

He turned the lock in the doorknob and left and I sighed, getting up and padding over to flip the rest into place before scurrying across the cold, cracked linoleum back to the area rug with my bed on it. *No heated floors here,* I thought to myself.

I fell back asleep in no time. The next time I woke up, was to the melody of Damien's ringtone. It took me a minute to find my phone. I picked it up on the third ring.

"Hello?"

"Hey Bright Eyes, how you holding up?"

"I just woke up," I said blearily and he sighed.

"I'll be there in just a few minutes, can you be ready?"

"What time is it?"

"After seven," he said softly.

"At night?" I pushed myself up, muscles protesting.

"Yeah."

"Oh my god, I don't ever remember sleeping so long in my life!"

"Ten minutes, Ally. Open the door for me."

"Yes, sir," I said sheepishly, in response to his cold blue command, ringing even through the phone line.

I got off the phone and quickly went to the bathroom. That done, and feeling a little lighter, I opened drawers and rummaged quickly through them looking for things to pack. I straightened and looked around and sighed.

This wasn't *home*… this was just the place where I lived. I hadn't had a home since my grandmother went into that place. I felt tears mist my eyes and sat heavily on the edge of my lumpy mattress for a minute. I struggled to pull it together and managed, but just barely.

A knock fell at my door and I rushed to it calling, "That wasn't ten minutes!" I opened it to Dawnie standing there.

"Are you okay?" she demanded by way of greeting. "I came down here like three times today and you wouldn't answer the door."

"Yeah, I was sleeping, I guess."

"You guess?" She pushed past me and I let her, sighing.

"I was out cold; I didn't hear you knocking."

"That's weird for you."

"I know, I'm sorry."

It was her turn to sigh, "No, I am. What was that about ten minutes? Lover boy on his way to come get you?" She felt her way to my sewing table and made a face when her foot nudged one of the boxes and she nearly tripped.

"Shit, I'm sorry, Dawnie. I don't have any place else to put them. The bed was occupied."

"So is the chair, apparently," she said dryly, but she was smiling.

"Yeah, it is, and I need to pack."

"Ah, ten minutes… so lover boy is coming to get you."

"Please don't be disappointed," I said miserably.

"I like him, actually. He's hard to get a read on, even for me. I just wish that I could be with my best friend right now who's hurting."

"I know," I said softly, moving around the room quickly, finding clothes and getting dressed. I threw other clothes into one of my totes.

A light knock fell at the door and we fell silent. I went over to it and checked the hall this time, and sure enough, it was Damien. I let him in quickly and he pulled me to him, covering my mouth with his in a swift but sweet kiss.

"Hey, Romeo," Dawnie said glumly, and he turned.

"Hey," he greeted back. "How are *you* doing?"

"Wishing you weren't taking my bestie away just yet."

"What are you doing tonight?"

"Thought I was hanging with her."

"Well, you're welcome to come, too, for a few hours. I can send you back here in a cab later tonight."

"Really?" she asked, perking up.

"Really."

"Can I go get some things?"

"Sure, hurry up. I drove the Escalade."

I cringed. "Was your car okay?"

"Just fine," he said. "I just haven't driven the Escalade in a minute."

"Wow, I'm impressed. You left an expensive car out there overnight, and no one took it or stripped it?" Dawnie asked.

"Probably thought it was someone's that they shouldn't be messing with," he answered. "They were right."

"Escalade isn't quite so flashy, so it's probably in more danger," I remarked.

"True."

"Right, I'm gone. Back in a flash." Dawnie said, and her cane unfolded with its rattling snap.

"While she's gone," he said, when a moment or two had passed, "I don't want to upset anyone further, but I got in touch with the funeral home. There are some things we will need to go over."

"Okay," I said, morosely. I didn't want to *go over* anything. I didn't want any of this to be real.

He gripped my elbow and gave it a light squeeze, and said, "Do you want me to just take care of it for you?"

I rolled my lips and thought, *Yes;* out loud I said, "No, I need to do it. I just…"

"I know you don't want to, Bright Eyes." He pulled me against his chest and sighed, a heavy thing that told me just how much he wished he could take the pain away. I swallowed hard and cuddled into him, letting go only when he did.

"Let's get your stuff together; I want you to stay with me for the next few days. What do you want to bring?"

I sighed and said, "I wish we could bring the sewing machine."

He eyed the table and asked, "Is it all one piece?"

I laughed, "No, it lifts out."

"Okay, then bring it."

"You're serious," I said, wide-eyed.

"Dining room table will have to do, but why not? You're going to have to have something to do."

"No, really. It's okay," I said but he wouldn't hear anything of it. He helped me pack my sewing machine and extra bits and bobbins up in its case. By the time Dawnie had returned, he had already been out to his Escalade with it and was about to take the rest of my things. It honestly felt unnervingly like I was moving out. Not unnerving because I felt like I was moving out, that wasn't right. More, it was unnerving how much I ached for that to be precisely what I was doing.

I didn't want to be alone, and I knew that I wasn't, that I had Dawnie and that Damien and I were solid, but I don't know, everything was tossed in the air and still falling for me, and I didn't know where things were going to land. It was awful and confusing, and I felt like I was being pulled and pushed and I just needed something to grab onto to pull myself up.

"Okay, that's it," Damien said, returning from a second trip out to his car. "Got your keys?" he asked me, and I nodded and held them up. We went out into the hallway and I locked my door behind us. He took my hand, twining his fingers between mine and I blinked, realization coming a bit late to the party.

"I thought you were coming from work," I said, frowning.

"What's that, now?" Dawnie asked me.

"He's wearing jeans and a tee shirt."

"So? Oh, wait. Never mind." She turned in the general direction of Damien and said, "Yeah!" like she was agreeing with a much stronger point than what I was trying to make. Damien's lips twitched in amusement and I laughed lightly.

"I went home and changed first, is that a crime?"

Then brought the Escalade and practically half moved me out of my apartment. I kept mum about it for now, though. I didn't want to upset Dawnie. Still, it was something to think about and I needed to talk to him. I mean, *really* talk to him. I didn't want to do anything for the wrong reasons when it came to our relationship. Gran's death rocked me. I felt like I was going to second-guess everything and that I *should*. You know? I didn't have my guiding star anymore. I was on my own.

We took the stairs silently, and I was glad he didn't try to make me take the elevator. We came out the stairwell and drifted up the hall and I frowned slightly when I realized that it should be dark, but there was light coming through the front windows to the building's little vestibule. I mean, it wasn't big enough to be considered a lobby and I couldn't think of another word for it.

My mouth dropped open when we rounded the corner in front of the glass doors with chicken wire in them. My grandmother's garden, the converted fountain, was aglow with hundreds of white candles. I let Damien hold the door for me as I stepped out into the Point Side's courtyard.

"Hey Ally," I turned to see Julio, one of the Point Side kids like me, step on the end of his skateboard. It popped up and he grabbed it by the wheel's base and came over.

"Hi," I murmured.

"Real sorry to hear about Ms. Sylvia."

"Thanks."

"Hey, you that prosecutor, right?" he asked, jerking his chin up at Damien.

Damien cleared his throat. "That's right."

"He with you?" he asked me.

"Yeah," I said softly. "He's with me. He paid for my grandma's stay in that place."

Julio nodded and said, "That's what's up." He looked around to make sure no one else was out here with us, and said, "You might wanna bounce. Not everybody around here is gonna be so understanding; you know what I'm sayin'?"

"Read you loud and clear, man. Just give my girl a minute. K?"

Julio nodded and said, "Y'all should keep better company. I worry about you girls."

Dawnie snorted, "Right, thanks for the pro-tip, Julio. Now stop actin' like you all hard." You could hear the eyeroll in Dawnie's voice. Julio's lips peeled back from his teeth, and he made a derisive noise, almost a hiss, at her.

I mouthed an apology to him and Dawnie jerked on my arm, crying "Don't apologize to him!" *What had she heard? Jesus!* It was creepy how she did that.

"Man, you just pissed I hurt your feelings. All one of 'em, you stupid bitch!"

I closed my eyes and asked for strength, but Damien was there, right in front of Julio, looking up at him. The lanky skater sneered down at my boyfriend and my heart was in my throat.

"One, apologize to the lady," Damien said, his voice a creeping cold I had only heard once or twice before and hoped would never be directed at me. Even Dawnie shivered, despite the warmth coming from the tiny flickering mass of candles.

Julio looked like he was going to be tough for a minute, but something in Damien's eyes made him back down, but only halfway. "Man, whatever, you all better get the fuck up out of here before shit gets real."

"Damien, let it go…" I begged softly and he did, but he only backed down halfway, too. His posture relaxed marginally, but he didn't budge; he made Julio go around him. I felt the tension in my own body ease when Julio slammed through the Point Side's front doors and disappeared around the corner opposite of the direction we had come from.

"Come on; we'd better go," Damien said, and I nodded.

"Yah think?" Dawnie asked, and let me go. I reached into my pocket for my phone.

"Go, I want to take a couple of pictures."

Damien nodded and went to collect Dawnie and guide her to the car. "Come on, let's get you squared away, Trouble."

"Peachy," she said, but let him guide her around the fountain-turned-memorial to his waiting SUV at the curb.

I got my pictures and a little clip of video and trotted after my two favorite people left in this world. He started the Escalade as I shut the door. It was quiet out here. I was pretty sure Julio was just grandstanding, but when it came to the people of the Point Side, you never could tell. I turned my head to stare as long as possible at the beautiful flickering memorial to my grandmother and felt tears wet my cheeks.

I knew she was a special lady here, but I don't think I realized just how many other people she touched, you know?

31

*Y*ale…

She was quiet on the drive over. I kissed her inside the door and let her set up the dining room how she would like it. When I came back from the second trip, she was guiding Dawnie around the apartment, helping her get used to things. I watched the blind woman a moment and I think I caught a glimpse of what Ally loved in her. She walked around, her cane preceding her, Ally at her hip.

With her other hand, however, she touched. With every light graze of her fingertips against a new texture, the wood of my table, the grain of the leather of my favorite chair, the plaid throw on the back of my couch, a slight smile shaped her lips and I realized it wasn't often she had the time or ability to explore a new space so thoroughly.

"Nice place, Lover Boy," she said to me with a crooked smile, and I felt an answering one touch my lips.

"If you're going to call me something obnoxious, might as well streamline it. Call me Yale." I set down Ally's totes by the door and

228

Dawnie paused from lightly touching the back of one of my dining room chairs, gauging distance between them.

"Is that where you went to school?" she asked.

"No, he went to Columbia," Ally said and turned with the cord to her sewing machine to find a nearby wall socket for it.

"Then why do they call you Yale?" Dawnie had one eyebrow raised, and I realized how different she looked without her glasses, staring at something fixed in front of her, without seeing a thing.

"Because I had every opportunity to go and I didn't."

"Why?" she asked like it was crazy, and for a lot of people, it was.

"Because it pissed off my mother," I said honestly.

She laughed, "Oh, my God! You're serious."

"Yes, he is," Ally declared, straightening.

"Not something I am especially proud of in hindsight, but yeah."

"Holy crap, okay. Your mom a piece of work or something?"

"Dawnie!" Ally barked, exasperated.

"What? I thought we were getting to know each other, here."

"Enough sharing-is-caring for now," I said. "I have some things to do over here in the home office. You girls do whatever it is you do, okay?"

"What, just like that?" Dawnie asked.

"Yes, Dawnie! Just like that!" Ally cried and I chuckled, letting them bicker.

I think Dawnie and I understood each other a little better in that unspoken way. She smiled at me and schooled her face into one of a petulant teenager before she turned to argue with her best friend. Intentionally aggravating Ally mildly was a bit manipulative, but, any port in a storm. Anything that could distract her from her grief for even a short while would be a welcome distraction indeed.

I worked late, Ally sewed, and Dawnie sat curled on one of my two couches, her back to me as she crocheted, with the hook and yarn right in front of her eyes as if she could see it. Ally had told me that something about the accident had severed Dawnie's optic nerves, plunging her into total darkness. It had a tendency to affect her sleep and other things about her life, but for the most part, she had adapted remarkably well.

"Sorry, girls," I said softly, when I just couldn't tolerate reading another single brief. "I do still have to get through my day tomorrow before the weekend." I stretched and said, "I'll order you an Uber and get you home, Dawnie."

"Thanks, I'll call my dad and have him meet me at the curb there."

I pulled up the app on my phone and Ally hugged her best friend at the door. "I'm going to clean up, up here."

"Okay, call me tomorrow?"

"Absolutely."

"Come any time you'd like," I told her, and Dawnie smiled in my general direction.

"Thanks."

I walked her down and helped her into the back of the car, as she called her dad. She waved and I smiled, not bothering to wave back. Back in the apartment, I found Ally neatly piling and laying aside strips of material. The skirt she was working on looked like it was nearly completed.

"Looks nice," I murmured, and she smiled.

"Thanks."

"Come here," I ordered softly, and she came to me.

I kissed her and let it linger probably a little longer than would be considered appropriate, given the circumstances.

"You said there were paperwork and things I had to do…" She trailed off unhappily and I sighed.

"Tomorrow morning. I'm going to work from home."

"You can do that?"

I nodded, "I have a login; I can prepare briefs just as easily here as I can at the office. I don't have court tomorrow and no meetings with any opposition that I know of. I may get called in, but we'll see."

"Okay."

She looked up at me, eyes glassy with tears, and said, "I'm going to miss her so much."

"I know, baby. I know." I held her tightly, but she didn't dissolve immediately like she had yesterday. She held it together quite admirably.

"I feel like I'm drowning," she said, and her voice was hollow, drained, and I understood perfectly well how much it cost her to make the admission. How much she trusted me to make such a confession. We had grown up worlds apart, but one thing we had in common was the knowledge that you couldn't tell *anyone* anything personal. To do so meant trust on a monumental scale.

"Trust me to take care of you?" I asked.

"Of course," she said dully, her emotional exhaustion coloring her voice in muted tones.

"Come into the bedroom with me. Strip. I need to gather a few things," I said to her, and she looked up at me, drawing back to do so.

"Okay," she agreed, and I kissed her forehead and let her go.

She moved past me for the hall and I watched her go, before pinching the bridge of my nose. I was tired, but she needed an escape, one that only I could provide, so it would be coffee tomorrow – copious amounts of coffee. I pulled my shirt over my head with a sigh and went after her. She stood at the foot of my bed, mutely taking off her clothes, her long tee falling to the floor, her leggings peeling down her legs. I went into my walk-in closet and discarded my own tee in the laundry basket.

I kicked off my boots and put them back where they belonged. Socks to the laundry hamper as well. I left my jeans on for now and went into one of the drawers in the wall unit, sorting through the rope I had there. I skipped the hemp rope and went with the softer bamboo, pulling out two thirty-foot lengths. The rope I had chosen was a beautiful cobalt blue. I selected a black satin sleep mask out of another drawer and returned to the bedroom.

Ally was on her knees, legs parted, seated back on her heels, hands resting on her thighs in the slave rest position I had taught her, and I felt my cock stir. Her submission was beautiful to me and I had every intention of rewarding her for the gift she brought to my heart which swelled with a fondness and love for her like no other.

"Stand up for me," I ordered. She did, and I gave a further command: "Turn your back to me, Bright Eyes." She turned away from me. "One giant step to the left." I needed her away from the bed so I would have the room I needed. She obeyed beautifully, and I set the rope on the foot of the bed. The mask I retained, and went up to her back, pressing a light kiss to her shoulder. She sighed out and I murmured, "Close your eyes," against her skin. I felt more tension ease from her as she submitted to my will.

I gathered her hair down her back– it reached nearly to her waist now. I loved her long hair, her supple skin, her light breaths as she waited in anticipation of what I would do to her next. I slipped the mask over her eyes, and she sucked in a sharp breath before letting it out in a trembling sigh. She was so stressed, so distraught, that this was going to take some work.

"Put your hands behind your back, palms together, lace your fingers, like this." I guided her arms gently to where I wanted them to be and pressed her forearms together, doing some light stretching. "Is that too much?" I asked.

"No."

"Are you comfortable holding this stance, like this, for a while?"

"I think so."

"You know your safewords, tell me if at any time it becomes uncomfortable."

"Yes, sir."

I undid the first bundle of rope and flung it out to the side. It unraveled and slapped the carpet and she jumped slightly at the unfamiliar sound. I made a soothing sound and started a loop at her thumbs, holding the rope at the bight. I smoothed the length between my hands and wound it around her wrists, creating a wrap-cinch, binding her wrists together. I used the extra rope to bind her in a double column from wrist to elbow, her shoulder blades sharply pulled together. It would have a similar effect when I got to fucking her from behind as it would if I pulled her arms back to drive into her. This would only be slightly less intense and would leave my hands free, though.

I turned her and she went willingly with the motion. I shoved her forward and she yipped slightly as she fell face-first into the mattress. I helped her up onto the bed and said, "Wait for just a moment. I'm still here; I'm not leaving you or going anywhere. Just hold that thought."

I went and grabbed my wedge pillow from just inside the closet door and brought it to the bed. I helped her to her knees, set it in front of her and laid her back down. The wedge, under her lifted her hips and took some of the pressure off. It also allowed her to breathe a bit better. Just flat to the bed she would be face-planted into the mattress, which could be claustrophobic or unpleasant.

I was going for bound, helpless, and at my mercy, but I didn't want to go too extreme for our first time engaging in serious rope-play and bondage. I went to the foot of the bed and unfurled the next set of rope, mimicking what I'd done to her wrists with her legs, binding her from ankle to knees, so she was trussed and safe. So she would just need to take what I gave her, feel everything, with no other choice.

God, I was hard. I admired my handiwork, how she lay helpless, her head turned to the side, her lips parted as she took deep, steady breaths. She was calm and sinking fast into sub space, as if her overwrought mind had simply switched off, finally.

I smoothed a hand over her exposed skin, touching her lightly but firmly, sweeping my fingers and palm over her body and watching the goosebumps raise on her. I took my time stripping out of my jeans, undoing my belt, letting her hear everything. Letting her listen as I opened the drawer on what had become my side of the bed when she was here. The sound of tearing the condom packet off the string of them. The crinkle of the wrapper as I tore it open. The subtle sounds of me rolling it down my length.

Every bit of it was more erotic than the last. Every subtle noise, every shift in air current against her skin, every shift of the mattress as I straddled the backs of her thighs, ramped up the anticipation. The tension so thick with *what next* you could slice it with a razor. Her breath was already coming in soft, short little pants the more I touched her.

I pressed on her glorious ass, pressing it out of my way to her entrance and, of course, found her body slick and wanting me. She never disappointed me on that front. I pressed my fingers inside her and massaged her walls, finding and exploiting that rough patch just a few inches inside and down. She whimpered and writhed against my hand as much as her bonds would allow and I smiled to myself.

"I'm going to fuck you," I told her, and she clenched around my fingers. I grinned and went further, "I'm going to fuck you and you're going to come all over my dick. I'm not going to stop fucking you either. I'm not going to stop until *I'm* satisfied."

I slapped her right ass cheek with a sharp report and she let out a low, gasping cry, and came lightly around my fingers. I felt a wicked grin curve my lips and said to her, "That's it. That's my good girl," as I teased another orgasm out of her. A stronger one, this time, with my fingers. She bit her bottom lip, whimpering, body relaxed and languid beneath mine. When she reached that point and she was super wet and ready, I plunged my cock into her warmth.

I wasn't easy on her, but I wasn't as rough as I could be, either. I stroked inside deeply and thrust just that little bit more and she cried out, a wailing, begging sound that was music to my ears. I set a rhythm that was just this side of punishing and rode her body into the mattress and wedge and she screamed, *"Yes!"* and angled her hips as best she could to both accept my body into hers and thrust hers back onto me.

It was hot, she was so far gone from her worries and concerns for the moment, and I had successfully gotten her there. I sighed out and worked my body into hers and let myself go and really *feel* her; let my body make the decisions for me in a pale imitation of what I had already stripped her down to.

The pressure built, things tensed and I thought I would explode and then I did in the best way possible. My balls contracted, my cock jumped inside her and I filled the damn condom so hard I thought it might very well be to the damn brim

"Oh, god! Ally!" I cried and collapsed over her, chest and belly scraping over the ridges of soft rope holding her at my mercy.

We panted, lying spent for several minutes while I tried to find the strength to push myself up and work her bonds loose. Slipping the rope free from its quick-release knot at the top and loosening things from elbow to wrist, I managed to pull the lot of it free, sliding it off like a sleeve.

I took my time, massaging life back into her hands and admiring the lattice of rope imprints in her delicate skin. She moaned softly, groaning when she took her arms back and moved them forward to lay flat on the bed.

"I'll get your legs, just lay still."

I pressed fingers to the root of my softening cock and slid out of her, holding the condom on and walking backward on my knees to either side of her so that I could step off the end of the bed and deal with it quickly before I got to unbinding her the rest of the way. She lay limp and in a perfect state of bliss while I threw the condom in the trash and wound the rope from her arms back into a neat bundle. I unlaced her legs and wound that rope too, while she basked in her afterglow. She didn't move once she was free and I smiled to myself, glad she'd liked it.

I set the rope aside on the nightstand and pulled back a triangle of blankets and sheets, saying "Come on Bright Eyes. I need you to move under the covers with me."

She pushed herself up slowly, languidly, and I pulled the wedge out from under her and set it aside. She stretched luxuriously, like a cat, and crawled to the top of the bed, sliding beneath the covers. I chuckled and got into the bed with her, reaching up and switching off the bedside lamp, plunging us into darkness. She sighed and settled against me, cuddling as close as she could get, putting as much of her warm, silky skin against mine as she could.

"I love you," she breathed and I kissed the top of her head, understanding the importance of sharing those three little words. Understanding the importance of sharing them back, as quickly and as often as possible.

"I love you, too, Bright Eyes."

You never wanted to waste the opportunity to tell the ones you loved that you did, or just how much. You never knew when it might be the last opportunity and what's more, the world we lived in needed as much love and positive energy as anyone could muster to put out into it.

The truth was, I needed this as much as she had. The briefs and case-files scattered on my desk in the next room weren't going to soon be far from my thoughts, just as the pile of funeral arrangement paperwork for her grandmother wasn't going to be, either.

32

$\mathcal{A}$lly…

Damien helped me so much in the next few days. He helped me fill out the funeral paperwork and to pick the best option. My grandparents had believed in cremation and so we'd done that. I couldn't help but wonder if that was what it was because it also happened to be the vastly cheaper option between cremation and burial.

When we went to the funeral home to give them the paperwork, he'd held my hand, and when they asked me if I wanted to see her, he had been the voice of reason, turning me to him and saying softly, "Speaking from experience with numerous families whose loved ones have died victims… you don't want to do that, baby. You want to remember her alive and vibrant. Don't let this be the memory of the last time you saw her." The pleading in his eyes convinced me and I told the funeral director, 'no.'

Likewise, the funeral director asked if there would be a service and I shook my head dejected. I couldn't afford what they were asking, and I honestly didn't see anyone but Dawnie, Mr. Comey, and myself attending. Even with the candlelit shrine in my grandmother's garden, the Point Side residents and funerals were a fickle thing. They were likely to turn out and show up for a banger killed by another banger or the cops, but when Mr. Dodds had had his heart attack? It'd just been his family, my gran, and Dawnie.

Damien had taken me home after that. Had fixed us lunch while I quietly sulked on the couch and tried not to let myself fall completely into the pit of my despair. He'd brought the two plates of sandwiches and chips to the living room and handed me one, taking up a seat in his favorite chair.

"Turn on the news for me, babe?" he'd asked since the remote was closer to me. I took it up and turned on the television and the midday news flickered to life on the screen. More terrorist attacks overseas. More hate, more tragedy, more despair. I broke down and cried softly, overwhelmed.

The remote was taken from me, the television switched off, and gentle hands smoothed my tears away while intense dark eyes tried to assess how to help. Problem was, I didn't know the answer to that.

"Okay, I want you to eat and then I want you to take a nap while I get some work done," he said. I nodded, ate, and he tucked me in, laying with me until I fell asleep. It was one of the sweetest, kindest things I ever remembered a boyfriend doing for me.

When I got up, he was dressed in jeans and a tee, his biker jacket and motorcycle vest on the back of one of the dining room chairs opposite the wreckage of my latest sewing project that was under construction.

"Did you go somewhere?" I asked.

"Nope. It's *where* we're going."

I frowned and he said, "Dress to ride. Casual, comfortable."

"Okay," I murmured.

I was curious and it *was* a Friday night, so why not? Maybe the 'wind therapy' of a ride, or so he called it, would do me some good. Who knew?

I dressed carefully, in jeans and boots, a thick sweater, and over it all, a more fashionable than functional leather jacket that I owned. When I came out, he smiled at me and said, "You're lovely." He held out his hand and I took it and we went down to the garage together. The ride was soothing, the cooler fall air a balm to the constant burning ache that had taken up residence in my soul.

He pulled into the alley by the 10-13 and tapped my knee. I got down and he backed his bike into the line of them that always seemed to be there. I sighed and he took my helmet from me and grabbing up my hand, we went around the corner.

A printed sign hung in the front glass of the door that read 'Closed tonight for a private event' which made me falter, tugging on Damien's opposite hand as he reached for the door.

"The sign," I said, and he turned to me.

"I know, we're good," he jiggled our combined hands reassuringly and pushed open the door, leading me in past him.

"I smell Yale, is Ally with him?"

"I'm here," I told Dawnie, blinking in surprise.

"Just so you know, you're supposed to wear cologne, not bathe in it. At least if you don't want the blind girl calling you out," she said, past me, in Damien's direction.

Oz, who was beside my best friend, started cracking up laughing, and I admit I kind of laughed too. Dawnie turned in Oz's direction and said pointedly, "I don't know what you're laughing at, buddy. You're guilty of it, too."

"Oh, you're funny!" Oz declared, his amused grin intensifying rather than diminishing.

"I'll be here all week," Dawnie declared sarcastically, "No, really, I will. That seems to be how long it's going to take me to get a drink around here."

"Relax, sweetheart. Leave the salt on the glass," Skids said, pressing a margarita into her hand.

"Thank you," she said happily, and sipped from the rim, ignoring the two little straws. "Mm, Skids, was it?"

"Yeah."

"That's some good shit, thank you."

"Anytime," he said, laughing, and made his way back around behind the bar.

"What is this?" I asked softly.

"This, is your grandmother's wake," Damien said gently in my ear and I blinked, realizing pictures were playing on the bar's television. Photographs of my grandmother. Well, photographs of photographs…

"How did you?"

"Took pictures of the pictures in your photo albums you brought with you," he said gently. "Robbed some out of your phone when you weren't looking."

Different tears sprang to my eyes and Chrissy, who was standing nearby, said, "Awww! Don't cry."

"Precious, it's her grandmother's funeral," Youngblood pointed out, and she turned and gave him a light smack against his chest. I laughed through my happy tears and Damien led me to a seat at our familiar tall table.

"I got a story for you," Golden says after swallowing a sip of his beer and setting his bottle down and I said, "Okay."

"Oz, you can back me up on this one," Golden says, and Oz hung his head, shaking it laughing and said, "Oh, Lord!" like he knew what was coming.

"Okay, so we pick up this guy, a drunk and disorderly call, and as we go to put him in the car, dude's like 'I call shotgun!' and the first responding unit let me know, 'Hey, we ain't searched him yet' and me, I'm like 'Thanks, assholes' 'cause now I gotta do it. So we search him, we ain't find nothing on him, and I go to shove him in the back of our patrol car and dude be like, 'Hey, I'm like 100% sure that I just called shotgun! Why are you shoving me in the back?' Of course, that's how arrest works, right?"

Already people were starting to laugh, and I could already tell this was going to be pretty funny. Golden says, "So my partner, being the dumbass strait-laced motherfucker he is, tries to explain to this guy he's being arrested, right? Without missing a beat, and as drunk as this fucker is, he turns to Westin and is like, 'Yeah, I know I'm being arrested, but the rules of shotgun are pretty clear, man!'"

The table laughed, and I couldn't help but join them. Oz just sat there shaking his head, laughing and said, "No, look! No, look! This guy bitched about this all the way through central booking. It was crazy, man. That dude was funny as hell, though!"

"I have a pretty funny arrest story…" I said and the table turned.

"Oh god, the one with your gran?" Dawnie asked.

"Your grandmother got arrested?" Golden asked, frowning at me like I was crazy.

"Okay, you have to understand, this was like a long time ago, the fifties or the sixties or something, right? So my grandmother and my grandfather had just gotten married, they hadn't been married for very long, and my granddad was this troubleshooter for this hotel downtown here in Indigo City."

"Okay, what's a troubleshooter?" Oz asked.

"It's like a bouncer," I answered. "So, anyway, my grandmother is a seamstress, right? And she'd lent money to a girl staying at the hotel. So she goes to the hotel to get it back and she's sitting with the woman at the hotel bar when the police swoop in and arrest her. She was a prostitute, and my grandmother had *no idea.* Well, they arrest my grandmother too, and she's screaming at my grandpa, 'Mace! Tell them who I am! Oh my, god, Mace! Tell them I'm your wife!' but my grandpa is *laughing* so hard he can't say it and they got her all the way into the back of the paddy wagon about to take her to jail!"

Everyone erupted into laughter and I glanced up at the television where a picture was sliding by of me sitting on my grandmother's knee, my mom next to us on the couch. They were all gone now and I missed them all so much… My heart swelled so big with my pain that I felt like some of my ribs cracked. Tears sprang to my eyes and I crumbled around the edges and Damien was suddenly there, propping me up, holding me tight until the rainstorm passed.

"Sorry," I said, at the pleasant but somber faces around the table.

"Don't be, it was a good story," Golden said, and held up his glass. "To Mace! Poor bastard probably slept on the couch for a week after that shit."

"To Mace!" Everyone cheered and drank. I laughed and said, "I don't know how long she stayed mad at him for that one."

The door opened and I turned; a cluster of people from the Point Side was gathered in the doorway. I could see Mr. Comey at the back, and one of the young people at the front, Yvette, asked, "Hey yo, this where Miss Sylvia's wake is supposed to be?"

"It surely is," Skids called from the bar.

"Yo, this is a *cop* bar!" a male voice shouted from the back. I think it was Julio.

Damien looked at the group and said back, "Not tonight, it's not."

Several of them in the doorway exchanged looks, and Skids called out, "Food's about to be up; I ain't heating the whole of Indigo City. Either you're in or you're out."

"Yeah, we're in," Yvette smiled at me and ushered everyone forward, and new happy tears kind of formed.

"Thanks," I said softly and she said, "Man, I'm really sorry about Miss Sylvia, baby girl." She came over and hugged me and everyone else followed suit.

"We were just listening to one of Ally's stories about her; you got any?" Golden asked.

"Yeah," Yvette said smiling. "A lot of us called her the Saint of the Point Side. She helped a lot of people, whether we done wrong or not."

"Oh, yeah, what'd she do for you?" he asked, and one by one the stories started to come out. Some I knew, some were new to me, but all of them were much the same. My grandmother loved everybody. She loved her community, and she wanted everybody to be safe and happy in a place that was inhospitable to both.

I turned to Damien and met his eyes, smiling, and mouthed 'thank you.'

"Anything for you," he murmured into my ear and I believed him. He didn't say it if he didn't mean it. I knew that about him. I loved that about him.

"Hey man, I ask you something?" Julio said a time later. Damien looked back at him over his shoulder and gave a nod.

"Sure," he said.

"You and Ally a thing?"

"Yeah, Julio, we're a thing," I said, gently.

He nodded, but regret sort of took over his expression. "You gonna take her out of the Point Side?" he asked.

"Why?" Damien asked, picking up on something I hadn't.

"'Cause, man. You're the city's prosecutor, dude. You're on the news and shit. There be bangers and guys at the Point Side that'd hurt Ally just to get to you." Julio looked at me and his face was a mix of sad and something else I couldn't quite define.

"I like you, Ally Cat. I liked Ms. Sylvia. I don't want to see nothin' happen to you." I nodded and took his warning to heart.

"We'll have her moved this weekend if we have to," Skids said, from behind the bar.

"Always knew you'd get out," Yvette said. "I'm happy for you."

I swallowed, things moved so fast, were moving so fast… I didn't even know where I was going to go!

Yes, you do, stupid. He's got you half moved in already.

I looked to Damien who reached up and caressed a light thumb across my cheek. Then I looked past him to Dawnie, who was visibly upset but trying to contain it.

"Oh, Dawnie, please don't cry!"

"I'm sorry!" She put a fist to her mouth, pressing it to her lips for a moment and finally pulled it away and said, "I always knew you would get out, too. I just didn't think it would all happen at once like this, you know?"

"Dawnie, she's going to move, sure, but we have a little time for that and she's not leaving your life completely. She's still here," Damien let her know and I loved him so much right then for trying to comfort my salty, distressed friend.

"He's right, you know," I said. "I can't do anything without my best friend."

"I know you can't," she warbled, "You'd be lost without me. Now get over here, bitch, and hug me."

I went and hugged her tight, and had nothing to say to make it better for her. We were caught in the same storm, but on opposite ends of it. It was as if my whole world had shattered and the pieces were tossed in the air. They were still coming down and hadn't all landed, but as soon as I was able to snatch a piece, it felt like, I was able to fit it to the one next to it. Like, even though everything was broken, with Damien's help, I was piecing it back together at a whirlwind speed.

It was much the same the rest of the wake, passing by at the speed of light. Laughter and tears, a roller coaster of emotion. When the last person had left and the doors were shut and locked, I sagged against Damien with relief.

"I think my girl has officially reached pumpkin status," he said, with a light chuckle.

"To be expected," Reflash said and I smiled at him. He'd cooked all of my grandmother's recipes for the food. That was more sneaky-sneaky from my boyfriend, taking pictures of her recipes and sending them to Reflash to ponder over and expand.

"I'd like to buy a couple of them recipes for the restaurant," he'd said and we were supposed to work out a deal later on. It would be nice to put some money aside for a rainy day, and I wasn't opposed to it. My grandmother loved to cook and feed people, so it felt right, actually.

"You go on and get out of here," Skids called. "We got clean-up just fine."

"I can't even begin to imagine what this cost you," I told them.

"Nothin'." Reflash leaned against the bar. "Your man there paid for it."

I turned to Damien and he kissed my forehead in that way that made me melt. "I meant it, I'd do anything for you. Plus, money is really no object for me."

I sighed, too wrung and turned-inside-out to argue or pitch any 'but's' out there.

"Let's go home," he murmured, and I nodded. I wanted to go home. I wanted a bed, and I know it was probably wrong of me, but I wanted the escape Damien's body in mine provided.

We said our final goodbyes, I gave hugs and my profuse thanks, and we were on our way back to the Calvert building by way of the garage next door.

We were silent all the way back up to his apartment. I didn't even object to using the elevator. I mean, not that I ever did, but this time I didn't even feel the usual accompanying anxiety that came with an elevator ride.

"How are you feeling?" he asked me.

"Empty," I replied softly as we stepped through his front door. I didn't want to give him the idea I wasn't up for anything before bed, though, so I said, "I don't suppose you would mind filling me up?"

He smiled and laughed at my crude joke and said, "Not at all; come here."

He drew me into his arms and kissed me with one of those kisses of his that scorched the earth and made it all just fall away. I kissed him back and let my hands run over his fit body underneath his jacket and what he called a cut. The heat radiating off of him was addictive after the chilly ride home, and I wanted to warm myself by him like he was the fire missing from my soul.

I only hoped I could reignite next to him and he was, it would seem, determined to make that happen. His mouth was hungry, like he would swallow my sadness whole. His hands were just as starved, moving over my body, desperate to touch, desperate to feel every inch of me.

It was like we lost ourselves in one another. Hands divested bodies of clothes, without a hope or a prayer of ever reaching the bedroom. He laid me down, right there against the warm hardwood floors, mouth traveling all down my body, hands following. I ran my fingers through his hair as he kissed the apex of my thighs and I arched when his tongue licked out decadently along the seam of my sex.

"Oh, god! Damien…" My voice died on a lust-filled gasp and he growled his approval against me. My hips lifted at the sound and thrill of vibration and I gave myself over to his tender loving care.

33

*Y*ale…

"You really want me to move in with you?" she asked suddenly, as we were lying in bed. We'd eventually made it back here, and we'd made love again. It'd been a three-condom night and I was good with that, utterly spent and on the verge of sleep when her voice had sweetly disrupted the silence.

I paused and thought about what she was asking. I didn't give her any platitudes or immediately jump to a 'yes, of course, I do' because that wasn't what she was looking for. She wanted the truth, and I swore I would always give her that. I couldn't expect total honesty from her if I wasn't willing to give it in return.

"Yes," I said, finally. "Everything about you makes my life better. I want to share it with you; I want you in my space. I want it to be *our* space."

She dragged herself up and straddled my hips, her hands resting on my stomach, and peered down at me, searching my face.

"I guess I'm surprised," she said after a while, deciding I was sincere.

I smoothed my hands over the tops of her thighs and met her level, somber gaze. Those green eyes of hers gave me no quarter.

"I tried to deny you, Ally. I tried keeping you out of my heart and keeping it just about meeting physical needs with you, but you weren't having any of it." I reached up and cupped her cheek, and she turned her face into my hand, kissing the heel of it as I grazed her soft skin with my thumb.

"I don't understand why you were so determined," she murmured.

"I'm not a good man," I said, swallowing hard. "I know how to move through the world and fake it, but I'm a deviant. I'm sexually depraved and I –"

Both of her small hands covered my mouth and she leaned down, nearly nose-to-nose with me. "I happen to like it, and you *are* a good man. Look at how you take care of me," she whispered, and she moved her hands and replaced them with her lips in a soft, sultry little kiss. I let my fingers dig slightly into her hips, surprised that my cock stirred where her pussy rested against it. Shit, I might have another round in me, after all.

"The least I could do for corrupting you so thoroughly," I murmured against her mouth.

She smiled and said back, "I like how you corrupt me."

"Yeah?"

"Yeah."

"I'll carry on, then." I sat up and rolled her onto her back, the sudden movement making her shriek and laugh. I loved the sound of her laughter after so many tears and so I nipped at the sensitive spot on the side of her neck, growling against it, tickling her with my beard.

She kicked ineffectively and laughed harder, her hands pulling me closer rather than shoving me away and I just couldn't stand it. I turned that laughter into a moan as I slid into her. I needed to get a condom, shit, but just for the moment, oh god, she felt so good.

I went to stop after just a couple of strokes, but she locked her legs around me and whispered, "Just a moment longer?"

"I shouldn't have even started –"

She interrupted me. "I don't think I've ever felt closer to you. I know it's stupid –"

"It's not." I interrupted her. It wasn't. I got it, even if no one else out there did; I did and that was what mattered.

Still, I wasn't ready for children, and though she had gotten on the pill, it was my responsibility to take care of us. Her pregnant, right now, would be too much, with every other major life change going on. So I withdrew, quickly got a condom on, and fervently picked up where we left off.

She was warm, soft, and everything I needed, and I loved having her here and in my bed. I wasn't upset at all by the confluence of events that brought her here to stay – except for the fact that they made her hurt. Her grandmother had been sweet and kind, but she'd known it was her time.

When Ally had gone to use the restroom on our last visit to her gran, Mrs. Blaylock had put her gnarled hand on mine, had looked me straight in the eye, and had told me she didn't think she had long and to please take care of Ally when she was gone. Then she had begged me not to tell her granddaughter, pleaded with me not to upset her.

I promised, because how could I not? I had every intention of taking care of what was mine, and make no mistake; Ally Blaylock *was* mine. Of course, unless there was ever a day that she didn't wish to be anymore. Then again, what kind of man would I be to give her just cause to walk away from me?

Call me an over-achiever, but that would never happen. I would make sure of it. I would love her, care for her, honor and cherish her. Someday this woman would be my wife, but there was plenty of time for all of that later.

It was a special moment, a special thing to know you had found the one that was for you. The one you knew, unequivocally, that you would be spending the rest of your life with. I loved Ally Blaylock with every part of my damaged heart and soul. She completed me – soothed the hurting, aching, broken bits of me in a way that no one or nothing ever had before. She believed in me to the point that I had to believe in myself, that I had to give myself more credit. She undid so many of the doubts that my parents had instilled in me and how, after all of that, could I not love her in return?

"Tighten up that pussy," I ordered and she complied, and I could stay here like this, in her, with her, forever. I stroked in and out of her in an easy cadence, her breath soft and her arms around me, her hands on my ass, encouraging me. Not that I needed the encouragement. Not when it came to her. I made her come twice before I concentrated on my own pleasure.

I laughed; it felt so good, but I couldn't get there. I think I was just too damn spent. I just didn't have one more in me, but it damn sure wasn't for a lack of trying. This last session of sex for the night ended with both of us laughing, holding each other tight and kissing as I cursed my inability to finish and Ally bemoaned how badly she felt that I couldn't.

It didn't matter. It really didn't. It was everything just to have her in my bed, in my arms, as we both finally fell asleep.

34

*A*lly…

I lived at Damien's for the whole following week, until the weekend, when all of the Indigo Knights helped us move the important things and sell or donate the rest. It'd been both a heartbreaking but super fun day, and I was beginning to feel like I had a different sort of family.

The rest of October wore on into November and the days turned rainier and colder. It was like the skies echoed my mood and I could almost believe I controlled the weather some days. Damien's love made me feel powerful, but I didn't think I was *that* powerful. At least, not really.

One rainy November day, I woke up to find his half of the bed empty, and pushed myself up, confused. On our days off, I almost *always* got up before him.

"Damien?" I called out softly, and I heard him padding barefoot over the hardwood down the hall. He appeared in the door to our bedroom, shirtless and delicious in just a pair of black pajama pants, hair still tousled.

"Morning," he greeted me, and stopped, looking at me much the same as I looked at him. A warm glow took root in my chest and grew, bursting to life and into full bloom as a smile on my face.

"What are you doing up before me?" I asked, pushing my hair back off my face, smoothing it behind my ears.

He smiled at me softly and said, "Hold that thought, I'll be right back." Then, sterner, with a hard look that said he meant business, he declared, "Don't you dare move."

"Yes, sir," I said mildly amused, my curiosity eating me alive.

He came in with a tray laden with breakfast, and my heart melted a little, he set it across my lap and put pillows behind me, and I looked at him with such love and asked lightly, "You didn't have to do this, what's the occasion?"

He laughed and said, "You serious?" He came around the bed and lay on his side, propping his head on his hand and I looked at the beautifully-cooked eggs, bacon, and toasted English muffin, alongside fresh coffee and orange juice.

"Yes, I'm serious." I blinked in confusion and his face fell slightly, and I felt color rise in my cheeks.

"It's your birthday, Bright Eyes."

I blinked in surprise and blurted, "Nuh-uh! It's not the twenty-second already, is it?"

"It is," he said, gravely.

"Oh, my god!" I laughed, embarrassed. "Who forgets their own birthday!?"

He laughed with me, "Apparently you do, but I didn't." He pushed himself up to his hands and knees and kissed my forehead, then drew back and saying, "Eat. I have a present for you."

I nodded and began to eat my breakfast. He came back in the room with a white garment box, tied with a giant indigo-blue, sheer gift ribbon. It was lavish and beautiful, and I almost felt bad that I would have to untie it. I plucked my phone off the bedside table and opened the camera, and he laughed at me and asked, "What are you doing?"

"The bow is so pretty, I want to take a picture before I ruin it."

"You're adorable, you know that?" he asked, snatching my phone out of my hand.

"Hey!"

"Eat your breakfast, baby. I've got this."

I did what I was told, eyeing him as he took several photos of the box, me, and, I was guessing, me stuffing my face. I kind of couldn't wait to see what was in it. Excitement fizzed through my blood as I put away the rest of the delicious meal he'd made me.

When he was satisfied I'd eaten enough, he took the single rose in its fluted vase off of the tray and put it on my bedside table for me before he took the tray and set it aside. He came back around to his side of the bed and sat down, lightly setting the box in my lap. I licked my lips and pulled gently at the ribbon, which slid easily, and artfully unraveled into a pile on top of the gleaming white surface of the box.

I lifted the lid, folding it back, and gasped. Inside was a beautiful crushed-velvet evening gown, such a deep blue as to almost be black. Sitting on top of it was an elegant, laser-cut, silver metal mask.

"They're beautiful."

"They're just the beginning, for what I have planned for you today."

I smiled; we hadn't been back to Indigo Nights since the first time, but

I was looking forward to a return trip and seeing what he had in store for us.

"When are we going, now?" I asked, and he laughed.

"No, tonight, after dark. I have other plans for us today."

"Like what?" I asked simply, but genuinely curious.

"Like I thought we could go for a ride."

"It's raining!"

"A short thunderstorm. I checked the forecast."

"Hmm, where are we going?"

"Well," he moved the box off of my lap and drew me in for a kiss. Resting his forehead against mine, he murmured softly, "I figured we could spend the morning in bed, then we'd go for a ride and get some lunch."

"Mm-hmm," I murmured happily.

"Then we could come back here and get ready, head down to the sex club, and go from there."

"Sounds like a perfect day."

"Oh, you have no idea," he growled, and covered more than my mouth with his. He nipped the side of my neck with a growl and I yipped, laughing, which quickly turned into a desire-filled little moan as he pressed me back into the bed and ripped the blankets from my naked body.

It was a most excellent start to my birthday, but I was really curious about how it would end and what he had planned for that ending. I could barely contain myself. The ride was freeing and only slightly damp. He took us across the bridge towards Baltimore and a restaurant that served some of the best crab bombs in Maryland. We had lunch, laughed, talked, and even did some dreaming for the future.

"If you could have anything, what would you want?" he asked softly.

"Nothing, I have you, which means I have it all."

"Surely, you don't want to work at the café for the rest of your life." He seemed surprised by my answer.

"I like the café, but no, you're right. I guess some day I would like to, hopefully, open a funky little boutique with mine and Dawnie's creations. Maybe co-op with some other local artisans. Some jewelry makers and artists. You know, a little gift shop in Old Town or along Bayside Park."

He nodded slowly. "How long would you need to get enough things together to make a go of such a venture? Like, how much stuff would you need to make?"

"Wait, you think we should do it?"

He shrugged, "Why not? Save all your money you make from the café; you have all the money from selling off your furniture and from selling your grandmother's recipes. Keep saving; it could be your startup money."

"You're serious," I said, shocked.

"I said I would take care of you, Bright Eyes. I meant it; and while we're on the subject, there's no reason why, if I'm taking care of you, you can't put your own money into this."

I sat back in my seat, my crab bomb forgotten. "You're really serious."

"Have you ever known me not to be?" he asked, levelly.

"Oh, my god…" I felt tears start in my eyes and had to sniff them back. It was like my whole narrow world just suddenly opened up wide in front of me.

"It's going to get really crowded in the apartment," I said softly, "with all of the things I am going to make."

"You have the whole spare bedroom; we'll cross those bridges when we come to them." He shrugged nonchalantly.

"You're dead serious right now," I said in disbelief, and he laughed and shook his head.

"Yeah, beautiful, I am."

All I could ask myself was *how did I get so lucky?* It was the best birthday present I'd ever gotten.

"Finish your lunch," he reminded me and I did, though I was so excited I could barely eat.

We rode back across the bridge and took the scenic route through the city, looping back in on our route on our way back to the Calvert building; *back home*, I reminded myself.

It was still hard for me to reconcile the new digs as *home*. Home had always been where my grandmother was, and though we'd received her urn of ashes and she sat alongside my grandfather in one of the rich wooden nooks around the television, the built-in light shining down above them, it was still a far cry, you know? I was still trying to come to grips with all of the abrupt changes.

Damien was amazing, patient and kind through all of it, and I didn't let on that there was still discord within me. I didn't want him, for even a single moment, to think it was him. It wasn't. It was me, and possibly just the need for more time. I honestly didn't know.

I got ready as dusk fell, standing in front of the bathroom mirror in my stockings and garter, matching panties in place until Damien walked into the bathroom, lavishing me with his dark gaze in a strong, slow look from head to toe. I paused, recognizing immediately his displeasure.

"What?"

"Those weren't in the box," he said simply.

Oh, no, it would seem I had mis-stepped. I smiled faintly and said, "My apologies, sir. I will get rid of them."

He nodded, buttoning the cuffs on his crisp, white shirt. "Do that," he said directly and with a check in the mirror, tied the deep indigo silk tie that matched the dress waiting, lying on the bed, to perfection. I got rid of the stockings, garter, and was half-tempted to leave the panties on, to test him. He'd never punished me before; of course, I never defied him. Not when we played and I could feel we were sliding into that dominant-and-submissive power dynamic, even now.

I knew where the lines were. It wasn't something we had ever overtly discussed, but all the same, we were in tune with one another that way. I instinctively *knew* and so did he. It just worked for us, and if it wasn't broken…

I put the things I had on back and felt a certain arousal and thrill as I slipped the satin lining of the gown over my skin. It was a long, tight affair. Backless, the front tapered up into a high collar around my throat, buttoned with three shank buttons at the back that could very well have been black pearls.

It covered my front, tight to my body, flaring slightly at the waist and dropping into a floor length skirt with a few inches of train. I looked elegant and sophisticated, especially with how I had curled and artfully piled my hair into an up-do with my grandmother's silver and freshwater-pearl combs.

I smoothed my hands over the bodice of the dress and smiled. I was beautiful, he made me feel beautiful with his thoughtful gifts. He came up behind me and put his hands on my waist, kissing the back of my shoulder reverently. I closed my eyes and sighed contentedly, and he murmured, "I can't wait to get this off you and fuck you in front of everyone." I shivered with anticipation and he smiled against my skin.

He helped me put the mask on, carefully and securely tying the ribbon behind my head. We stared at each other in the mirror for a long minute, and I felt he was committing this to memory, every fine detail, as much as I was.

The drive to the club was peaceful, despite the anticipation. Damien wore a laser-cut, black-metal skull mask with deep, dark blue stones littered across its surface like dark stars. He pulled up to the stairwell to the club's basement door and a man in tails with a simple leather black mask came to take the car, getting my door for me.

Damien and I went inside and he lifted my cloak from my shoulders and handed it to the man behind the cash wrap, taking the ticket and waving off a locker key. "No need tonight," he said and the man behind the black, solid, blank face mask said, "Of course, Mr. Silver. You and Angel enjoy your evening."

"Thank you," I said softly and the man's glittering brown eyes flicked to my masked face. I couldn't tell if he smiled or not behind the blank, expressionless black mask, but the slight crinkling at the corners of his eyes where I could see them through the cut eye holes suggested that he did.

"Come on, Angel, with me," Damien corrected gently.

"Yes, sir." I followed along at his side, into what I knew was likely a den of wolves.

He murmured, "You're too sweet sometimes."

"Would you like me to change?" I asked, and he chuckled.

"Not for the world, love. That's why you have me." I smiled as we swept back into the bar and masked faces turned to us, some nodding in greeting. He took me over to the bar and ordered two glasses of champagne before we retired to the same seating area, where he took up a seat in a black velvet wing-back chair, pulling the ottoman to his side and gesturing I should take a seat on it to protect my dress but still remain at his feet.

I could feel the power exchange, the shift in dynamic, as an almost palpable thing between us as his hand drifted to the back of my hair, resting on it lightly. He sipped his champagne, and I sipped mine while he made light conversation with some of the other men in the room.

"May I address your girl?" one of them, a man in a stylized big bad wolf's mask asked, and Damien's lips twisted in a cruel smile.

"I would rather you didn't."

"Ah, understood. Disappointing to be sure, but I look forward to the show nevertheless."

Damien inclined his head and the man in the wolf's mask made his way elsewhere. I gave Damien a questioning look but he simply saved his genuine smile for me and I trusted he knew best. I'd gotten a slimy feeling from the man in the wolf's mask anyway.

We finished our drinks and he had me take the glasses to the bar, then met me in the hall between it and the seating area. He took my hand and led me toward the stage. It was different from last time, in that there were already people taking their seats. Still, I was confident, having him there and having already done this once before.

Instead of a chair and the high hanging hook, there was a small table with lengths of rope neatly arranged on its top and a sparkling steel ring spinning lazily under the stage lights. The same chair was there too, but mostly, I think, as a place to set our clothes, like last time.

Damien smiled at me and came to me, kissing me as his hands smoothed over my body through the velvet of the dress. I let my hands sneak around his neck and kissed him back and he drew back and said, "Palms together, behind your back like this," and he showed me what he wanted. I nodded and did as he asked, and he selected some of the rope, dyed to match my dress, off of the table.

I closed my eyes and let out a breath as he walked around me, contemplating his next move. Finally, he came to me and re-positioned my hands so that I was gripping each opposite forearm, up near the elbow, my chest thrust out. He bound my arms and took his time. The rope sliding against my skin a sensual thing. I could feel the heavy press of the small, but increasing crowd's gaze and felt the heat build between my legs. Heat that only increased when his fingers went for the shank buttons at the back of the collar holding my dress up.

He peeled the velvet off my body, the cooler basement air of the club caressing my skin and sending my want into overdrive. I stepped out of the pool of the dress at his command, and he took my shoes, low velvet pumps that matched the dress, from my feet and left me standing there with just the mask and rope between me and their eyes while he set things over the chair and on the floor beside it.

He walked around me slowly, loosening his tie, and I could see the critical thinking going on in his eyes behind the mask as he swept me with his gaze, considered the rope on his table, and did what looked like mental math when he looked at the slowly-spinning ring above us. A thrill went through my veins when I realized what he might do with that ring.

He selected more rope after he took off his tie and rolled back his sleeves. He faced me towards the audience by my shoulders, and, starting at my bound arms, began making a chest harness with the new length of rope. Lashing between and under my breasts, the rope lifted them slightly for better display as he went around me, making decorative angles, a sensual web to accentuate my curves. I felt myself begin to slide back into that warm, pleasurable space where I gave myself over to him completely, and I sighed in contentment.

He slid a mat out from under the table and positioned it under the ring, and snapped his fingers, pointing.

"Come kneel," he ordered and I did as he asked, facing the crowd. He selected more rope and knelt beside me, parting my thighs with a gentle touch, bringing me into a more upright position with a gentle pat on the ass. He began winding the rope carefully around one thigh and asked me, "Do you love me, Angel?"

"Yes," I answered.

"Do you trust me?"

"Yes, of course."

"Would you commit to me?" he asked cinching the rope down.

"I already have," I answered him and turned my head to meet his eyes.

"I was thinking something a little more permanent, something with a little more meaning."

"Are you asking me to marry you, sir?"

Light tittering laughter swept through the audience.

"I am asking you to be my submissive, formally, of course. Though, yes, at some point I will ask you to be my wife," he said. I closed my eyes and smiled as he cinched the rope around my other thigh and guided me down to my stomach. I lay on the mat and let him continue his elaborate work, excitement burning in the middle of my body, turning my heart to a ball of flame as it beat, a small sun in the center of my chest, filling me with warmth and light.

"What do you say?" he asked me, and I smiled at the floor, unable to turn my head far enough to see him.

"I say I was already yours; it's a little silly to be asking now." I yipped at the sharp slap that landed on my bare ass.

"Don't be pert," he ordered, and before I could be a smart-alec again, he hoisted on the ropes which strained against my body, uncomfortable at first. I gasped, but it was too late; I was airborne and rising as he hoisted me up, tying things off efficiently, bracing me against his thigh and body with a practiced ease.

Endorphins and adrenaline raced through my veins and I swallowed hard. He chuckled darkly and said, "So, is that a yes, Angel?"

"Yes, that's a yes," I murmured, and he came around in front of me, bent down and kissed me sweetly.

"Good girl," he breathed against my lips, and then I let out a shriek of surprise as he sent me spinning.

The room passed in a blur of dark and light, dizzying as I spun wildly in one direction, slowed and then picked up speed the other direction.

"Oh, my god!" I cried, and I couldn't help the crazy laughter bubbling out of me. It was fun, stupidly, obnoxiously *fun* and my heart was so light I couldn't stop giggling even if I wanted to.

When he stopped me, he was nude, and he knelt to meet my eyes, a metal collar, beautiful silver scroll-work, like lace made from metal, rested in his hands. The bright gleaming metal was studded with sapphire cabochons. He flexed it open and pressed it to the front of my throat.

"Bow your head, that's it." I complied as he threaded black ribbon back and forth like a corset through the loops and tightened it – snug, but not choking – tying it off into a neat bow.

"Good girl," he breathed again, and, running his fingertips along my body, raising goose bumps on my skin, went around behind me, stepping between my open legs. I heard the crinkle of a wrapper and closed my eyes, bowing my head, waiting for him, breathless with anticipation.

He took me roughly, plunging into my wet and ready cunt, balls-deep. I cried out, breathless, passionate, and did the only thing I *could* do, trussed and dangling like I was. I squeezed down around him. He gripped the rope at my thighs and used it as leverage to fuck me in front of our audience.

I let him; I wanted to show these people, shout it from the roof tops;

tell the whole world that he was mine as much as I was his. I loved him, I loved being with him, and I reveled in our mutual darkness. Even depravity could be beautiful, if done right and from a place of love.

THE END

ALSO BY A. J. DOWNEY

The Sacred Hearts MC

1. Shattered & Scarred

2. Broken & Burned

3. Cracked & Crushed

3.5 Masked & Miserable (a novella)

4. Tattered & Torn

5. Fractured & Formidable

6. Damaged & Dangerous

The Virtues

1. Cutter's Hope

2. Marlin's Faith

3. Charity for Nothing

The Sacred Brotherhood

1. Brother to Brother

2. Her Brother's Keeper

3. Brother In Arms

4. Between Brothers

5. A Brother's Secret

Indigo Knights

1. Her Thin Blue Lifeline

Paranormal Romance (with Ryan Kills)

1. I Am The Alpha

2. Omega's Run

3. Hunter's End

ABOUT THE AUTHOR

A. J. Downey is the international bestselling author of The Sacred Hearts Motorcycle Club romance series. She is a born and raised Seattle, WA Native. She finds inspiration from her surroundings, through the people she meets and likely as a byproduct of way too much caffeine.

She has lived many places and done many things, though mostly through her own imagination…An avid reader all of her life, it's now her turn to try and give back a little, entertaining as she has been entertained.

Stalking Links

www.ajdowney.com
aj@ajdowney.com

Praise for *My Heart Is Human*

"Transness, bodily autonomy, and AI sentience intersect with razor-sharp precision to create a heartfelt declaration of what it means to be human."

— Al Hess, author of *World Running Down*

"Hogan deftly weaves moral questions about identity, humanity, and self-sacrifice throughout the narrative without losing a drop of tension."

— Sarah J. Daley, author of *Obsidian*

"Reese Hogan's *My Heart Is Human* is a passionate, well-written look at found family, identity, freedom, and love with a dash of punk rock and a reminder that the apocalypse is only the beginning (usually of another apocalypse)."

— R.W.W. Greene, author of *Mercury Rising*

"An exciting and thoughtful exploration of what identity means for AI and human alike."

— Ginger Smith, author of *The Rush's Edge*

"*My Heart Is Human* is a smart, exciting, near-future adventure that attacks the deepest questions of personhood, identity, and the impending confrontation with the technologies we've created. An intense rampage that leaves you both breathless and pondering the nature of self."

— Chris Panatier, author of *The Phlebotomist*